I0952741

# SNOW ANGELS

# SNOW ANGELS

## JAMES THOMPSON

G. P. PUTNAM'S SONS

*New York*

Prescott Valley Public Library

PUTNAM

G. P. PUTNAM'S SONS
*Publishers Since 1838*
Published by the Penguin Group
Penguin Group (USA) Inc., 375 Hudson Street, New York, New York 10014, USA • Penguin Group
(Canada), 90 Eglinton Avenue East, Suite 700, Toronto, Ontario M4P 2Y3, Canada (a division of
Pearson Penguin Canada Inc.) • Penguin Books Ltd, 80 Strand, London WC2R 0RL, England •
Penguin Ireland, 25 St Stephen's Green, Dublin 2, Ireland (a division of Penguin Books
Ltd) • Penguin Group (Australia), 250 Camberwell Road, Camberwell, Victoria 3124, Australia
(a division of Pearson Australia Group Pty Ltd) • Penguin Books India Pvt Ltd, 11 Community
Centre, Panchsheel Park, New Delhi–110 017, India • Penguin Group (NZ), 67 Apollo Drive,
Rosedale, North Shore 0632, New Zealand (a division of Pearson New Zealand Ltd) • Penguin Books
(South Africa) (Pty) Ltd, 24 Sturdee Avenue, Rosebank, Johannesburg 2196, South Africa

Penguin Books Ltd, Registered Offices: 80 Strand, London WC2R 0RL, England

Copyright © 2009 by James Thompson
First edition: WSOY 2009
First American edition: G. P. Putnam's Sons 2010
All rights reserved. No part of this book may be reproduced, scanned, or distributed in any printed or
electronic form without permission. Please do not participate in or encourage piracy of copyrighted
materials in violation of the author's rights. Purchase only authorized editions.
Published simultaneously in Canada

Library of Congress Cataloging-in-Publication Data

Thompson, James, date.
Snow angels / James Thompson.—1st American ed.
p.    cm.
ISBN 978-0-399-15617-5
1. Police—Finland—Fiction.   2. Murder—Investigation—Fiction.
3. Finland—Fiction.   I. Title.
PS3620.H675S66     2010                    2009030948
813'.6—dc22

Printed in the United States of America
1   3   5   7   9   10   8   6   4   2

BOOK DESIGN BY NICOLE LAROCHE

This is a work of fiction. Names, characters, places, and incidents either are the products of the author's
imagination or are used fictitiously, and any resemblance to actual persons, living or dead, businesses,
companies, events, or locales is entirely coincidental.

While the author has made every effort to provide accurate telephone numbers and Internet addresses
at the time of publication, neither the publisher nor the author assumes any responsibility for errors, or
for changes that occur after publication. Further, the publisher does not have any control over and does
not assume any responsibility for author or third-party websites or their content.

# SNOW ANGELS

# 1

I'M IN HULLU PORO, The Crazy Reindeer, the biggest bar and restaurant in this part of the Arctic Circle. It was remodeled not long ago, but pine boards line the walls and ceiling, like an old Finnish farmhouse. Nouveau rustic decor.

Even though it's early afternoon, a couple hundred people are here. The bar is crowded and noisy. It's minus forty degrees Celsius outside, too cold to ski. The rush of wind from racing downhill would cause instant frostbite on even the smallest patch of exposed skin. The lifts are closed, so people are drinking instead.

My wife, Kate, is the general manager of Levi Center, a complex of restaurants, bars, a two-hundred-room hotel and an entertainment arena that holds almost a thousand people. Hullu Poro is only part of a massive operation in the biggest ski resort in Finland, and Kate runs it all. I'm proud of her.

Kate is behind the bar, talking to Tuuli, the shift manager. I'm eavesdropping on their conversation because I'm a cop, and Kate may want to have Tuuli arrested.

"I think you played with the inventory on the computer," Kate says. "You transferred liquor to other sales points, made it look like it disappeared from other bars, but you brought the bottles here, sold them out of this bar and pocketed the money."

Tuuli smiles and replies in Finnish. In a calm voice, she unleashes an eloquent stream of vicious invective. Kate has no idea of the ways in which Tuuli has insulted her.

Kate is five foot ten and slim. She's wearing jeans and a cashmere sweater. Her long cinnamon hair is swept up in a chignon. Men around the bar sneak glances at her.

"Please speak English so I can understand you," Kate says. "If you can't explain where the liquor went, you're fired. I'm considering pressing charges against you."

Tuuli's face is unreadable. "You don't know what you're talking about."

Kate is an expert in ski resort management. The owners of Levi Center wanted to expand the resort, so they brought her here to Finland from Aspen a year and a half ago to oversee the changes.

"I checked the dates and times on the computer system," Kate says. "The inventory transfers are consistent with times you were on duty. No one else could have done it. Six hundred euros worth of liquor went missing last month. You've been working here for three months. Want me to check the other two months?"

Tuuli mulls it over. "If you give me a week's pay and a letter of recommendation," she says, "I'll resign without protesting to the union."

Kate folds her arms. "No severance pay, no letter. If you file a protest, I'll prosecute."

Tuuli fingers a bottle of Johnny Walker on the shelf. The dull shine of her eyes tells me some of the stolen booze has been going down her throat. I know drunks. She's considering bludgeoning Kate with the bottle. She glances at me and I shake my head. Tuuli takes her hand off the bottle and tries the conciliatory approach. "Let's sit down and talk about this."

Kate signals to the bouncer at the front door and he comes over. "This conversation is over," she says. "Take Tuuli to get her things, then escort her out. She's banned from the bar."

"You're a cunt," Tuuli says.

Kate smiles. "And you're unemployed. You're also banned from every bar in Levi owned by this firm."

That's most of them. In effect, Tuuli is ostracized. She clenches her teeth and fists. *"Vitun huora."* Fucking whore.

Kate looks at the bouncer. "Get her out of here."

He puts a hand on Tuuli's shoulder and guides her away.

When Kate turns to me, she looks ice-calm. "I have to do a couple things in the office, I'll just be a few minutes."

I lean on the bar while I wait for her. A tourist asks Jaska, the bartender, "Just how far north are we?"

Jaska puts on the condescending face he reserves for foreigners. "You Australians aren't too good with . . . " he can't find the word and reverts to Finnish. *"Maantiede.* Drive that way for one day and you reach the Barents Sea, the end of the world." He's pointing west.

"Some Finns aren't too good with geography either," I say. "That way is toward Sweden." I turn ninety degrees. "The North Pole is that way." I point east. "Russia is over there. We're a hundred miles inside the Arctic Circle."

"Inspector Vaara and I went to high school together," Jaska says. "He got better grades than me."

"Thanks for the lesson," the Aussie says. "It's hard to get oriented when it's dark all the time. You're a policeman?"

"Yeah."

"Have one on me officer. What are you drinking?"

"Lapin Kulta."

"What's that?"

"Beer. We had a gold rush in the Arctic a little over a hundred years ago, and the brand name means 'The Gold of Lapland.'"

Jaska makes drinks for the tourists and chats about skiing conditions. It's supposed to warm up to minus fifteen tomorrow, still bitter cold, but safe enough so that with proper clothing skiers can hit the slopes again.

It's good for me to make my presence felt here, to discourage locals whose idea of a good time is to get drunk and beat up or otherwise harass tourists. I look to the other side of the room. The Virtanen brothers are here, prime candidates for such behavior. By the end of the night, like as not, they'll pull knives on each other. One of these days one will kill the other, and the survivor will die of loneliness.

Jaska hands me my beer. *"Jotain muuta?"* Anything else?

"A ginger ale for Kate."

While Jaska gets it for her, I go over to the Virtanen brothers' table. "Kimmo, Esa, how's it going?"

The brothers look sheepish. My presence makes them nervous. "Fine Kari," Esa says. "How's your gorgeous American wife?"

My marriage to a foreigner causes suspicion and consternation among the less progressive thinkers of our small community, but also envy, because of Kate's success and good looks.

"She's good. How are your mom and dad?"

"Mom can't speak since the stroke, and—you know how he is—Dad is Dad," Esa says, and Kimmo nods drunken agreement.

Esa and Kimmo and I grew up in the same neighborhood. Esa

means their father has been drunk for weeks. Every winter he stays tanked on cheap Russian medical alcohol through *kaamos*, the dark time, until spring, and even then his sobriety is measured only in relation to his alcohol-induced winter coma. I wonder if their mother can't speak, or if she's so worn out that she has nothing left to say. "Give them my best. You two stay out of trouble tonight."

Kate comes out from the back room. I get our drinks and we go to a table in the nonsmoking section.

I set her ginger ale on the table in front of her.

*"Kiitos."* Thank you. She can't speak Finnish yet, but she tries to use the few words and phrases she knows. "I could use a beer right now," she says, "but I guess I'm going to have to wait seven months for my next one."

Kate is pregnant with our first child. She told me two weeks ago while we celebrated our birthdays. We were born two days shy of eleven years apart, on opposite sides of the world.

Kate has put away her tough facade. She's trembling. "Tuuli," she says, "is not a pleasant person."

"She's a thief. Why didn't you have me arrest her?"

"Recovering the small amount she stole doesn't balance against the bad press associated with theft by an employee. Word will get around. That's why I fired her in front of Jaska. If anyone else is stealing, they'll stop."

"You have the day off tomorrow?" I ask. "You could use one."

Kate manages a coquettish smile. "I'm going skiing."

I don't want her to, but can't think of a reasonable objection. "Do you think you should?"

She takes my hand. Before I met Kate, I didn't like public displays of affection, but now I can't remember why. "I'm pregnant," she says, "not crippled."

In fact, we're both slightly crippled. Me from a gun shot, Kate from a skiing accident that shattered her hip. We both limp. "Okay, I'll go ice fishing."

She closes her eyes for a second, stops smiling and rubs her temples.

"You feeling all right?" I ask.

She sighs. "When I first came to Finland to interview for my job, it was summer. The sun was up twenty-four hours a day. Everyone here seemed so happy. I met you. They offered me a lot of money to run Levi, a great career opportunity. The Arctic Circle seemed exotic, an exciting place to live."

She looks down at the table. Kate isn't given to complaining. I want to know what's on her mind, so I prod her. "What changed?"

"This winter, I feel like the cold and dark will never end. I get it now that people weren't happy, just drunk. It makes me depressed. It's terrible. Being pregnant in Finland seems scary, makes me homesick for the States. I don't know why."

It's two thirty P.M. on December sixteenth. We won't see daylight again until Christmas day, and then only a glimmer. She's right. That's the way things are here in winter. A bunch of depressed hard drinkers freezing in an endless night. *Kaamos* is tough on everyone. I can see how being pregnant here would make her feel vulnerable and frightened.

My cell phone rings. "Vaara."

"It's Valtteri. Where are you?"

"In Hullu Poro with Kate. What's up?"

He doesn't speak.

"Valtteri?"

"There's been a murder, and I'm looking at the body."

"Tell me who and where."

"I'm pretty sure it's Sufia Elmi, that black movie star. It's bad. She's in a field on Aslak's place, about thirty yards off the road."

"Anybody there with you?"

"Antti and Jussi. They were the responding officers."

"Anything that requires immediate attention, like a suspect?"

"No, I don't think so."

"Then seal off the crime scene and wait for me." I hang up.

"Problem?" Kate asks.

"You could say that. Somebody's been murdered in a snowfield on Aslak Haltta's reindeer farm."

"You mean where we met?"

"Yeah."

She looks at me and I read pain in her eyes. "I wish you didn't have to go," she says.

I didn't realize how much she needs me right now, and I don't want to leave her. "Me too. Can we talk about this later?"

She nods but looks sad as I kiss her good-bye.

# 2

I STEP OUTSIDE INTO the dark, and the cold makes my face burn. I take a deep breath to clear my mind, feel the hair in my nostrils freeze, check my watch. It's two fifty-two P.M. I call Esko Laine, the provincial medical examiner, tell him there's been a murder and to meet me at the crime scene. He's getting ready to go to sauna, sounds a little drunk and less than pleased.

The car skitters on the ice as I pull out of Hullu Poro's parking lot. I light a cigarette and crack the window, despite it being minus forty. Nicotine and cold are a good combination for thinking.

Finland has a population of only five and a half million people, but a lot of violent crime. Per capita, our murder rate is about the same as most American big cities. The overwhelming majority of our murders are intimate events. We kill the people we love, our husbands and wives, brothers and sisters, parents and friends, almost always in drunken rages.

This is different. In a country as sensitive to insinuations of racism as Finland, the murder of a black, female public figure will explode across national headlines. It's never happened before. If the actress, Sufia Elmi, has been murdered, I've got a big problem.

Finns are sensitive about race relations because by and large we're closet racists. As I once explained to Kate, it's not the overt racism of the American kind she's accustomed to, but a quiet racism. The passing-over of foreigners for promotions, a general disregard and disdain. I compared it to politics. Americans ramble on about politics but have a low voter turnout. Finns seldom talk about politics, but around eighty percent vote in presidential elections. We don't talk about hatred, we hate in silence. It's our way. We do everything in silence.

I've heard jokes about Sufia, local rednecks snickering over their beers, talking about how they'd like to do it with the knockout nigger movie star, but never anything threatening. If we're lucky, Sufia's killer is a tourist and we can avoid cultural implications. I hope it's a German. Germans are a petty hatred I inherited from my grandparents, who despised them for burning down half of Finnish Lapland during World War II.

During the war, my grandmother found a German soldier frozen to death on a mountainside and dragged him down to show her friends. She told me it was the happiest day of her life. In my work, I find them a terrible annoyance. German tourists will steal anything. Silverware, salt and pepper shakers, toilet paper.

I know a little about Sufia from the newspapers. Looks as much as talent have earned her a minor career as a B-movie starlet in Finnish film, and she's wintering here in Levi. The first time I saw her, I found myself staring. I was embarrassed at first, but then I noticed she inspired that reaction in everyone, even women.

Sufia wore a cocktail dress that didn't do much to conceal spectacular breasts. Her waist was so small I could have wrapped my hands around it, and high heels accented the slender legs of a gazelle. Her black skin was flawless and her angelic face bore a combination of youth, beauty and innocence. She had obsidian eyes and a look of perpetual amusement that charmed everyone around her.

Sufia is, or was, a physical anomaly, so beautiful that it didn't seem possible for a creature like her to exist. What seemed a gift may have drawn the wrong kind of attention and gotten her killed. The first inclination of so many people in this world, when confronted by beauty, is to destroy it.


I PULL OFF THE road onto the drive leading into Aslak Haltta's reindeer farm, park next to Valtteri's squad car and get ready for the hours I'm going to spend in the cold processing the crime scene. A winter field uniform is wadded up in the backseat of my Saab. Marine-blue police coveralls, they're lined and heavy, should keep me warm enough to do my job. I pull them on over my jeans, sweater and a layer of thermal underwear.

The neighborhood I grew up in starts on the other side of the road, about two hundred yards away. It will have to be canvassed during the investigation. No doubt my parents will enjoy acting like they're being accused of murder.

All I can see from here is snow. Valtteri's headlights are on to illuminate the crime scene, so I leave mine on too. They cut a swath through the darkness, and I see Valtteri standing twenty yards ahead of me with Jussi, Antti and Aslak. I leave the comfort of the heated car and take the two fishing-tackle boxes I use for a crime kit from the trunk.

Valtteri wades toward me through the snow. It's deep, frozen hard on the surface but powdery underneath, and trudging through it makes him lurch until he reaches the driveway. "Don't go over there yet," he says.

"Is it that bad?"

"Just take a second and brace yourself."

Valtteri is a devout Laestadian and to my mind overobsessed with his strict, revivalist version of Lutheranism, but he's a good man and a good officer. If having eight kids and going to church every Sunday and most evenings makes him happy, it's okay by me. I turn on a flashlight and start toward the crime scene.

When I get about five yards away, I see a naked corpse embedded in the snow. I'm certain it's Sufia Elmi. When I see what's been done to her, I understand why Valtteri warned me. I've investigated more than a few homicides, but never seen anything so cruel. I set down the fishing-tackle boxes and take a moment to steady myself.

Judging by the indentations in the snow, it looks like the killer parked, then either dragged Sufia or forced her to crawl away from the car. The snow is about three feet deep and she's sunk about half that distance into it. She managed to thrash enough to make a snow angel. Her black body is ensconced in white snow stained with red blood. In places, blood has spattered and sprayed two yards away from her. Her corpse is starting to cool, and silver frost is forming on her dark skin, making it shimmer.

A car pulls off the road and I figure it's Esko the coroner. The responding officers, Antti and Jussi, are standing there shivering, even though, like me, they have on heavy winter field uniforms and thick hats and gloves. They're looking useless and might pollute the crime scene tramping around, moving to keep warm. I tell Jussi to walk back up to where the driveway meets the road and look for discarded evidence. If there is any, it will be easy to find with the glare of his flashlight on unbroken snow.

Antti is our best artist. I take graph paper and a pencil from a tackle box and tell him to make sketches of the crime scene, not an easy task in this bitter cold. He puts chemical hand warmers inside his gloves to keep his fingers from getting stiff and starts drawing.

Esko comes over and nods hello, doesn't speak. I tell him to take a look around.

I get two cameras out of the tackle boxes, one film and one digital, a couple external flash units and a tape recorder. Winter here is an endless night, but the snow reflects what little light there is and casts everything a dim murky gray. I use a Leica M3 to shoot film photos of the surroundings. Old Leicas are well made and don't use batteries, so they almost never fail because of cold-weather conditions.

Snow photography isn't easy. If you use lights or flashes at more than a forty-five-degree angle, everything disappears in the glare. It has to be done with polarizing filters and lights at the level of the snow. I give the cameras to Valtteri. "You know what to do, right?" I ask.

Valtteri nods, starts setting up the external flash units. "I was going to take my boys deer hunting tomorrow," he says. "Now I don't think I have the stomach for it."

I wouldn't either. "Take photos with both cameras," I say. "I want the snow as intact as possible so evidence doesn't get mashed up in it, so try to walk in your own footprints."

I rub my gloved hands together, try to warm them up. It's seldom this cold, even here in the lower part of the Arctic Circle, and it creates an odd sensation. There's a feeling of both heightened and deprived senses. Exposed parts of the body first burn, then ache, then go numb. The senses of touch and smell disappear. The cold makes my eyes run and the tears freeze on my cheeks. I have to squint and it's difficult to see. Nothing moves, birds don't sing.

There would be silence, but cold has a sound of its own. The branches of trees freeze solid and crack under the weight of snow with sounds like muted gunshots. The snow freezes so hard that its surface contracts and takes on a pebbled texture. It crackles underfoot, even when I think I'm standing still.

We're in a field about thirty yards east of the main road. A barn with a pen outside it for sick and birthing reindeer stands twenty yards to the north. Aslak's reindeer number in the thousands, and they've earned him a handsome living. His house, an expensive ranch-style brick, is another hundred yards northeast. Christmas lights in the distant windows wink on and off. To the south and west are only barren fields and icy forests.

The atmosphere is one of isolation, of desolation. It seems an ideal spot for a murder. I picture the murderer turning off the main road, killing his engine and cutting his headlights, gliding to a stop a little way down the drive. The sky is cloudy, no moon or stars illuminate the dark afternoon. The nearest homes are a football field away in one direction, two football fields in the other. The murderer had privacy and time. If he heard noise or saw lights, all he had to do was start his car and drive away before being spotted.

Aslak looks down at Sufia, leans on a shotgun, smokes a home-rolled cigarette. I guide him a few yards away from the body and light one myself. "See anything?"

"Not much. I came out to feed the dogs and saw headlights.

I went back and got my gun"—he holds up a Mossberg twelve-gauge pump—"and came over to see what was going on. I got here in time to see a car drive away. Then I saw her like this. I had my cell phone with me and called the police."

"What kind of car?"

Aslak seems unperturbed. I've known him since I was a kid. He's a *Saame* reindeer herder, an aboriginal Lapland Finn and a tough old bastard. "It was pretty far away, some kind of sedan."

"How long ago did it leave?"

Aslak checks his watch. "Fifty-two minutes."

I look at Valtteri. "You didn't set up roadblocks?"

"The only thing I could think to do was call you."

"And I asked you if anything required immediate attention."

Fuckup number one. If this case goes wrong, not just Valtteri will be blamed, but me as well, since I'm in charge. He's embarrassed and I don't press it.

Valtteri and I get some sticks and drive them into the snow. We spool out crime-scene tape and seal off a few yards of the tire tracks, then do the same in a ten-yard square around the body. Footprints span a fifteen-foot distance between the body and the tire tracks. We tape those off too, so we can make spray-wax casts later.

The driveway hasn't been plowed for a couple days and has a few inches of powdery snow on it. Under the right conditions, tire tracks are as individual and identifiable as fingerprints. These look crisp enough to get the manufacturer and model, but maybe not the specific set of tires. The footprints are in deep snow and won't yield much, but we might get a shoe size. Esko waits until we finish before he starts his examination.

Sufia is beautiful no longer. What's left of her tells the story of an agonizing death. My first task is to describe this horror in detail. It makes me feel sad, and inadequate, because the only person able to describe such depths of suffering would have been Sufia herself. Valtteri starts shooting pictures. The flash pops every few seconds and lights up the blood and snow and Sufia, and I feel like I'm living in a grainy black-and-white photograph.

I start the tape recorder, and Esko takes out a notebook and pen. I'll do a verbal description while he does a written one, for the same reason that Antti draws while Valtteri photographs, to rule out the chance of documentation being lost. I kneel down in the snow beside her. "Let me know if I miss anything."

He nods. I run the beam of my flashlight up and down her body and start.

"General observations. A nude female body. The victim is black. A cord"—I take off my glove, reach over and touch it—"of silk or similar synthetic material, is around her neck, and ligatures suggest it was used as a means of control. The snow is disturbed in a five-yard line between the tire tracks and the location of her body. It appears she either crawled or was dragged from the vehicle to her present location."

"Dragged, I think," Esko says.

"The snow is unbroken outside the immediate vicinity of the body and drag line. Her arms are raised at forty-five-degree angles over her head. Her legs are spread, and the indentations in the snow indicate that she thrashed around as her killer assaulted her. Evidence such as other weapons or her clothing would be readily visible were they present. They're not. The victim is mutilated. Her face is brutalized, but I recognize her. She's the actress Sufia Elmi. The words *neekeri huora*, nigger whore, have been cut into her stomach."

My worst fears are confirmed. This is a hate crime. It's hard to believe anyone could have hated her so much. The question, despite the words carved on her stomach, is what could have inspired this kind of hatred? Was it her race, her beauty, or something else?

"A half-liter Lapin Kulta beer bottle has been broken off at the neck and inserted, broken end first, by means of twisting and cutting, into the victim's vagina. No glass shards from the shattered bottle are evident. The victim was hit with a blunt instrument, which left a contusion on her forehead."

Esko stoops down beside me. "She was struck twice. Probably with a carpenter's hammer."

I nod. "Probably with a carpenter's hammer. Her eyes have been gouged out, maybe with the broken bottle. A superficial piece of skin from her right breast, about three by four inches, is sliced off and located beside the victim, near her left shoulder. There's a long deep cut across her lower abdomen. Her throat is slashed. The clean cuts suggest the killer used an edged weapon, not the beer bottle, to inflict those wounds."

"He left the piece of her breast," Esko says. "Not a trophy taker."

"At least three instruments appear to have been used to mutilate the victim, one blunt and heavy, as evidenced by the two blows to the head, and two sharp ones, one the beer bottle and the other an edged weapon."

"I'd guess a serrated hunting knife," Esko says.

"Have I missed anything?" I ask.

"I don't think so."

Something glints in the beam of my flashlight. I get down close to her. "What's this stuff on her face?"

"Where?"

I point out three small streaks. "By her nose, on her cheek."

"I don't know," Esko says.

"Think he spit on her?"

"It doesn't look viscous enough for saliva."

"It wouldn't even be noticeable if she was white. Hard to see it as it is. Make sure you get a sample for testing. Anything else?"

Esko shakes his head no. He takes her hands, careful to keep from disturbing the snow lodged under her manicured fingernails, looks them over and puts plastic bags around them. He takes blood samples from various areas in the snow around the body, and a sample of the liquid on her face. "Listen," he says, "I'm out of my depth, I've never handled anything like this. This is going to be international news and I'm afraid I'll fuck it up."

I appreciate his feelings. It's been a long time since I conducted a difficult murder investigation. Plus, it's near Christmas and four officers from our force of eight are on vacation. We don't even have an evening shift—we're taking turns being on call at night. Even our dispatcher is on vacation. It's an ideal time to commit a murder. A local would know this, and it bothers me.

"We have tire tracks," I say, "and the body will yield a lot of evidence. We'll solve this."

We kneel in the snow and look at each other for a few seconds, both at a loss for words. From the pen outside the barn, a pregnant reindeer looks on with indifference. Aslak stands not far away, rolling a cigarette. I want this not to have happened. I want to be at home with Kate, to lay my hand on her belly and imagine our child growing inside it. I look across the snowfield. Aslak's house is a shadow in the distance. Almost a year and a half ago, Kate and I met in his backyard.

The *Saame* people, Laplanders, suffer a lot of prejudice here, like Eskimos in Alaska. Every year on midsummer, Aslak throws a lavish party, invites friends, neighbors and the more prominent members of the community. Maybe it's a way of proving to himself and everybody else how much he's achieved despite the odds against him. Maybe it's his way of saying, "Fuck you, I'm *Saame* and I'm richer than you are." He has his own midsummer tradition: roasting a whole reindeer on a spit like other people roast wild boar. I've never seen anyone else do that.

Kate and I met at Aslak's party. It was getting late, but this is the land of the midnight sun and in summer, especially after a few drinks, it's easy to lose track of time because of the constant daylight. It feels like early evening all night long. I heard a voice speaking English and saw it belonged to a tall redhead across the lawn. She was the most beautiful woman I had ever seen. Kate was standing in a crowd, talking to a girl named Liisa, an assistant manager at Levi Center. Liisa and I had gone out a couple times a while back, but it never amounted to anything. I walked over. They were drunk and giddy.

"Kari, this is Kate Hodges," Liisa said. "She's in Finland interviewing to be the new general manager of Levi Center. Kate, this is Kari Vaara. He's the chief of police here. His name means Rock Danger."

Kate burst out laughing. "Rock Danger, like a name in a bad movie?"

I had never thought about it. The idea made me laugh too. "It could mean that. Kari means rock, scar, shoal or reef. Vaara means hill, danger, risk or pitfall. So my name could be Reef Hill or Scar Pitfall. However you look at it, it sounds stupid in English. I promise it sounds better in Finnish."

"You speak excellent English," Kate said.

"Kari is a smart guy," Liisa said. "He speaks Swedish and Russian too."

"My Russian is weak," I said.

"I was just telling Kate about midsummer," Liisa said. "I explained that midsummer marks the summer solstice and is also Finnish Flag Day, that we have a tradition of going to sauna and having a big bonfire at midnight. Care to add anything?"

"Midsummer is the longest day of the year and a pagan festival of light," I said. "It was Christianized into a celebration of the nativity of St. John the Baptist. That's why in Finnish it's called *Juhannus*. For pagans, it was a potent magical night, mostly for young women seeking men or wanting children or both. The burning of the bonfire is associated with beliefs concerning fertility, cleansing of the soul and the banishing of evil spirits."

"Rock Danger," Kate said, "you sound like an educated man."

I smiled. "I'm a font of useless information."

Kate pulled Liisa away a few steps. They whispered back and forth. I stood in the middle of a group of drunk people munching roasted reindeer and potato salad off paper plates, watched Kate and thought again how beautiful she was. She and Liisa finished their palaver and came back. "So this pagan thing," Kate said. "Does it mean women can ask men out on midsummer?"

"I'm certain it does," I said.

Alcohol had worked Kate's courage up and, during their chat, Liisa had tried to teach her to speak a sentence in Finnish. *"Komea mies,"* she said, *"lähtisitkö ulos ja pane minua syömään?"*

Her pronunciation was strange, but what she said was clear enough. People around us burst out laughing. I felt my face turn red. She meant to say, "Handsome man, would you like to go out to dinner with me?" but what came out was something like, "Handsome man, would you like to go out and fuck me for dinner?"

Kate's face turned red too. "What did I say wrong?" she asked.

Liisa whispered it to her.

Kate's eyes fluttered like she was going to cry. She walked away from the people still laughing at her.

I went after her. She turned and looked at me, humiliated.

"I'd love to take you to dinner," I said.

Then she saw the humor, managed a smile.

"They're going to light the bonfire soon," I said. "Want to go watch it with me?"

"That would be nice," she said.

She took my hand, it surprised me. We started walking. "You limp," she said. "How come?"

"Somebody shot me. How come you limp?"

"I fell."

We held hands and watched the bonfire in silence. Afterward, I asked Kate if she would like to come over to my house for a drink.

"Where do you live?" she asked.

"About a *poronkusema* from here."

"How far is that?"

"A *poronkusema* is a Laplander measure of distance that means 'reindeer piss.' A reindeer can't urinate when it pulls a sled, and it gets a clogged urinary tract if you don't stop and let it pee once in a while. A *poronkusema* is about ten miles, around thirty minutes of riding on a sled."

"You really are a font of useless information," she said.

We went to my place. Six weeks later we were engaged. Nine months later we were married.

It's hard to believe that this place, the site of an event that led to such happiness for me, is now the scene of such tragedy. I look down again at Sufia's mangled corpse. "Esko . . . "

"Yeah?"

I need to ask the question but I'm afraid to hear the answer. "How much of what happened do you think she was conscious for?"

"She's such a mess that I can't say without an autopsy. I've been wondering the same thing. Still, it could have been worse."

"How?"

He stands up and brushes the snow off his pants. "She could have lived through it."

I look down at Sufia the snow angel. Her face changes and I imagine Kate naked and slaughtered, dead in a snowfield. The wave of sadness I felt earlier renews itself, and for the first time in my life I'm sorry that Finland has no death penalty.

# 3

THE CRIME SCENE HAS been processed. Sufia Elmi's body has been taken away. We've been going inside Aslak's house once in a while to warm up, but still I'm frozen to the bone. I'm the last one to leave and I stand alone shivering. I look up. Wind has chased the clouds away and the night is starry. There's enough light to see without my flashlight and I flick it off.

The black-and-yellow crime-scene tape looks out of place on a reindeer farm. The spot where Sufia's body lay is a bloody hole gouged in the snow, like an empty eye socket. The scene will be torn to bits soon, when forest animals smell the blood and come looking. It doesn't matter. It will be buried in fresh snow before long anyway.

Years ago, when I was working on my master's thesis, I went to New York for a semester as an exchange student. What struck me most was the sky. On that side of the world, so far away from the North Pole, the sky is flat and gray, a one-dimensional universe. Here, the sky is arched, and there's almost no pollution. In spring and fall the sky is dark blue or violet, and sunsets last for hours. The sun turns into a dim orange ball that transforms clouds into silver-rimmed red and violet towers. In winter, twenty-four hours a day, uncountable stars outline the vaulted ceiling of the great cathedral we live in. Finnish skies are the reason I believe in God.

It's just before ten P.M. Hours spent in the cold have left me so numb that it's hard to move. My bad knee has gone so stiff that I'm dragging my left leg more than walking on it. I limp to the top of the drive.

On the other side of the road and down a narrow lane is a neighborhood of sixteen houses called Marjakylä, Berry-Village. I walk the two hundred yards, as I have so many times, down the unpaved road. Snow banked up from plowing makes walls on both sides of me and they funnel me into the village. The people that live here seldom come or go. They exist in their own little world, year after year, in little wooden homes. The only thing that changes is their ages.

I go from house to house and explain that there's been a murder. People raise their eyebrows and say *"oho,"* our language's expression of surprise, then tell me they've seen nothing. Canvassing brings me closer to my parents and their neighbors, the people of my childhood.

Big Paavo's yard is lit up by work lamps that reflect off the snow and negate the effect of strings of Christmas lights scattered around. He's in a shed with a kerosene heater, and, as usual, he's building something. A two-stroke engine with a bad gasket stinks from burning oil and clunks, because one of the pistons isn't firing. I ask what he's working on. A clothes press, so his wife won't have to iron sheets. He's seen nothing.

I knock on the Virtanens' door. Through the front window, I see Kimmo and Esa's mother, Pirkko, sitting in an armchair. She doesn't move. I test the door and it's open, the place smells of must and urine. Both of them are incommunicado, Pirkko from her stroke, her husband Urpo because he's passed out on the kitchen floor. I say hello to Pirkko. Her eyes flicker recognition but she doesn't answer, so I leave. I'll have to speak to their sons about them.

Next I try Eero and Martta. They aren't home and if true to form are out walking.

Christmas candles burn in a front window. Tiina and Raila invite me in, but I know better than to accept. Tiina is forty-two years old and anorexic. All her teeth have fallen out as a result, and she can't afford dentures, but she's learned to smile in such a way that you can't tell. She walks around the village pushing a baby stroller with a doll inside it, and has since she was a teenager.

Raila, Tiina's mother, is an alcoholic. She was sober for twenty years, until her fortieth birthday party, when she decided to have just one drink. For the past thirty years, she's lived in a nightmare of alcohol psychosis coupled with religious fervor. When I was a kid, she would stand outside our house, point in the front window and shriek. Mom would tell me to pay no attention and pretend like it wasn't happening. I ask if they've seen unfamiliar cars today.

"This is a day of desolation," Raila says. "My life is a vale of tears."

Tiina smiles her funny smile. "We've been watching TV all day."

I save my parents for last. Their house is the same as it was twenty-five years ago, except for the addition of indoor plumbing. No more freezing trips to the outhouse in the morning. No more cold showers in an underheated outbuilding shared with the neighbors. Mom and Dad fought about it for years. He refused because of the expense, although he always had booze money, but she finally wore him down.

As a little kid, because it was so cold in the outbuilding, I would go two weeks without washing if they let me, and sometimes I accidentally peed on myself because opening my pants in the freezing outhouse hurt so much that I would hold it for too long.

There must be fifteen clocks hanging on the walls. I don't know why my parents are so concerned with marking the time. The syncopated drumming of all those second hands makes me crazy. They haven't put up any Christmas decorations yet. They always wait until the last minute. We sit in the kitchen, and I explain about the murder.

"Mom, did you see or hear anything unusual today?" I ask.

Mom doesn't work, Dad never would let her. She still calls me by my pet name from childhood. *"Ei Pikkuinen"*—No, Little One—he says.

"What the hell did you expect your mother to hear?" Dad asks.

"I didn't expect anything. This is a normal part of a murder investigation."

Dad isn't bad when he's sober, but when he's drunk, he goes one of two ways, either euphoric or mean. "You think your mother has nothing better to do all day than sit by the window and watch what goes on outside?"

"I don't think that."

"So you think your mother killed a nigger woman on Aslak's farm?"

I wonder if he's going to take off his belt, like when I was a boy. "No, I don't think that either."

Dad pulls out one of his favorite expressions. *"Haista vittu,"* sniff cunt. A colorful way of telling me to go fuck myself. His sodden mind veers off in another direction. "You heard from your brothers?"

My three brothers all moved away as soon as they were old enough. "Not for a while."

"You'd think they'd at least call, after all we went through raising them. And you."

Dad the martyr. "Christmas is coming, you'll hear from them."

Mom asks me if I'd like something to eat, and I realize I'm famished. She warms up leftover *läskisoosi*, fat sauce, a childhood favorite made from pork strips like bacon but less salty, and ladles it over boiled potatoes.

While I eat, Mom gossips about the neighbors and chatters about how well my brother Timo is doing. Timo served seven months in prison for bootlegging when he was young, and ever since, Mom has overcompensated by talking about him like he's a saint.

Dad nurses a water glass half full of vodka in silence. I remember that my sister died thirty-two years ago today, that's why he's being such a prick.

The cold came late that year, but when it did, it hit hard. I was nine and Suvi was eight. Mom was a regular brood mare, five children in seven years. Dad wanted to go ice fishing. Suvi and I asked if we could come along and skate. Mom warned Dad that the ice was still too thin, but he hushed her up. "Kari will look after Suvi," he said.

A lot of snow had fallen, but it was dry powder. The wind had blown it off the lake, and the ice was as slick and clean as glass. The afternoon was starry, and out on the ice we could see almost as if we had daylight. Dad drilled a hole in the ice and sat on a crate, fishing and warming himself with a bottle of Three Lions whiskey.

I tried to take care of Suvi. We were skating fast, toward the middle of the lake, but I was holding her hand. I heard a sharp crack, felt a jerk on my arm, and she was gone. It took me a second to understand what had happened, and then I was scared the ice would break under me too. I crawled to where Suvi fell through, but she was already slipping away. The last I saw of Suvi alive was her little fists thrashing, beating at the ice.

I was too scared to go in after her, and Dad was too drunk, so we did nothing. He sat there crying, and I ran for help. They drilled holes in the ice and dredged under it with fishing nets. It didn't take long, she hadn't drifted far. When they pulled her out, she had a look of surprise more than pain frozen on her face.

I've always suspected that Dad blames me for Suvi's death. Maybe that's why he was so quick to use his belt on me. I suspect that I blame him too. Maybe Mom blames us both. I eat the last bite of *läskisoosi* and set my knife and fork down on the plate. Mom is silent now, they both look lost in thought. I tell her it was delicious and hug her good-bye. I give Dad's shoulder a squeeze and tell him I'll see him soon.

On the way back to my car, I see Eero and Martta returning from their evening stroll, bundled up against the bitter cold. Eero is over seventy, well dressed, dapper and schizophrenic. He lived with his mother until she died twenty years ago, and then he hired Martta as his housekeeper. Whether their relationship is sexual in nature remains a mystery, as does where he gets the money to have a housekeeper.

By outward appearance, Eero is homosexual. Martta is dwarfish, gray-haired and squat. I meet them at the top of the road, across from Aslak's drive. They're walking their dog, a Jack Russell terrier named Sulo. Sulo is dressed in a blue-and-red sweater and tiny felt boots. I ask them about today.

"I was talking to a friend on the phone this afternoon and saw a car pull out of Aslak's place," Eero says.

There's a phone booth by the side of the road. The phone is disconnected and has been for years. Eero spends hours standing in the cold, talking to imaginary friends, sometimes for so long that his breath forms a sheet of ice over the mouthpiece. Martta kept cutting the cord in the hopes that Eero would quit pumping coins into it. The phone company finally gave up repairing it, but left it there so Eero could talk into it.

"What kind of car?" I ask.

"BMW, BMW, BMW."

He repeats things sometimes. I'm not quite believing. "What model BMW?"

"A new sedan, 3 Series, 3 Series."

"You know BMWs that well?"

"I like cars."

Eero always had a memory like no one else I've ever met. I check to make sure it's still true. "Eero, can you remember May sixteenth, 1974?"

"Oh yes."

"What happened?"

"Nothing special. It was a Thursday, warm. Two catalogues came in the mail. Your father got drunk and wrecked his bicycle."

I remember that. I'm impressed. "What color was the BMW?"

"I was talking, not paying attention. Dark-colored."

"And it was new?"

"Pretty new anyway."

"Did you see who was driving?"

"Too dark. Didn't see, didn't see."

"Okay. Thank you very much." I reach down and give Sulo a pet. "Do you mind if I come back to ask you about it again?"

"Not at all," Eero says, "glad for the company."

Martta takes his hand. "You're always welcome in our home."

It's a good lead. I tramp off down the icy lane, shaking my head, picturing Eero taking the stand.

# 4

I HAVEN'T SHOVELED my driveway for a few days, and when I get home I have to shove the car door hard through the snow to get it open. I pop open the hood of the Saab and take out the battery. If I don't, the car won't start in the morning. I go inside, set the battery on the floor of the foyer, then shut the door behind me and lock out the world.

Like every good Finn, I take off my shoes before doing anything else. Kate still sometimes forgets to take hers off when she comes in, and I have to ask her. Wearing shoes in the home is a habit that I find barbaric. Christmas tree lights blink at me from across the room. Most Finns trim the tree closer to Christmas Eve, but Kate wanted to do things the American way, so ours is already up. I have to admit it's cheery.

I was married once before. After my divorce, I was single for thirteen years, made pretty good money and had nothing to spend it on, so I bought this house and surrounded myself with nice things. Expensive Danish blond-wood furniture, a thirty-two-inch flat-screen television I hardly ever watch, loads of books and CDs, the new Saab out in the driveway. I thought I was happy, but I was only content. I didn't know what happiness meant until I met Kate. Or maybe I'd forgotten. After seeing Sufia Elmi's slaughtered corpse, my happiness seems wrong.

I peel off my coveralls, dump my pistol and wallet on the coffee table, get a beer out of the fridge and flop down on the couch. Kate pads down the stairs in panties and an oversized T-shirt. She's almost as tall as me and a sinewy one hundred and twenty pounds. She's twenty-nine years old and despite her limp moves with grace and elegance. I'm forty, going gray at the temples and built like the hockey player I used to be. I feel bearish by comparison.

"Did I wake you?" I ask.

"I wasn't sleeping. I wanted to wait up for you."

She sits down next to me, gives me a kiss, grasps my stubby fingers with her slender ones. Her eyes are red and swollen.

"You okay?" I ask.

"I've been reading."

I don't press it. *Kaamos* is hard on everyone. We all get depressed this time of year. Plus, she's pregnant and the hormonal change can't help.

"What about you?" she asks.

I don't know where to begin. "Sufia Elmi—the Somali girl in those bad movies—was murdered."

"You don't look good," she says.

I rub my face, try to smooth away the tension. "Somebody mutilated her, carved 'nigger whore' in her stomach."

She pulls her legs up under her and puts an arm around me.

"I've seen her in Hullu Poro. She was so beautiful." Kate's pronunciation of Finnish words is soft and strange, as if a sparrow tried to caw like a crow.

"I've seen murders before, bad car wrecks, nothing like this."

"Do you have any idea who or why?"

I take a swallow of beer. "Sex crime, race crime, maybe both. It's hard to say yet."

She looks at me, reads my pain. I don't want her to see it but don't know how to hide it. "I just don't get how one human being could do something like that to another."

She snuggles up closer. "Want to talk about it?"

We sit in silence for a minute.

"Was it really where we met?" she asks.

"It was in the snowfield about a hundred yards in front of Aslak's house, across from Marjakylä. After we processed the crime scene, I had to canvass my parents' neighborhood. That was a fucking thrill. Dad acted like I accused Mom of murder."

"He's always so polite when I'm around."

"You're a foreigner. He's afraid of what he doesn't understand. You intimidate him, and when you're around he stays on his best behavior to hide it."

She takes this in. "Something about him scares me too. How drunk was he?"

"Pretty drunk."

She looks pissed off on my behalf. Kate's father is dead now, but he was a drunk, so I don't need to say more. Kate had a tough childhood. She grew up in Aspen, Colorado. Her mother died of cancer when Kate was thirteen. Her brother and sister were seven and eight at the time.

The death broke her father's spirit, and although he wasn't

mean like my dad, he wasn't home much, spent his evenings in bars. Kate had to raise her brother and sister, cook, clean, beg her father for grocery money to keep them fed.

Her father managed to do one good thing for her. He was a mechanic, worked at a ski resort maintaining the lifts, and he got her free skiing lessons and lift passes. She became a fantastic downhill skier. She won several key events over the years and dreamed of competing in the Olympics.

When she was seventeen, she was in a race and going nearly a hundred miles an hour. She took a fall, broke her hip and spent weeks in traction. End of dream. She couldn't compete anymore and lost the only thing she loved. Still, she toughed it out, got a scholarship and an education, made herself into a successful career woman in the ski resort management industry.

Thinking about Kate's family makes me remember Suvi again. I've never told Kate about her. Maybe I'm afraid she'll blame me for Suvi's death too.

"Want me to make you something to eat?" Kate asks.

"Mom fed me."

She wraps her arms around me, kisses my eyes. "Let's go upstairs then."

Kate takes my hand and guides me to the bed. She crawls naked on top of me. Long white limbs tangle around me, long red hair hangs in my face. Despite today, I can't help but want her. I always want her. Maybe witnessing the aftermath of Sufia's death makes me want to celebrate life.

Kate's not showing yet, but kissing her belly reminds me of our child growing inside her. She presses her mouth to mine, runs her tongue along my lips. I feel myself stiffen and hear her breath go ragged.

We make love, and I fall asleep. The next thing I know Kate is shaking me awake. "You were having a bad dream."

The image is still lingering behind my eyes. I was nine years old, in the bedroom I shared with my brother. Sufia Elmi sat in a chair by my bed. My sister Suvi stood beside her. My father pulled my pants down and beat me with a belt. Sufia and Suvi held hands and looked on. Sufia, naked and mangled, mouthed words I couldn't understand.

"What were you dreaming?" Kate asks.

"I don't remember."

"I was having the most wonderful dream," she says. "I was sixteen, before I broke my hip. I was in a ski competition. It felt like I was flying."

I dread waking up in the morning and look at the clock. It's two A.M. I pull Kate close and try to get whatever sleep I can.

# 5

THE ALARM CLOCK GOES off at five thirty. Kate doesn't stir. I have a slice of rye bread with sausage and cheese and wait for the coffee. I haven't slept enough, but the investigation has to get rolling.

I pull on wool socks and a robe, go out on the back porch and look at the stars while I have a cigarette and drink coffee. The smoke doesn't bother me, but the freezing air takes my breath and makes me cough. The thermometer on the porch wall reads minus thirty-two. It's warming up.

I go back inside and get dressed. I usually wear jeans and a sweater, but today I might need to look official, so I put on a suit and drive to work through deserted, ice-laden streets.

It's a typical small-town police station. Six drunk tanks and two holding pens, my office and a room for the dispatcher, a common room with a couple desks and computers for whomever is on duty. I want the crime report done before the morning briefing.

I sit at my desk and write it, then set it aside until later. If

I wait a few hours before entering it into the Finnish crime incident database, it will be too late for newspapers to pick up on it, and I can delay the media storm for another day. I want Sufia's parents to be notified before releasing the report.

Cell phones are a difficulty in this regard. When people witness crime scenes, or learn of crimes and their details, they often call tabloids and sell information for a nominal reward. When canvassing Marjakylä, I didn't mention the name of the murder victim. Only the investigating officers, Kate, Aslak, Esko and my parents know Sufia was killed. I've told them all to keep quiet about it and managed to stanch the problem.

I download the crime-scene photos from the digital camera into the computer system, so we can look at them during the briefing, then start setting the investigation in motion.

Technically, I should go through the chain of command and call the regional police commander, but I don't like him and opt not to. The national chief of police and I have a history, so I call him instead. He's not in yet, so I ask for his cell phone number and call him at home.

He answers. "Ivalo."

"This is Kari Vaara, in Kittilä. Sorry to call so early."

"I'm shaving."

"It can't wait, I've got a situation you need to be aware of."

Silence.

"We have a murder investigation in progress. A young woman named Sufia Elmi was abducted and killed around two P.M. yesterday. She's a Somali refugee and she's also a minor movie star, the kind that's in the tabloids all the time."

"Fuck."

"Yeah, but it gets worse. The murder has the characteristics of a sex crime, but also of a race crime. It could be both. The girl was butchered. The killer carved the words 'nigger whore' on her stomach."

"Media frenzy."

"That's why I called."

"Got a suspect?"

I hear rushing water. He's taking a piss while we talk. "I have tire tracks and a lot of forensics."

"I can send a homicide unit from Helsinki or Rovaniemi. You know how it is around Christmas. I have to check who's available."

I'm not getting it yet. "You don't need to, I've got a good start."

"No doubt you have, but still, maybe you could use some help."

I'm surprised. No one has ever called my professional capability into question before. "Thanks, but I don't need it."

The rushing water stops, his toilet flushes. "Are you sure you want this case?"

"Why would you ask me that?"

"It's something you should consider."

"Of course I want it."

"Think about it. Maybe you should step aside for this one."

Finland is a provincial little country, but people in Helsinki act like they're sophisticates, while we here in Lapland are backwards-ass country shitheads. Sometimes they call us *poron purija*, reindeer biters.

"It's my jurisdiction," I say, "my case." My voice is getting louder. I tell myself to calm down.

"There's a lot riding on this," he says, "a lot of potential embarrassment for both of us. You might be out of your league."

"I've conducted other murder investigations."

"Years ago."

I call him by his first name and work the personal angle. "Jyri, you decorated and promoted me. Don't tell me you don't think I can do this."

"I decorated you for bravery, not your crime-solving ability."

I want to tell him to go fuck himself, but don't.

"I promoted you because you deserved it," he says, "but also because that bullet in your knee ruined you as a patrol officer. It was promote you or retire you. I did you a favor."

He did me no fucking favor, I earned it. I was a beat cop in Helsinki and answered an armed robbery call at Tillander, the most expensive jewelry store in the city, on Aleksander Street in the heart of the downtown shopping district. It was the middle of a gorgeous summer afternoon.

My partner and I got there fast, arrived as two thieves exited the store carrying backpacks weighed down with jewelry. They pulled guns and one fired a shot at us, then they separated and ran. I chased one of them down a street crowded with shoppers and tourists.

All of a sudden, the thief stopped, turned and fired. My pistol was in my hand but he surprised me. I was still in mid-sprint when the bullet hit me and blew out my left knee, which I had already wrecked playing hockey in high school. I sprawled on the ground. He should have kept running but, for what reason I can't imagine, instead he decided to kill me.

When he came toward me, I got a shot off first and the bullet caught him in the side. He went down, and for a second we both just sat there on the sidewalk, looking at each other. He raised his pistol to fire again. I told him to lower his gun. He didn't, and I blew his head off.

It turned out that he and his partner were gangsters from

Estonia on a crime spree. They had come from Tallinn to Helsinki on a day cruise. I guess they expected to rob Tillander and go home on the same boat that evening.

"If you take this case away from me," I say, "you're taking my career away with it. You might as well have retired me."

"Your career opportunities ended when you left Helsinki for Kittilä. You requested the transfer, why complain about it now?"

After the shooting, the department made a big deal about it, gave me a medal and promoted me to detective. Later, when I was promoted to inspector, I requested a transfer back here to Kittilä, my hometown. He thinks this is about my pride, but he's wrong, this is about my duty. "You either retire me right now or back off my case. Which is it?"

He can take a chance on me and the case, or get rid of me and explain why he forced out a hero cop. Bad press. I wait while he thinks.

"Okay, you win. However, should you decide that you want a homicide team to step in, I'll oblige you. I don't care who does it, I just want the case solved fast."

"Fair enough."

"Anything else I can do to help?"

"Locate Sufia Elmi's parents. Have a pastor and an officer go to their home and inform them about the murder." In this country, Lutheran clergy accompany the police when they notify relatives of the deceased. "And the autopsy will be later today. I could use twenty-four-hour turnaround on DNA sampling."

"Done. Call me with daily progress reports. And Kari, this is on your fucking head now."

I hang up, so pissed off I can barely breathe.

———

AT EIGHT A.M., I go out to the common room. Antti and Jussi, the only patrol officers I've got because the others are all on Christmas vacation, are lounging around drinking coffee. Their field uniform coveralls are rumpled. Antti looks so much like a stereotypical Finn that it's almost comical. Blond hair and a face shaped like a frying pan. Jussi is dark-headed, heavyset and serious. They look sleepy.

Valtteri looks tired too. Maybe he couldn't sleep after seeing Sufia's body. He's wearing his newest dress sergeant's uniform, starched and pressed. He knows today is important.

I lean against a cluttered desk. "I guess you all know this murder is the biggest case our department has ever handled. We're the crime team and the whole country will be watching, so we're not allowed to make mistakes."

"I've never investigated a murder before," Jussi says.

"You went to school. Just do what you were taught."

When I was coming up in the force, you just had to attend the police academy for a couple months. Now you need a bachelor's degree to be a cop. Antti and Jussi are young guys in their twenties: educated police officers.

"Besides," I say, "we have some good evidence, this might not be a tough one."

"My winter vacation starts the day after tomorrow," Antti says, "I'm off for two weeks."

"Not anymore. Your vacation is canceled until this is over."

He raises his voice a little. "Why?"

"Because it's your job. Other people are already on vacation, there's nobody else to do it. You were the responding officers, it's your case."

"I've got plane tickets to Thailand."

He's giving me a hard time because Sufia's murder will interfere with him fucking Thai whores on Christmas. "Sorry," I say.

I dim the lights, go to the computer and set the PowerPoint slide show at ten-second intervals. Images from the crime scene flash on the wall.

"I canvassed Marjakylä last night. It would have been the easiest thing in the world for someone who lives there to kill Sufia, drive the two hundred yards across the road and just slip back into his house." I hand Valtteri my notebook. "I want you to start by checking alibis."

He takes out a pocket flashlight and flips through it. "Your father is in here."

"Him too."

An image of Sufia's face and torso comes up and I freeze it. "We've got mutilation, including a broken beer bottle stuffed into her vagina. He may have raped her before he dumped her and killed her. Her eyes are gouged out, like he didn't want her to see him. It could mean he was ashamed. He cut off a piece of her breast."

Jussi looks sickened and interrupts me. "Who the fuck could do something like that?"

"He may be a psychotic sexual predator who hates women. We haven't had much in the way of serial murderers in this country, but you never know. If it is and he's a local, this is probably his first kill or we would recognize his modus operandi, and we can expect more murders to follow at intervals."

"There's a typical profile for this kind of serial killer, if it is one," Antti says.

"Yep. Typical serial killers are male, age twenty to thirty. Their usual motives are sex, power, domination and control. They roughly fall into two categories—organized and disorganized. The motive for an organized killer is most often rape. Organized killers usually have above-average intelligence and plan their crimes methodically. They tend to abduct their victims, kill them in one place and dump the bodies in another. Disorganized killers are most often motivated by sadism, are of lower intelligence, commit impulse crimes of opportunity and leave bodies at the murder site. For both types, a series of five or more murders with a cooling-off period between each is common. As like as not, a serial killer has been wrapped up in a sex-murder fantasy since his teens or even earlier. The reality committed as an adult may disappoint the killer, causing him to act it out again and again, trying to find a way to make the murders more satisfying."

"You know a lot about it," Jussi says.

"I did a lot of reading about serial killers while I was working on my master's thesis. This murder is atypical. Abduction, three separate weapons, including a bottle broken beforehand in preparation, and writing on the body all meet the criteria for a methodical, organized killer. But killing her on site and leaving her there instead of dumping her in a separate location point to a disorganized killer. I'll check out the crime database and look for similar crimes."

"What about the 'nigger whore' thing?" Jussi asks.

"That's our problem in determining motive. We can't say yet if the crime is the product of a deranged mind, or maybe a race crime dressed up to look like one. We need to figure out which one it is to focus our investigation. Maybe the autopsy will help. For now, we'll stick to the basics and work with what we've got until we can narrow down the field of potential suspects. We've got the tire tracks and the Lapin Kulta bottle he used on her eyes and vagina. I have a lead on the car. Eero Karjalainen claims he saw a BMW 3 Series sedan pull out of Aslak's driveway around the time of the murder."

Antti raises his eyebrows. "Eero?"

"Not a reliable witness, I know, but sometimes he can surprise you."

"If he testified, the court would laugh."

"True, but the tire tracks aren't too sharp. If they point to six different makes of vehicle, including a BMW, we can focus on the BMW. Everything helps."

"Have you got assignments for us?" Valtteri asks.

"Let's pray it isn't a local," I say. "Antti, get a list of tourists currently in Levi. Focus on Americans first, because they have far and away the world's highest rate of serial murderers."

"There are thousands of tourists," he says, "in six hotels and dozens of rental cottages."

"That's right. Call every place of lodging, have them e-mail or fax their guest lists. Call every vehicle rental agency. Match their rentals against the list of tourists. Divide the list into Finns and foreigners. Run the Finnish citizens through the computer and get their crime sheets and vehicle registrations. Call the border police and get the foreigners' identity numbers. Divide foreigners by home country, then call each of their embassies and request a crime sheet on every person that rented a car. It won't take as long as you think. The Finnish ones can be done in a day."

"This is a needle in a haystack."

"For the moment."

"You're going to ruin my vacation over a dead nigger refugee?"

I can't believe he said it. I try to check my anger and don't react. Valtteri solves the problem for me. He stands up, strides across the room and slaps Antti's face.

Antti is speechless. His face turns red from embarrassment and redder from the slap.

"Take your vacation," Valtteri says. "It might be longer than you think."

Antti looks at me. I shrug and back up Valtteri. "He's your sergeant."

I've never seen Valtteri lose his temper before, let alone hit anybody. I don't know if he did it because Antti was disrespectful to me or to Sufia. Either way, it's a bad way to start the investigation.

A few tense seconds tick by. "Inspector," Antti says. He always calls me Kari. He must be trying to say he's sincere. "I was disappointed about my vacation and said something I didn't mean." He looks at Valtteri like he's afraid he'll hit him again. "I understand how important this case is, and I'm happy to cancel my vacation to work on it."

I might dismiss him if I could do without him, but I can't, and I don't want him to file a complaint against Valtteri. "And in return for my ignoring a racist comment, in which you suggested that the victim in this investigation doesn't deserve justice because of the color of her skin, you'll forget about Valtteri slapping you for being a jackass?"

He nods.

"Okay with you Valtteri?"

He sits down, looks distressed. "Yeah."

I try to get us past a bad moment by acting like it never happened. "Jussi, work on the wax casts from the tire treads. They're our best lead. Use the database, find out what makes and models are possibilities. Shouldn't take too long. Do the best you can with the shoe prints too. When you get done, help Antti. In a day or two, we'll know who in Kittilä and Levi had vehicles that make them possible suspects."

Jussi nods.

"Get it now Antti?" I ask. "It's not that fucking hard."

He nods. "I got it."

"Valtteri," I say, "you work the local angle. Make a list of known racists and sex offenders. Find out where they all were. That shouldn't take too long either. I'll get the lot number off the beer bottle, and you can try to figure out where it was sold."

"Okay."

"Sufia's place of lodging is a potential secondary crime scene. I'll find out where she was staying, collect evidence and lift prints, then go to the autopsy. After that, I'll try to figure out where she was when she was abducted. Any questions?"

No one has any. Sufia's image hovers on the wall. She stares at us with empty eye sockets. I flip on the lights.

# 6

I GO TO MY OFFICE. Valtteri trails in behind me and sits on the edge of my desk.

"Did you kiss and make up with Antti?" I ask.

"No."

"Going to?"

"No."

I don't blame him. "Want to talk about it?"

"No."

They can't even laugh it off over a beer. Valtteri doesn't drink. His religion precludes it. It precludes a lot of things which for most of us are basic entertainment, like watching TV and dancing. Laestadians tend to live passive, rather ascetic lives. They keep to their own and don't associate much with people outside their church.

We have a large Laestadian community here in Kittilä. Valtteri is thirty-eight years old, two years younger than me, and has eight children. His wife is his age and looks fifty. They had their youngest child four years ago. Their religion also forbids contraception, so either one of them is sterile or Valtteri's sex life has come to a close.

As far as I know, Valtteri doesn't want to be anything besides a small-town police sergeant. Laestadians don't take part in any form of competition. He seems content to be part of his religious community and raise his family. We've been working together for a few years now, and he's the most tranquil person I know. Aside from hitting Antti today.

"Why do you want me to investigate your father?" he asks.

"Dad didn't kill anybody, it's just something we have to do. We look at everyone."

"Like you said, he didn't kill anybody. I don't see any need to look into your family."

I don't get why he's making a big deal about it. Maybe it's a Laestadian thing. Laestadians do a lot of things I don't get. My ex-wife was raised Laestadian, but it didn't take with her and she hated it. I'm starting to think Valtteri knows something about Dad. "Everyone."

Valtteri still looks bothered.

"He was probably at work."

Dad is a bartender in a dive near downtown. He has a bad drinking problem, but to my knowledge, he's never touched a drop while behind the bar. I've often wondered if all that alcohol surrounding him doesn't make him drool with craving while he's selling it to customers.

"The truth is," I say, "Dad was drunk and foul-tempered last night, and I didn't ask him where he was because I didn't want to fight with him. It's easier for me if you just check. Do you mind?"

"No problem. Did you know Antti is such a racist?"

"Antti was upset, he's no worse than most. He didn't kill the girl, he was on duty with Jussi."

"Still."

"Sure you don't want to talk about it?"

"There's nothing to talk about."

Valtteri never talks much, that's one of the reasons I like him. My phone rings, he leaves to give me privacy.

"Vaara," I answer.

"This is Jukka Selin from the Helsinki police department. You asked that the parents of Sufia Elmi be notified of her death."

"Yeah."

"A pastor and I visited them. It didn't go well. They want to talk to you." He gives me their names, Abdi and Hudow, and their phone number.

I call them right away. A woman answers the phone. I'm nervous and don't know what to say, so I just start talking. "Ma'am, this is Inspector Kari Vaara from the Kittilä police department."

"*Anteeksi?*" Excuse me?

Even that one word of Finnish is barely understandable. I repeat who I am.

"Sorry, I get man."

I'm worried they might not speak Finnish well enough for me to be able to make myself understood. Her husband comes to the phone. "Abdi."

"Sir, this is Inspector Kari Vaara. I'm a police officer in Kittilä. I'm told you want to talk to me about Sufia."

"What has happened to her?"

Still at a loss for words, I restate what he already knows. "Sufia is dead sir. She's been murdered."

Seconds tick by in silence. "Who killed her?" he asks.

"I don't know yet. I'm doing everything in my power to find out."

"You are responsible for finding out?"

"Yes."

"Then you do it. Give me your phone number."

I give him my work and cell phone numbers.

"My wife and I will drive from Helsinki and be there tomorrow, to see our daughter. And you."

I call Jaakko Pahkala. I've known him since I was a cop in Helsinki. He's a freelance writer for the Helsinki daily newspaper, *Ilta-sanomat*, and also for the gossip magazine *Seitsemän Päivää* and the true-crime rag *Alibi*. There's little about the goings-on of our celebrities that Jaakko doesn't know.

"This is Kari Vaara. Sufia Elmi is vacationing in Kittilä. Do you know where she's staying?"

"Yes, and I'll tell you if you tell me why you're asking."

"Because she's dead." I didn't mean to be so gruff. This day isn't going the way I had hoped.

"Jesus," he says, "I'm sorry. How?"

He doesn't sound sorry, he sounds itchy for details. Jaakko loves his work. "She was murdered yesterday. I'll give you the scoop and fax you the police report before I enter it into the crime database if you help me out."

"Sure. She's at—she was at—Pine Woods Cottages."

I know the place. It's walking distance from the main ski slopes. I thank him and get his fax number.

"I'll come up on the evening flight," Jaakko says.

"You don't need to, I can keep you informed."

"See you soon." He hangs up.

I have the feeling Jaakko is going to be a pain in my ass, but at least now I know where Sufia was staying. I make some phone calls, get a search warrant for her hotel room and subpoenas for her bank and phone records, then head off to see what I can learn from Sufia's cabin.

I'M TIRED, so I stop at a gas station and get a big takeaway coffee to sharpen up. The gas station is in the middle of a snowfield with a two-lane road running through it. In the dark, big neon signs reflect off the snow like crayon marks on a sheet of dirty white paper. I lean against the car, smoke, sip at the scalding coffee, and through the steam rising off it, watch the signs flash, flicker on and off.

My next stop is Pine Woods Cottages. It may be that Sufia was abducted from her room, and good investigative work could solve her murder here and now. I go to the manager's office and get the keys, tell him Sufia's place is a crime scene and no one else can enter until I say otherwise. He tells me the maid hasn't cleaned it for five days, Sufia didn't want anybody in her room.

I take the crime kit fishing-tackle boxes from the trunk of my car, stop and look around. It's not a cottage, more like a motel. Twelve units are housed under one roof with a log facade. It's a nice-looking place. A ski vacation in Levi is expensive. Even a place like this runs a few hundred euros a week. The lift pass and ski rental is about a hundred euros, a beer is five. If you want to do something like go on a dogsled run around a reindeer farm with lunch included—exotic if you don't live here—it's a hundred and fifty for three hours. At those prices, tourists expect things to be done right.

It's warmed up to minus fourteen now, and the ski runs are

open again. Blazing lights cut through the dark and illuminate them, and from Sufia's door, I have a good view of the slopes. Hundreds of black dots rush down the mountain. Still, there's a degree of privacy here. An abduction could have been carried out if she was subdued, not kicking and screaming. A knife and the noose around her neck could have sufficed.

There aren't any footprints in the snow leading up to her door. The last snowfall ended yesterday around noon, so she was away from here for at least two hours before she was murdered. My hope is to find a bloody mess, signs of a violent struggle. If I can type the killer's blood and get a DNA sample, I'll have gone a long way toward solving her murder.

There's a DO NOT DISTURB sign on the door. I go in and do a walk-through. It's spacious, nicely decorated. There's a living area and bedroom, a bathroom with a sauna. It's also got empty beer and liquor bottles all over the place. Maybe because she was a Muslim, using alcohol embarrassed her, and Sufia didn't want the maid in to clean it until she got rid of them first.

An overflowing ashtray sits on a coffee table. I sift through the butts: they're all Marlboro Lights. I take a long minute to let it sink in, to get a sense of what might have happened here. Nothing broken, no bloodstains evident. It's just a little messy.

I take out the cameras and start snapping photos. The sheets are stained with semen, but nothing that might link to Sufia's murder presents itself.

Two books sit on the nightstand beside the bed. One is *The Shock Doctrine: The Rise of Disaster Capitalism* by Naomi Klein. Sophisticated reading, and in English. Sufia must have had good language skills. The other—in Finnish—is *Nalle ja Moppe: The Life of Eino Leino and L. Onerva*. It's about two Finnish writers, both most famous for their poetry, the stories of their lives and their on-again/off-again love affair. Romantic stuff, but only of interest to someone with intellectual inclinations. Her address book is on the nightstand by the other books. I slip it into an evidence bag. I had hoped to find her purse and cell phone, but it's better than nothing.

On television, crime-scene investigators just hose down everything with Luminol, and—abra-cadaver!—invisible blood pools are exposed, crimes solved, murderers brought to justice. In fact, Luminol reacts with lots of chemicals, household bleach among them, and can destroy other crime-scene evidence. If the room had been professionally cleaned before I processed it, I might use Luminol, but for me, it's a last resort.

I lift fingerprints from the doorknobs, the desk, the bathroom sink, every surface that will hold them, then I start bagging evidence. First I do detail stuff, collect pubic and other hair from the bed and toilet. Then I move on to bigger things. I strip the dirty sheets off the bed and fold them inward to keep evidence intact before bagging them.

In a closet, I find several pairs of dirty panties in a hamper, most of them semen stained. I bag the cigarette butts and liquor bottles. When the floor is clear, I spend an hour on my hands and knees going over the carpet, focusing on hairs and fibers, angling a flashlight low to make them stand out.

I finish and look at my watch. I'm supposed to meet Esko for the autopsy in forty-five minutes. As far as yielding evidence goes, the place is a mixed blessing. There's nothing here to bring the case to a quick conclusion, but a lot that may help me down the road. I sit down on the edge of the bed for a minute to form a

SNOW ANGELS \ 53

mental image of the person who's been living here. There's been a lot of drunken fucking going on.

The murdered have no privacy, their flaws and secrets are held up to scrutiny in an effort to bring them justice. Because of the circumstances of her death, I had canonized Sufia slowly but surely over the past day. Sufia, the snow angel—that was a mistake, I know nothing about her. To get at the truth, I need to see her as she was. This room is a beginning. I hope the autopsy will tell me more.

# 7

ESKO HANDS ME a cup of coffee and tells the morgue attendant, the diener, to bring him Sufia's body. We wait in the examination suite, and I look around to pass the time. Photos of Esko's family hang on the walls: his daughter's wedding, one of him and his wife at a summer picnic. I browse through a tray of surgical tools. Among the saws and scalpels, chisels and forceps, I find a set of garden shears. "What are these for?"

"This place runs on a tight budget," he says. "A pair of rib-cutters from a surgical-supply company costs three times as much. It's not like my patients bleed to death if they get a nicked artery from a less-than-perfect instrument."

He comes over to the table and picks up a piece of cutlery from the collection of scalpels. "Discount stores are great. This is a bread knife I picked up on sale at Anttila. Perfect for making thin organ slices. It's got way more cutting surface than a scalpel and does a better job at a fraction of the cost. You gotta think of this stuff if you want to run a backwater government facility."

The diener, Tuomas, wheels in Sufia's body on a gurney. "Want me to do anything?" he asks.

Esko scratches at his gray beard. "Break the seals on the bag and photograph the body while I finish my coffee."

The diener unzips the body bag. Sufia is exposed, naked and violated, swathed in shiny black plastic, like an offering to an angry god on the glittering steel altar of the gurney.

Esko has dark circles under his eyes. "I guess you didn't get much sleep either," I say.

"I'm knackered," he says.

An interesting choice of words, given that Sufia was knackered, like a farm animal, with a hammer.

"I've been province coroner for seventeen years," Esko says, "and I've never seen anything like this, let alone autopsied a body so mutilated for a murder investigation. Like I told you yesterday, I'm scared I'll fuck it up. I stayed up most of the night reading forensics journals because I was afraid I'll forget something."

"You won't," I say.

The diener finishes snapping photos. He sits down on a stool in the corner, pulls off his surgical cap. Lank blond hair falls in his face. He starts reading a magazine. I don't bother to say hello. When I've spoken to him in the past, he never answered, just nodded and went on with what he was doing.

Esko examines the body while it's still in the bag, before it's cleaned up. He turns on a tape recorder. He states that he's positively identified the victim as Sufia Elmi from dental records, then notes her race, sex, hair color and length and her age. He takes the bags off her hands and scrapes under her fingernails, enters the scrapings and the bags themselves into evidence. He takes samples for DNA analysis from her lips and inside her mouth with swabs, and continues.

"There's a cord with a simple slipknot around the neck, located above a laceration in the throat." He lifts her head and removes the noose. "The ligatures aren't deep, the esophagus isn't crushed. Asphyxiation wasn't the cause of death."

He looks the body over for hair and fiber samples, for any kind of foreign materials. The only hair samples he finds most likely belong to her, unless the killer is of African descent, and we don't have many black people in Kittilä, neither locals nor tourists. He picks up some fibers, maybe from her own absent clothing.

He goes over the body with a UV light to make secretions fluoresce, then draws blood samples with a syringe for toxicology. Although he's done it once already, he takes blood samples from various areas on the corpse. A single drop of the killer's blood might expose his identity. He doesn't find anything else and starts looking at her injuries.

"I'll start with her eyes," Esko says. "Puncture wounds have penetrated the cornea, iris, sclera and vitreous humor. Little ocular fluid remains. Rough, irregular intrusions suggest an imprecise instrument, and corresponding circular wounds around the eyes suggest he used the broken beer bottle, still embedded in the subject's vagina, as the instrument."

I stand up and look into Sufia's eye sockets. Yesterday, she could see through those bloodstained maws. I find myself wishing I had taken the national police chief's advice and bowed out of the investigation. I sit down again, and Esko goes on.

"Upon examining the scalp, there's ecchymosis in the right and frontal areas, a subarachnoid hemorrhage on the right side and small hemorrhagic areas in the corpus callosum."

Meaning the two hammer blows to her head caused heavy bruising and internal bleeding.

"The throat is incised. The esophagus, internal carotid artery and superior laryngeal nerve are severed. Aggressive compression and shearing from one cut resulted in a wound that reaches to the spine, which was nicked by the blade."

Esko is saying he nearly cut her head off.

"To go so deep and through cartilage without sawing, the instrument must have been sharp and of some length, and so not a scalpel. He used a knife with a curved blade. A skinning knife comes to mind. I see an irregular laceration and superficial loss of skin from the right breast. The tissue loss is more or less square in outline and measures three and one-eighth inches transversely and three and a half inches longitudinally. The manner in which this skin from her breast has been removed, with two unidirectional slashes rather than with a sawing motion, reinforces my opinion about the cutting instrument."

I want Esko's examination to tell me the story of her death. "Can you give me the order of attack?"

"Hang on until I finish, I'm trying to figure it out."

"The words 'nigger whore,'" Esko says, "have been written, one below the other, with a series of cuts on the body's midsection, between the breasts and the umbilicus. Each letter is approximately three inches transversely and one and a half inches longitudinally. The writing is precise and the wounds are shallow. If a curved blade were used, it would have been awkward to use the tip to cut the words into the body while holding the knife by the handle. I think he held the knife by the tip, like a pen. The words are intersected by a light cut, interrupted by other wounds, that runs from the throat to the pelvic area." He turns her over. "The body is nicked in other places, on the thighs and buttocks, and once in the center of her back, by a blade with similar characteristics."

"How long do you think it took him to cut 'nigger whore' into her belly?" I ask.

He shrugs. "Grab a scalpel and a pad of paper and try it for yourself."

I take a scalpel from the instrument tray and paper from a shelf, hold the blade like a pen and time myself while I scratch out the letters. "Forty-nine seconds."

Esko moves on. "The trunk is lacerated by an incision that travels almost straight through the abdomen, severing the intestine at the duodenum and through the soft tissues of the abdomen. The incision is deep and nearly reaches the intervertebral disk between the second and third lumbar vertebrae."

"It almost looks to me like he tried to cut her in half," I say.

He considers it. "Maybe."

He examines her pubic area and tries to remove the broken Lapin Kulta bottle from Sufia's vagina. It doesn't want to come out. He uses both hands, gives it a jerk, and it comes free. He examines her vagina and the wound inflicted by the bottle. *"Mitä vittua?"* What the fuck? "Come over here and look at this," he says.

I go to the other side of the gurney. All I see is a mutilated vagina. "What?"

"Her vagina is damaged," Esko says, "but not just in the way you think. Look again."

I get down close to look and feel embarrassed, but now I see. Her clitoris and part of the labia minora are missing. "You think the killer is a surgeon?"

"No, I think her family had it done."

I overlooked the scar tissue because Sufia's vagina is smeared with dried blood and damaged by the beer bottle. I'm shocked, but I shouldn't be. Back in the nineties, when we took thousands of Somali refugees into Finland to help them escape genocide, I made an effort to learn a little bit about Somali culture. The vast majority of Somali women have undergone clitoridectomy as a rite of womanhood.

"You ever see one of these before?" I ask.

"Only in pictures. This is what they call a Type II clitoridectomy. Because of the absence of the labia minora and clitoris, the anterior perineal structures have an unusual contour."

"It looks ungodly painful."

"In my medical opinion, it hurt like screaming fucking hell. They dug her clitoris out at the root, down to the bone."

I think about her cottage and the semen-stained sheets and panties. "Could she have derived enjoyment from sex?"

"Not the kind of physical pleasure usually associated with it."

"Learn anything about the sexual assault with the bottle?"

"Not much, he pushed it into her while twisting and cutting. There's semen present, but that doesn't prove anything. The killer did so much damage with it that I can't tell if she was raped or not. Makes me wonder if he's as smart as he is brutal. She could have had intercourse a day or two before her murder."

The external examination is complete. The diener finishes an apple, throws the core in the trash and puts down his magazine. He weighs and measures the body. "Five feet and eight inches, ninety-six pounds," he says.

Dieners are an odd lot, tend to stay in their low-paying jobs for decades. They live in the cool quiet of the morgue, moving and washing bodies. Makes me wonder about them. The diener moves Sufia's corpse while Esko takes a break. He and I drink more coffee. He looks lost in thought, so I stay quiet to let him sort things out.

The diener moves Sufia to a slanted aluminum autopsy table. It has raised edges, faucets, gutters and drains to rinse away blood and drek. The diener washes the body. If there was any evidence left on her, it's gone down the drain. He places a body block, a rubber brick, under her back, to make her chest protrude. It will make it easier to cut her open.

I remember the first time I went deer hunting. My oldest brother, Juha, and some of his friends took me. Hunting dogs cornered the deer, a six-point whitetail buck, and since it was my first time, they let me take the shot. The bullet went behind the shoulder and through the heart, a clean kill. Juha handed me a knife and told me what to do. I zipped the buck open from the sternum to the genitals and plunged my hands in to pull out the organs. The morning was bitter cold, and the heat inside the dead animal made me sigh with pleasure.

"Isn't working with chilled bodies uncomfortable?" I've attended quite a few autopsies, but never thought of this before.

"You get used to it, like anything. Refrigerated flesh is easier to work with. Warm flesh is squishy, harder to cut."

Esko goes back to work. He makes a Y-shaped incision from each shoulder to the bottom of her breastbone, then from the breastbone to her pubic bone. He pulls her skin away in flaps. The chest flap hangs over her face so that I can see her bones and muscles.

He removes her rib cage and detaches her esophagus and larynx by cutting arteries and ligaments. He cuts the attachments to the bladder, spinal cord and rectum, then flops out her internal organs in one go. He takes his bread knife and slices organs for tissue samples.

"How does her liver look?" I ask.

"Pure as the driven snow."

"What about her lungs?"

"Pink as the day she was born."

I try to see Sufia as she was. "I processed her cottage today, there were booze bottles and cigarette butts everywhere."

"Unless she has new vices, they weren't hers."

"We get twenty-four-hour turnaround on DNA. The evidence bags from her room are in the trunk of my car. When you get done, we'll send them and your samples to Helsinki on the next plane. We might know whose they are in a day or two."

Esko opens her stomach. The smell is less than pleasant. He dumps the contents into a container. Then he zips a scalpel around Sufia's head, across her forehead and from ear to ear. He pulls her skin away in two flaps. "Blows to the head from the blunt instrument caused a fracture in the frontal cranium," he says.

He cuts into her skull with an electric Stryker saw, then pulls off the top like he's taking off her hat. He cuts her brain's connection to the spinal cord and lifts it out, slices it with the bread knife for samples. When he's done, Esko flops into a chair, exhausted. The diener starts sewing her back together.

"We've got this girl," I say. "She appears to be a chain-smoker living in alcoholic squalor, but she doesn't drink or smoke, so I think she has a boyfriend who does."

"A fair guess."

"She has sex she doesn't enjoy. She's sexually mutilated both in life and in death. There might be something to that, some kind of symbolism."

"Could be."

I mull it over. "Paint me a picture of what you think happened."

"That's your department."

"But I'm asking you."

He takes a second. "I think he kidnapped her somewhere, used the knife to intimidate her and the noose to control her. Cut her to scare her into submission. Maybe raped her somewhere along the line."

"The semen. You're sure there's no way to tell if it was his, if she was raped?"

He shrugs. "She's so torn up, I can't tell you more. I wish I could. I just don't get it," he says. "The way he butchered her suggests an agenda, but I can't imagine what it was."

"Let's try to sort it out," I say. "What do you think happened before he took her to the snowfield, and what did he do after he got there?"

"We know what he did there because of blood loss into the surrounding snow. He attacked her eyes, removed a section of skin from her breast, made a deep laceration in her lower trunk and inserted the bottle into her vagina."

"She was awake at least part of the time," I say, "because she thrashed around in the snow."

Esko goes quiet for a minute, then covers his face with his hands. "I think I got it," he says, lowers his hands and looks at me. "He abducts her using the knife and the noose. Maybe he rapes her, maybe forces oral sex on her, maybe he doesn't do either. Anyway, he hits her in the head with the hammer and knocks her out. He drives her to the snowfield. When he drags her out into the snow, she's still unconscious from the concussion, maybe he even thinks she's dead, and he goes to work. He cuts off a flap of skin from her breast, gouges out her eyes with the bottle and inserts it into her vagina. Then he makes the deep incision in her abdomen, maybe intends on cutting her in half."

I see where he's going. "You can't mean it."

"Yeah, I mean it. He's cutting her in half, and she wakes up, starts flailing around, screaming and making noise. It scared him, so he cut her throat to finish the job."

"Jesus," I say. "She woke up to find herself blind and being cut in half? That's when she flailed around and made the snow angel?"

"I can't be certain of the exact order of events, but it looks that way. Before he kills her on Aslak's farm, he cuts off her clothes and strips her—that's why she's got the nicks on her body—and writes 'nigger whore' on her with the knife."

"Then he drives her to the reindeer farm, drags her unconscious out of the car and kills her. Sounds premeditated," I say.

"Yes it does. There weren't any fragments of broken glass at the scene. He broke the bottle beforehand and brought it along."

I try to take all this in. "There's a lot of hate here," I say.

Esko nods. "A lot of hate."

The diener finishes sewing her up. Sufia's next stop is the funeral home.

# 8

I GET BACK TO the station at nine P.M. Antti and Jussi are still at their desks. They've put in long days too. Antti is calling realtors, asking for occupant lists. Jussi stares at his computer screen with bleary eyes. He looks up at me. "I got something for you."

"I'm all ears."

"The tires on the vehicle used in the murder were Dunlop SP Winter Sport M3 DSST snow tires mounted on seventeen-inch rims."

I clap him on the back. "That's great."

"There's more. That particular make is a factory option on the BMW 3 Series sedan. Maybe Eero didn't imagine it after all."

There can't be many new 3 Series sedans in a small town like this. The car will break the case. "Good work. The next thing is to get online with vehicle registration. Check out every 3 Series owner, both private and rental agency, in Kittilä and Levi. Tomorrow, we'll inspect each one and find out which of those BMWs have the same model Dunlops on them."

"I'm already working on it," Jussi says. "Oh yeah, and the foot-prints were size tens."

The break with the tires is heartening, but this may still be a long haul and I don't want them to burn out yet. "Listen guys," I say, "I appreciate your hard work, but maybe it's time to call it a day."

Antti puts a hand over the mouthpiece of his phone. "In a little while."

I go to my office. Before doing anything else, I figure I'd better pursue the possibility, unlikely though it may be, that Sufia's murder is the work of a serial killer. I sit down at my computer and log on to the crime database, working from the nearest countries outward. Serial killers at large in Finland: none. In fact, we've only had one convicted serial killer in over a hundred years. Antti Olavi Taskinen killed three men by poisoning and was sentenced to life in prison in 2006.

Serial killers at large in Sweden: none. Again, only one con-victed in recent history. Thomas Quick, a child molester, com-mitted his first murder at age fourteen. Committed to closed psychiatric care in 1990, he confessed to thirty murders and by the year 2000 had been convicted of eight murders. At large in Norway: none. Denmark: none. Iceland: none. And also very few in the histories of those countries. Serial murders are a rarity in Nordic and Scandinavian cultures.

Russia has a few serial killers at large, but crime details don't suggest connections. I check Germany and Japan, countries known for breeding sexual deviance with a murderous bent. Again, a few are at large, but the crimes don't fit the profile.

I save the United States for last, because the list is so long. Around eighty-five percent of the world's serial killers are

Americans, and the rate in the U.S. has risen nine hundred and forty percent over the past thirty years. Of course, this may also reflect increased accuracy of crime statistics.

The most conservative estimates claim there are around thirty serial killers active in the U.S. at any given time. Some analysts claim as many as five hundred roam free. They base this on an average of ten to twelve murders per killer, five thousand unsolved murders per year, and they figure that a fair percentage of the hundreds or thousands of women and children that go missing every year are victims of serial killers.

I try to keyword-search and connect American crimes to Sufia, but there are so many murdered women in the States with their eyes gouged out or broken bottles stuffed into their vaginas that it's a waste of time. It occurs to me that the U.S. has a tradition of this. The actor Fatty Arbuckle was accused of killing a woman by raping her with a Coca-Cola bottle in 1921. If any American tourists have crime sheets, I'll search again by geographic location to narrow down the field.

Sufia's cell phone and banking records for the past year arrive by fax. Antti comes in and lays them on my desk. Same-day service. This is the way an investigation is supposed to go. I take my time and sift through them. Sufia was well-connected. I find the numbers of Finland's foreign minister, a high-ranking member of *kokoomus*, the Finnish Conservative Party, some other politicos and movie stars and, the biggest surprise of all, the phone number of Jyri Ivalo, the national chief of police. He failed to mention that he knew Sufia when we spoke this morning. I wonder why.

I keep looking through her records. Sufia received many calls from a particular cell phone while making few calls to the same number in return. She did, however, send a quantity of text messages to the number, and this suggests to me that she wasn't supposed to call it directly.

She made only eighteen hundred euros from *The Unexpected III*, her last film, and she had no other source of earned income, no permanent residence. She'd been receiving injections of cash into her account for the past couple months from a private source, and hasn't been paying the rent on her vacation cottage herself. Sufia Elmi was a kept woman.

I call Pine Woods Cottages and get the credit card number used for payment. I run checks on the credit card, bank account and cell phone. One name comes up. Seppo Niemi.

My ex-wife left me for Seppo thirteen years ago. Seppo is from Helsinki. He's rich and owns an expensive winter cottage here, bought it before he intruded on my life. He doesn't visit Levi often. We've seen each other in Hullu Poro a few times since then. We never speak, but when we make eye contact, he cowers. I suppose keeping the cottage is a way of trying to convince himself he's not intimidated by me.

I check his vehicle registration myself. He owns a BMW 330i. I'm shaken. The irony is so great that I'm not sure whether to laugh or cry.

I call Jyri. "I have a suspect," I say. "His name is Seppo Niemi. He funneled money into her bank account and paid her rent. Odds are good the car used in the crime was a BMW 330i, and he owns one. How do you want me to handle it?"

"You mean the rich guy from Helsinki?"

"Yeah."

He considers it for a minute.

"Another thing," I say. "She knew a lot of important people, including you."

"So what? I have an active social life."

"I just thought I should mention it."

"I've heard a few things about Seppo Niemi," Jyri says. "By all accounts, he's an ignorant piece of shit. Bring him in, treat him as a dangerous suspect."

"No interview first?"

"Nope. Fuck him. Arrest him first. And there's no reason to mention Sufia's more important friends to the press."

"Okay," I say.

"Let me know what happens." He hangs up.

Given the nature of the crime, it's within the boundaries of the law to drag Seppo's ass to jail without checking his alibi first, but Jyri's reaction makes me think maybe he has reasons of his own for handling the arrest like this. I apply for arrest and search warrants, and request subpoenas for Seppo's phone records and financial information.

I go back out to the common room where Jussi and Antti are still hard at it. "Go home," I say, "get some sleep and be back here at eight in the morning. We're going to make an arrest."

Antti brightens. "Who?"

My cell phone rings. "Vaara."

"This is Dr. Jukka Tikkanen from Kittilä Health Center Emergency Services. Your wife has had an accident."

My heart pounds and the phone trembles in my hand. "What kind of accident?"

"She took a fall while skiing and fractured her left femur."

"Is she all right?"

"All things considered."

"I'm on my way."

Jussi and Antti are staring at me, wondering what bad news I've received. "Kate broke her leg, I've got to go."

I run to get my coat and then remember Antti's question as I button it. "Oh yeah, we're going to arrest a guy named Seppo Niemi."

I PULL UP TO the emergency room entrance and leave the Saab in a no-parking zone. An old man sits outside smoking a cigarette. I bump into his wheelchair and apologize. The automatic doors slide open too slow and pushing them doesn't help. The admissions desk has a line. I'm supposed to take a number and wait my turn. I go to the window and flash my police card. "Kate Vaara. Where is she?"

The receptionist pretends like I'm not there and keeps talking to her current client. I slap my hand on the desk. "Now."

She starts to get angry, then puts on a bureaucratic face and checks her computer. "Katherine Vaara is in room 207. Officer."

I find Kate in a hospital bed, her left leg in a cast that goes from the bottom of her foot to high up on her hip. Her already pale skin is waxen, her lips are pursed tight. She holds out her arms for me to hug her. When I do, her mouth presses against my ear and I hear her suppress a whimper. "I want to go home," she says.

"Tell me what happened."

"Later."

I can't ask the next question, but she reads my thoughts and lets go of me. "They did an ultrasound." She pauses, manages a demure smile. "There's not just one baby, there are two."

"Two?"

"We're having twins, and they're both fine."

I lay a hand on her belly, overwhelmed by joy and relief. "Kate, that's wonderful."

She doesn't say anything. I can't tell if she thinks it's wonderful or not.

I ask a stupid question. "Are you okay?"

Kate's trying hard to keep herself under control. "No."

"Are you in a lot of pain?"

She shakes her head. "Not now."

"Are they going to let you go home?"

"I don't know."

I find her doctor. "She's lucky," he says. "She fractured her femur, but it's not that bad. If it were closer to the hip or a deeper fracture, she'd have to stay here in traction for the next couple months. She already has a pin in that hip. If she'd broken it again, she might have been permanently disabled. I'm putting her on sick leave."

"Can I take her home?"

He shrugs. "Sure."

They give Kate crutches and we get her checked out of the hospital. She has a hard time fitting into the back of the Saab with the cast. I try to talk to her on the way home, but she's not ready.

When we pull up to the house, she won't let me help her, says she has to learn to get around by herself. She pushes herself out of the car. I put an arm around her, but she shrugs it off and manages to hobble inside. Because of the cast, she can't negotiate the couch and starts to tip over. I scoop her up and lay her down, take off her shoe.

She starts to cry. "I fell. I took a steep back trail down the mountain, full of rocks and trees, and I hit an ice patch and I fucking fell."

This has to be traumatic for her. A reminder of how she shattered her hip as a teenager and had her dreams of becoming an alpine ski champion destroyed. I sit on the floor beside her so I can stroke her hair while I listen.

"I went ass over end and barreled into a big rock and broke my leg and I couldn't move and I was afraid I killed the baby and I lay there for forty-five minutes before another skier came by and another thirty before they came with a snowmobile and got me."

I try to hold her hand, but she shakes it free.

"And I got to the hospital and the nurses wouldn't speak English to me and I didn't know what was happening or if the baby was alive, and while they examined me they shoved me around like I'm an animal. And then I found out there are two babies."

"Kate, they probably just don't speak English." In truth, they probably just deal with everybody that way. Sometimes Finns are like that.

"They shouldn't have treated me that way."

"You're right, they shouldn't have, but aren't you happy about having twins?"

"Of course I am, but that's not the point."

She squeezes her eyes shut and tears of frustration slide down her cheeks.

"Damn it." She slams the glass top of the coffee table with her fist. "Damn it." She hits it again. The next time she screams. "Goddamn it!" Pound. "God fucking damn it!" Pound.

"Stop it Kate—that's dangerous."

Now she's yelling for all she's worth. "And now I can't go skiing!" Pound. "And I can't go to work!" Pound.

"Stop it Kate."

"And I can't speak Finnish!" Pound.

I don't want to manhandle her, but I don't want her to hurt herself, so I'm considering it. "Kate, stop it, goddamn it."

She stops and bursts into tears. "I'm sorry Kari. I'm just so frustrated. I'm helpless and trapped in this house."

With both hands, she lifts her broken leg up to rest it on the coffee table. She drops it too hard, and the cast shatters the glass tabletop. Glass flies. The weight of the cast going through the table makes her pitch forward onto the floor. She breaks her fall by jamming her right hand into the broken glass on the rug. When she holds it up in front of her, blood streams out of it down her arm.

I rip my white shirt down the front. I whip it off and wrap it tight around her hand, then take her in my arms. She presses her face into my shoulder. Her chest heaves and tears explode out of her in big racking sobs. We stay that way for a few minutes until she calms down. Blood has soaked through my shirt and drips on the rug.

"I don't want to go back to the hospital," she says. She starts sobbing again.

I unwrap her hand. Some glass shards are stuck in it. She has about a dozen puncture wounds, but none of them need stitches. I get antiseptic, tweezers and bandages from the bathroom. She winces as I pick out the glass, but she doesn't cry anymore.

I bind up her hand. "It's going to be okay," I say. "A couple weeks at home, then you can go back to work. In a few weeks, the cast comes off. A couple months after the babies are born, you'll be back on the slopes."

"But I can't do anything. I can't work, can't take care of the house, can't shop."

"We'll work it out. I'll get somebody to help you."

Before long, she passes out from exhaustion. I call a neighbor, wake her up, explain things and ask her to check on Kate in the morning. I clean up the glass and blood, rearrange the living room, then take our bed apart and bring it downstairs. Even the buzz of the electric screwdriver doesn't wake her when I put the bed back together. We have a small bathroom next to the foyer, so at least she won't have to worry about the stairs now.

The clock reads two A.M. I won't get much rest again. I pick her up, put her in bed and crawl in beside her. Kate's eyes open. "What happened with your murder investigation?" she asks.

"The case broke."

"Who did it?"

It's late, I don't want to talk about it and I don't want to upset her. "I'll tell you about it tomorrow," I say.

# 9

WE HEAD OUT IN two squad cars, Antti and Jussi in one, Valtteri and me in the other. It starts to snow. On the way, I tell Valtteri about the evidence against Seppo and my conversation with the chief. "So you're going to arrest Seppo Niemi," he says. "The Lord does indeed work in mysterious ways."

He doesn't take it farther than that. It's a subject people don't broach with me.

We roll up on Seppo's winter cottage. It's bigger than my house and set on a two-acre lot. It cost a lot of money. We park behind a gray BMW 330i. I get out and look at the tires with a flashlight: Dunlop Winter Sports. Valtteri calls for a wrecker to drag it to the police garage. The four of us go to the door together and I knock.

My ex-wife, Heli, opens the door. I haven't seen her for thirteen years, since she left me for Seppo. I was in the hospital for a few days after getting shot. She never came to see me, wouldn't answer the phone. When I got home, her things were gone. She refused to ever see me again, or even to speak to me. After a few weeks, I got the divorce papers in the mail.

She's sweaty, in tight workout clothes, and techno music is playing. We caught her in the middle of exercising. She was a good-looking girl when we were together. Even then, she worked hard at it. It's difficult to reconcile the image of the girl I was married to with the woman before me. A combination of dieting, exercise and bulimia have taken their toll. She's tiny, looks old, tired and undernourished, a gym hag with bleached hair and a fake tan, like she was somebody's idea of pretty once.

She shakes her head and squints her eyes, like I'm a ghost. "Hello Kari, what brings you . . . " she looks around, "and your friends here?"

"I have an arrest warrant for Seppo Niemi and a search warrant for the premises. Please step aside."

She doesn't move. "Are you fucking kidding me? Arrest for what?"

"I'll take that up with Seppo."

She laughs at me. "If you wanted to see how I'm doing, it would have been easier to drop by for coffee."

"Please step aside."

"This is a joke, you're a goddamned joke. Go home Kari."

She tries to shut the door but I straight-arm it. It flies and smacks the inside wall. "I asked you to step aside ma'am."

She looks frightened and takes a step backward. The four of us pour through the door. "Valtteri, keep her here," I say.

He drops into Laestadian-speak. *"Jumalan terve Heli."* God's greetings to you Heli.

A pair of men's shoes are on the floor of the foyer. I pick them up. Size tens. I look around: expensive furniture, expensive everything.

A pack of Marlboro Lights sits on an end table. Antti, Jussi and I draw weapons and search the downstairs for Seppo, then we move upstairs together. I open a bedroom door. He's sleeping naked in a fetal position with his mouth open, the covers kicked off and his hands around his dick. Antti and Jussi come in and we surround him. I snap cuffs on his wrists, he snaps awake.

"Seppo Niemi, you're under arrest."

His face radiates fear and sleepy confusion. Then he recognizes me and panic sets in. "Not you."

I smile at him. "Me."

"Under arrest for what?"

"You think this is an American cop show? Next you'll want me to read you your rights. You'll be given information as provided by law, within the time allotted by law."

We look at each other for a moment. I think both of us are having a difficult time getting used to what's going on here. "Can I get dressed?" he asks.

"I can't allow you to touch anything right now, because I have a search warrant for the premises and I don't want you disturbing evidence. We'll get you a blanket out of the cruiser."

"You're going to haul me naked out of bed and put me in jail, and you won't tell me why?"

"A good summation."

I change my mind and decide not to be cruel. I go through his closets, pull out a suit and a white shirt. They're still in dry cleaner's plastic and the tags date the cleaning at before the day of the murder. "Let him put these on."

I leave Seppo with the others and go back downstairs. Heli is giving Valtteri a hard time about the search warrant. She doesn't want us touching her things.

Valtteri knew her when they were kids, from church. "I'm sorry Heli, this is the way it has to be. We'll be respectful and get it over with as quick as we can. Try to be patient with us."

She turns to me. "You goddamned loser. After all this time, this is the best you can do to get even? It won't fucking work. You'll pay for this Kari. I'm going to sue you. I'll have your job for this."

Heli and Seppo never married. After she divorced me, she went back to her maiden name. "Ms. Kivinen, we mean to cause you no unnecessary inconvenience, but for the moment this house is considered a crime scene. I'll release it to you as soon as possible. Please cooperate with us."

Her face turns crimson as she works herself up. She slaps me and spits in my face. "You stupid sorry fuck. I'm glad I ditched your sorry loser ass so I didn't have to spend all these years watching you limp around this miserable hick town playing sheriff and making an ass out of yourself. Fuck you Kari."

I'm surprised that I feel so little upon seeing her again. "Cuff her."

Valtteri pulls her hands behind her back and pops handcuffs on her. She doesn't resist. I wipe the spit off my face and rub it on her workout jacket. "I understand that being intruded upon in this manner is disturbing, and for that reason I'm going to overlook this, but if your behavior doesn't improve, I'll charge you with assaulting a police officer."

"Fuck you."

"When you calm down, I'll let you get some things if you want them. I hope to turn this house back over to you before the day is out. Until then, I want you to shut the fuck up."

She does.

Antti marches Seppo down the stairs, looking smart in a

thousand-euro suit. Valtteri uncuffs Heli, and Jussi goes with her while she throws some things in a bag. When she's done, I leave Antti and Jussi to start searching the house, and the rest of us step out into the dark. Snow is drifting down in big flakes almost half the size of my hand. Heli looks at Seppo. "I'll call our lawyer. This bullshit won't last long." She starts toward the BMW.

"Nope," I say, "that car is impounded. Give me the keys."

She gives me a deadpan look of hatred, drops them in my hand, gets into the Honda beside it and drives away.

I PUT A HAND on Seppo's head and guide him into the back of the cruiser, then take the driver's seat. Valtteri gets in beside me. I pull out onto the road between Levi and Kittilä. The headlights bore into the dark and illuminate an icy two-lane road that cuts through the middle of a vast snowfield. It's like driving through a moonscape.

Seppo is silent. A confession would simplify matters. I watch him in the rearview mirror. "Seppo, why did you kill Sufia?"

He winces, goes stricken, the blood drains out of his face. He doesn't answer right away. "Sufia who?" he asks.

He doesn't seem to get it that I've already connected them. "Your girlfriend Sufia."

Another pause. "I want to speak to a lawyer."

"You can, after you're charged. I've got seventy-two hours before I have to do that. You're caught Seppo, get used to it. You're look- ing at life and will probably serve twelve years of it. If you confess, maybe show some remorse, you'll get a lesser sentence. If you can demonstrate that you killed her because of emotional problems or other extenuating circumstances, you could get it down to seven.

After the way you butchered her, it shouldn't be hard to do. That's five years of your life back."

"You know I didn't kill anybody," he says.

"We can begin that way if you want, but we both know better."

"After thirteen years," he says, "now you want to get even with me. Why?"

Some time goes by. I see him in the rearview, working himself up. He shifts in his seat. "I fucked Heli. She loved me instead of you and I fucked your wife. I took her away from you. I won and you lost, and we both know that's what this is about."

He's trying to press my buttons. I think about how Heli looks and acts now. "And what a lucky man you are."

He goes silent again.

"That was all a long time ago," I say. "I'm arresting you because the evidence suggests you killed Sufia Elmi, not because of personal animosity. As far as Heli goes, you're welcome to her. Which did you cut first, Sufia's face or her vagina?"

He recoils like I just slapped him and clamps his eyes shut. It takes him about thirty seconds to recover. He leans forward, presses his face into the grill that separates us. "I saw you at Hullu Poro with the redhead. They tell me she's your new wife."

I don't say anything.

"She's a good-looking girl."

"My wife is off-limits to this conversation," I say.

"Since you arrested me for no fucking reason except you hate me, I don't think anything is off-limits to this conversation."

He struck a nerve, and I've given him ammunition. He taunts me. "Is that what this is about? You afraid I'll fuck her too? In a couple days, when I get free of this bullshit, maybe I'll pay her a visit. I bet we'll hook up, what do you think?"

I see Sufia in the cold and dark, naked in the bloodstained snow, staring at me with empty eye sockets. Sufia turns into Kate, her face and body tortured and desecrated. First, my vision goes hazy, then it's like a swarm of tiny black flies are in my eyes and I hear a high-pitched whirring. My left arm starts to hurt like I'm going to have a heart attack. I manage to get the car over to the side of the road.

I feel like I'm outside my body looking down. The long flat stretch of road and the empty snowfields surrounding it reflect starlight, makes them shimmer a murky silver. Valtteri's face registers concern. Seppo is sitting behind me, on the driver's side of the patrol car. I turn around and look at him. He sneers at me.

I get out of the car, unholster my Glock and jerk his door open. Seppo is rigid, stares straight ahead, like he's pretending I'm not there. I crawl past Seppo and sit down beside him, on his right. I chamber a round in my Glock, put my left arm around him and press the muzzle of the pistol to his temple. "You son of a fucking whore."

Valtteri gets out of the car and comes around to the driver's side, gawks at me through the open rear door.

I push the muzzle harder against Seppo's head. He whimpers.

"The last time I killed a man they gave me a medal and promoted me. If I kill a sick fuck like you, they might do it again. I might even get a career in politics out of it. What do you think?"

Seppo looks out the door at Valtteri. "You're seeing this, you're seeing this."

Valtteri doesn't say anything. A car comes toward us and flashes its headlights. I left the high beams on and they're blinding the driver. Valtteri reaches into the open driver's door and cuts the lights, then stands beside the car and watches me.

"If you ever get near my wife," I say, "you're a dead man. You ever even say anything like that again, you're dead. You say it while you're in custody, you'll hang yourself in a jail cell. If a lawyer weasels you out of this and you get near my wife, I'll murder you on the spot and serve my sentence. Whatever happens, you leave Kittilä and never come back. Put that fucking winter dacha of yours up for sale, because if you use it again, you're fucking dead. We clear?"

He looks at Valtteri, doesn't answer.

"I count down from five. You don't agree to my terms, I blow your brains out."

He starts to cry.

"Five, four, three . . ."

His voice is shrill like a child's. "I agree, I agree."

"Too late, you fucking cunt. BOOM!" I shout it in his ear.

Seppo faints and slumps over in a puddle of his own piss.

Valtteri and I look at each other through the open door. "Let's go," he says, "it's cold out here."

I stumble past Seppo out of the cruiser. "You better drive," I say.

We get back on the road. "If you feel like you have to report what I did, I won't hold it against you."

"You did what you felt you had to do to protect your wife. I understand that."

"I wouldn't ask you to lie for me."

"You wouldn't have to ask me."

Valtteri is surprising me more and more every day.

# 10

WE ARRIVE AT THE police station. Valtteri turns off the squad car's engine. I sit still for a minute and try to compose myself before dealing with Seppo again. Valtteri exits the car before me. "I'll process him," he says, and ushers Seppo from the car into the police station.

I get out of the car, light a cigarette and exhale. Smoke and frozen breath pour out into the dark in a great plume. The street is empty and silent. I'm tired. I want some peace and quiet. Hard-packed snow crackles under my feet. Every surface is sheathed in ice and snow. I feel like I live in a vast frozen hell.

I made a mistake threatening Seppo. He made a mistake bringing Kate into the equation. Questioning him will be harder now. I'll wait, give us both some time. A few hours in a jail cell might make him consider what it would be like to live in one and encourage him to confess.

My cell phone rings and destroys my thoughts. "Vaara."

"This is Sufia's father. My wife and I are in Kittilä. We wish to see you, and we wish to see our Sufia."

I'm still shaken by my confrontation with Seppo and unprepared for Abdi's call. "Sir, perhaps we could meet at the police station. I could bring you up to date on the investigation and ask you a few questions about your daughter."

"No, we will not. Where is Sufia?"

I give him the name of the funeral home.

"We will meet there, and in her presence, you will tell me all that you know, how you intend to find her killer, and how he will be punished."

I don't want Sufia's parents to see her ravaged corpse, and I don't want to see it again either. "Sir, I don't think that's for the best. Please consider that it might be better to remember Sufia as she was, not as she is now."

His voice rises a notch. "Sufia is our daughter. We will decide what is best and how we shall remember her. When can you meet with us?"

I have no choice but to respect his wishes. "I'll leave for the funeral home right now."

Abdi and Hudow pull their car up to the front of the funeral home just as I arrive in my Saab. I watch their silhouettes through the window as they step out into the snow. Abdi stands more than six and a half feet tall. Even in his winter coat he looks gaunt, thin as a razor.

Hudow is short and fat. She observes hijab, traditional dress for Muslim women. A loose brown dress hangs below the hem of her coat to her ankles. A scarf is wrapped around her head so that only the outline of her face is visible. Atop this arrangement sits a thick fur hat.

I get out of the car, go over to them and offer my hand. "I'm Inspector Kari Vaara. I'm sorry for your loss."

Hudow looks uncomfortable. I forgot that she probably doesn't shake hands with men. Abdi doesn't look uncomfortable, he just doesn't want to shake my hand. We stare at each other. I'm six feet tall, but I have to look up at him.

"My wife is cold. We should go inside," he says.

We file through the front door. A bell rings, and a few seconds later the owner comes out of the back room. He's a small man, about sixty, in a charcoal-gray suit. What's left of his hair is gray. He looks at the three of us, and I see his confusion. The chief of police has arrived with two black people, one of whom is a giant. As like as not, a black person has never crossed the threshold of his establishment before. But then he registers understanding, must have remembered who his latest client is.

"I am Jorma Saari," he says. "Nothing can ease your suffering, but please accept my condolences, and know that whatever is in my power to help you through this most difficult of times, I will do. You have only but to ask."

This isn't just industry patter for Jorma. I've known him since I was a kid and dealt with him on many occasions because of my work. He's a nice man. He offers his hand. Abdi doesn't take it.

"Good," Abdi says. "Thank you. We wish to see our Sufia."

Jorma looks unsure how to continue. He must have seen Sufia's body. "Mr. Elmi . . ." he says.

Abdi raises a hand and silences Jorma. He has a commanding presence that derives from more than just his height. "My name," he says, "is Abdi Barre. You have mistakenly referred to me by my daughter's surname. We are Somali. As is our custom, my daughter's surname is matriarchal."

"I apologize," Jorma says.

"Do you understand what I have asked of you? We wish to see our Sufia. Please take us to her."

"Mr. Barre, of course this is your right, but I would spare you needless suffering. Sufia has not been prepared for viewing, and in my opinion cannot be. At this moment, embalming is taking place."

Abdi raises his hands, presses his fingertips together. His fingers are long and slender, twice the length of mine. His face is scarred. He has the air of a holy man, as if a lifetime of suffering has hollowed him out and left him a creature of spirit.

"In Finland," Abdi says, "I own a cleaning service. The people that work for me vacuum the floors and empty the trash in businesses such as yours. My language skills do not allow me to pass the Finnish medical boards, but I studied at the Sorbonne and in Somalia I was a physician. I assure you that whatever has happened to my Sufia, it is nothing that I did not see in my practice in Mogadishu. My wife saw Sufia as she came into this world, she can see her as she leaves it."

Abdi's Finnish is stilted but excellent. Maybe he doesn't write it as well as he speaks it.

"May I have my technician make Sufia ready for you?" Jorma asks.

Abdi peers at Jorma over fingers like tendrils. "No."

Jorma wrings his hands, as if absolving himself of responsibility.

We walk downstairs to an embalming room in the basement. A machine hums. Sufia is naked, on the same kind of table as the one used during her autopsy. The machine is draining the remainder of her blood. The embalmer is sipping a Pepsi. He looks shocked to see us, like we've violated his space. He shuts off the suction machine.

In silence, we look at Sufia. The torment she suffered, the hurt done to her, both pre- and postmortem, is as clear as if the story were written down. Still, I've never seen a body look less human, so devoid of life. I can't understand why Abdi insisted on this.

Hudow chokes back a scream. Abdi puts an arm around her. She turns her head and vomits on the floor. When she's done, she stands upright and tries to salvage what remains of her dignity. She speaks in broken Finnish. "I sorry. I clean up."

Jorma folds his hands in front of him. "That's not necessary."

Abdi looks at me. "Now, in the presence of myself, my daughter and her mother, you will tell me how you intend to prosecute the investigation of our daughter's murder, and how her murderer will be punished."

He wanted to make a point and he's done it well. Since my first glimpse of the crime scene, this case has held tremendous gravity for me. Now though, I feel like all our lives depend on it. I look at Sufia, then at Abdi and Hudow. Her head is held high. She's regained her composure and looks like a font of strength and nobility.

The smell of vomit mingled with chloroform is overwhelming. I try not to react to it. I give Abdi what he wants and start at the beginning, tell him everything that was done to Sufia, everything that has been done to find her murderer, and about Seppo's arrest.

When I'm finished, Abdi asks, "How is it possible that you do not know if Sufia was raped?"

"As I told you, and as you can see, there has been excessive damage to the genital area."

Abdi bends over Sufia's body, looks for himself. "As I hope you realize, Sufia underwent the rite of womanhood as a child. Had she not been raped, she would be intact. It is clear that prior to being assaulted with the bottle, she was not intact. Please do not ask me to be more explicit in the presence of her mother. She is not intact, therefore she was raped."

Abdi wanted truth, but now we're on new and dangerous ground. I can't find it in myself to tell him what I know about Sufia's sexual relationships. I'm afraid it might be more than even he can bear. "I can't discount the possibility that Sufia might have had sexual intercourse of her own volition."

Hudow looks down, looks around. The embalmer is cleaning up the floor with paper towels. "I know people say things about daughter," she says. "Those things not true. We no watch movies, not want see, but Sufia actress. Movies acting. Sufia good girl. Abdi and I no like her be in movies, but we proud for who she was. I proud her. She keep her good even around bad people."

"I need not say more," Abdi says.

I can't destroy her beliefs and I wonder if Abdi shares them, or if the scene we're playing out has been in some measure a charade designed to maintain them. "I will proceed accordingly," I say.

"This man, are you certain of his guilt?" Abdi asks.

I want to be careful here. I don't want to make a false promise, raise false hopes. "I can't say with certainty, but the evidence gathered thus far is convincing."

"Given your professional expertise in these matters, please express your opinion in terms of a percentage."

Abdi inspires truth. "Better than ninety."

"How will he be punished?"

"If convicted, and if no mitigating circumstances weigh in his sentencing, he'll likely receive life in prison."

"Mitigating circumstances?"

"Incapacity, such as mental illness."

"In this instance, how long would his prison term be?"

"In my experience, five to seven years, perhaps served in prison, perhaps in a mental hospital, the cure of his illness a prerequisite to release."

Hudow raises her hands, turns her face upward. A ceiling with a bank of fluorescent lights is above her, but she beseeches the heavens. She wails. "Look my angel. This no justice."

Abdi puts a consoling arm around her. "Hush," he says, "your screams will bring her grief."

He turns back to me. "And if there were no mitigating circumstances, how many years would this man serve in prison?"

"Life means life," I say, "but in common practice, murderers serve ten to twelve years, after which they receive presidential pardons and are released."

"Look at Sufia," Abdi says. "Do you believe that a sufficient penalty?"

I don't need to look. "No."

"Inspector Vaara, see to this man's punishment, pallid though it may be. In the Koran, Surah 5:45 tells us: 'Life for life, eye for eye, nose for nose, ear for ear, tooth for tooth, and wounds equal for equal.' In Islam, it is permitted that the closest living relative exact justice in such a matter, but in this country it is not permitted. I abide by the laws of this country, and as such, you must act as my surrogate. I hold you responsible. Now, leave us alone with our daughter, all of you."

I leave, feeling like I may be punished if Seppo walks free, like somehow I'm already being punished, but I don't know what I've done to deserve it.

# 11

I RESPECT ABDI'S GRIEF, but melodrama won't solve his daughter's murder. Routine police procedure will. Seppo's car is in the police garage. I park next to it, take the cameras out of my fishing-tackle boxes and start snapping photos.

The BMW is a gorgeous vehicle, graphite with satin chrome exterior trim and star-spoked wheels. I open all the doors, walk around it and look for anything inside that might stand out. This car just says money. The interior is leather trimmed with matte black stainless steel and variegated poplar. It has automatic climate control and a LOGIC7 sound system. To avoid touching anything, I use a flashlight and a mirror to look under the seats. I find no evidence, but see three subwoofers. They give me an idea.

This kind of work makes me feel confident, in control. I can use this time to be alone, to do my job in peace. A rack under the dash holds around twenty CDs, mostly techno crap. I lift fingerprints from the steering wheel and dashboard, then go back to my car and choose music appropriate for this type of work. I decide on Miles Davis, *Kind of Blue*. I load it into the LOGIC7. The garage throbs with cool jazz.

I divide the interior into quadrants and go through the car inch by inch. In the backseat, I find pubic hair, fibers and small semen stains. I don't find blood, so I use Luminol in the area of the semen, but just a touch. Traces light up. My mood is much improved. I've gotten everything I could ask for and more. Now maybe Seppo and I will have something to talk about.

It occurs to me that I haven't checked on Kate today. I feel guilty and hit the speed dial on my cell phone.

"Hi Kari," she says.

"Sorry I haven't called. This investigation is keeping me busy. How are you?"

"Fine. I was hoping I would hear from you. I wanted to tell you I'm sorry for last night."

"For what?"

"For breaking the table."

"It was an accident, and anyway, I don't care about the table."

"For behaving like a child over a broken leg."

"Jesus Kate, you lay on the side of a mountain worrying about our child—our children—in screaming pain. Anybody would have been traumatized."

"Well, I'm not anymore. I'm getting used to the cast and crutches. Mrs. Tervo came by today to check on me. She brought me smoked whitefish and potatoes with cream sauce for lunch. They were delicious. Thanks for calling her and for moving the bed."

"Do you need anything?"

"It's pretty hard to get around and moving still hurts some. You mentioned finding someone to help with errands."

"I'll take care of it this afternoon."

"You're a love. Hey, didn't you say you broke the case?"

I can't help it, I don't want to talk to Kate about my ex-wife and her affair with Seppo. She knows the basics, but I've never discussed it beyond that. I guess she knows it makes me uncomfortable and so never pressed it. "I'll tell you about it later."

"You sound like you're in a hurry."

All I want right now is to be with her. "Yeah, I have to go. I'll be home as soon as I can."

"I love you Kari."

Finns seldom tell each other they love one another, and we seldom call each other by name without cause. The two in conjunction is so intimate that I'm moved every time she does it. "I love you too Kate."


I GO BACK INTO the police station. Valtteri is staring at a computer monitor in the common room. I sit on the edge of his desk. "How are things?"

He looks up at me. The circles under his eyes are so dark that they look like bruises. "Okay. You?"

"Good. I processed the BMW. It's a gold mine. Blood, semen, everything."

He looks surprised, smiles. "That's great."

"You check on Seppo lately?" I ask.

"No. He didn't say a word while I processed him. I figured I'd let him stew for a while."

"I'll pay him a visit, let him know how the case against him is progressing."

"Want me to come along?"

I guess he's worried because of what happened earlier. I don't blame him. "I'm close to a hundred percent certain he killed Sufia. When he threatened Kate, I pictured him doing the same thing to her and I lost it. It won't happen again."

He nods. "Okay."

I also guess he's afraid that I can't separate this case from what happened years ago, but doesn't want to broach the subject. I don't want to either. Still, I open the door in case he feels he needs to. "Do you think I should give up this case?"

He stares at the desktop, considers it. "No, but some people might think otherwise."

Enough said. I change the subject. "Listen, before I forget, Kate's having a hard time with her broken leg and could use some help at home. Running errands, shopping, a little cleaning. Think one of your kids might be interested in making a little extra spending money?"

"My boy Heikki can do it. He's been out of sorts lately, it'll give him something to do. I'll call and tell him to go over this afternoon. He was disappointed when we didn't go hunting. Some extra money might cheer him up."

"I appreciate it. Do you know if Antti and Jussi finished processing Seppo's house?"

"Antti called about half an hour ago and said they're done. They've got a lot of stuff to be analyzed, but nothing definite."

"Then I need to release the house to Heli. Give her a call and tell her to come pick up the keys."

We sit in silence for a minute. Valtteri looks thoughtful. "You, Heli, Seppo, this case," he says. "You shouldn't give it up. No matter what. It's the will of God. It has to be."

I leave Valtteri, still seeming reflective, thinking that even for him, it seemed like an odd thing to say.

THE DETENTION CELLS ARE in the basement. My timing is good. As I walk down the stairs, I hear Seppo screaming, "Hey! Hey! Somebody let me out of here!"

It took all of three hours to break him. The cell door is steel. I slide open the observation port and look in. His face is pressed against the inside.

"Can I help you?" I ask.

"Please let me out. I can't stand it in here."

"Stick your hands out the window."

He looks like he's afraid I'll rip them off, but he does it. I handcuff him. "Now move away from the door."

I unlock it and step inside. He almost falls backing away from me. His piss-stained expensive suit is gone, along with his bravado. He's wearing jeans and a T-shirt, both way too big for him.

"Where did you get the clothes?" I ask.

"The sergeant gave them to me. I was expecting an orange prison jumpsuit or something."

"You've been watching too much American TV."

Valtteri's Christian charity applies even to psychotic murderers. They're his own clothes. The T-shirt is tucked into the jeans and accents Seppo's beer belly. His face is red from broken blood vessels. It takes years of hard drinking to acquire that look. I can bench-press two hundred and fifty pounds. Seppo doesn't look like he could bench-press a vodka bottle.

"Want a smoke?" I ask.

"Are you going to hurt me?"

I sit down on a metal cot bolted to the wall and shake a cigarette out of the pack. "No."

He reaches out to take it, his hands tremble. I try to light it for him, but he's shaking so hard that I have to hold him by the manacles to steady him. He inhales and coughs. The cell is sixteen by twenty-four feet square. Former occupants have scrawled names and dates on the gray concrete walls.

"Drab surroundings compared to your winter dacha," I say.

He sucks on the cigarette like he'll never get another.

"Let's talk about Sufia."

He coughs again. "I don't know any Sufia."

"Sufia Elmi, murdered forty-nine hours ago in a snowfield. You were having an affair with her. If you're going to murder someone, you shouldn't leave documentation. You gave her money, paid her rent."

"I didn't kill her."

"I just spent a couple hours collecting evidence from your BMW. I found blood, hair and semen. Are you going to tell me they won't connect you to Sufia?"

He purses his lips, like he's trying to decide something. "Can I talk to you straight, without you hurting me?"

"If you want to get out of here, that's the best thing you can do for yourself."

"I didn't kill anyone, and I think you know it."

"I'm ninety-nine percent convinced that you did."

"There's been a murder, and you found a way to link me to it. After all this time, you're getting even with me for my affair with Heli."

"That's not true."

He starts to cry. "Can't I just apologize? I'm truly sorry that Heli and I hurt you. I didn't know you. All I knew was that I loved Heli."

This note rings false. People have affairs all the time and I doubt he cares who he hurts. Seppo is a sack of shit. He's begging, just spewing whatever he hopes will get him out of this mess. I don't say anything.

He sniffles. "And I'm sorry for what I said about your wife. I was trying to be brave."

"Ancient history has nothing to do with this murder investigation."

"I know what Heli did to you was awful. I didn't make her do it, I told her to decide for herself who she wanted to be with."

"Let's move forward in time thirteen years and talk about Sufia's murder."

He dries his tears. "I don't know anything about it, and I don't think I should discuss it without talking to a lawyer."

"You want out of here? Come upstairs with me. I'll show you something that might change your mind."

We go up to the common room. It's empty. I give him my pack of cigarettes and lighter. "Keep them. Have a seat."

He sits and smokes. I douse the lights and start the PowerPoint slide show of the murder scene. He watches Sufia, I watch him. He shakes, then sobs a little. After a couple minutes, he's weeping like a child. Finally, he holds himself, rocks back and forth, mutters "No, no," over and over.

I think he'll confess now. I freeze the projector on a close-up of Sufia's ruined face.

"Please charge me," he says, "so I can have a lawyer."

"Not yet," I say. "After the DNA samples come back from the lab."

"I'd like to go back to my cell now."

He wanted out of the cell. I guess he didn't enjoy his taste of freedom. I take him back downstairs.

"Thank you for the cigarettes," he says.

I slam the steel door shut and the clang echoes through the corridor. "You're welcome," I say.

# 12

I GO BACK TO my office, write a detailed summary of events and e-mail it to the national chief of police. A photocopy of Sufia's address book is in a plastic sleeve on my desk. I have coffee and a cigarette and browse through it again. I recognize more names familiar from the tabloids. Sufia must have liked to surround herself with famous people.

I start dialing numbers. I introduce myself and say I have a few questions concerning Sufia Elmi. The media picked up on the murder through the national crime incident database and word has gotten around. People express shock. The interviews are all the same. No one knew Sufia well. The men say they went out a couple times, had some fun. The women say they hung out in nightclubs, went dancing, had some fun.

Valtteri comes in. "I called Heli," he says. "She doesn't want to see you and asked if I could bring her the keys."

"Tell her no. Seppo's car is a crime scene and she had access to it. I have to talk to her."

"She won't come."

"Then arrest her and lock her up."

"Are you serious?"

"Yeah."

He hands me a magazine. "I thought you should see this." He walks out.

The front page of *Alibi* is splashed with the headline: "MURDER! SOMALI SEX GODDESS SLAUGHTERED IN SNOW-FIELD!" When I open the magazine, I'm outraged. Two photos side by side occupy a quarter-page each. One is a still from her last movie, a display of her beauty. The other is a photo from the morgue, her corpse on a gurney in an unzipped body bag. She's nude and ravaged, once again violated. Smaller but no less grisly photos are underneath.

Jaakko has written an article that refers to Sufia Elmi as Finland's Black Dahlia. He's managed to paint Sufia's murder as both a race and sex crime and called to mind a legendary Hollywood murder. I wonder if Sufia's murder will also pass into legend, if she will forever be Finland's Black Dahlia. I find this disturbing. It's as if the tragedy of her death has been forgotten before it was even recognized, trivialized in favor of tabloid glitz and the terrible romance of celebrity murder.

I didn't want details of the crime released. The fucking diener must have sold Jaakko the photos. I'll charge him with obstruction of justice.

My cell phone rings—it's Sufia's father. We must have been looking at the morgue photos of her at the same time. I answer. "Vaara."

"Inspector, this is Abdi Barre. My wife is in tears. Can you imagine why?"

I can imagine. "The photos."

"Her friend called and told my wife that revolting photos of her murdered daughter were published in a filthy magazine. She went to a newsstand and bought that filthy magazine. She is devastated and humiliated."

"I'll press charges against whoever sold the photos to the magazine."

"You have failed to protect my daughter."

He has my pity, but I'm tired of taking shit from him. "You can't expect me to be responsible for security at a government facility over which I have no control."

"I hold you responsible for all matters relating to my daughter."

Once again, he's treating me like I'm on trial for Sufia's murder. I don't know why and it's not fair. "You have my sympathy for the pain the photos caused you and your wife. I'll deal with it today. I can't do anything more."

"The Koran tells us Inspector Vaara, that 'when the sky is rent asunder, when the graves are hurled about, each soul shall know what it has done and what it has failed to do.' For my wife and I, the sky has been rent asunder. Do not fail in your duty."

He hangs up. I feel like he just punched me in the head.

Before I can recover from Abdi's accusations, Valtteri knocks on my door and enters. "Antti and Jussi are back"—he hands me Seppo's house keys—"and Heli's here."

He walks out, she walks in.

Apart from this morning, we haven't spoken since she left me so many years ago. I didn't think it would, but being alone in a room with her makes my pulse quicken. I light a cigarette, try to hide my discomfort. "Thanks for coming," I say. "Have a seat."

She hangs up a chinchilla coat and matching hat. "You didn't leave me much choice."

She puts her hands on her hips and looks around, like she's looking for something to criticize. If so, she can't find anything. I have a polished oak desk, nice art on the walls, a Persian rug on the floor. I paid for them myself. One of my theories of life is that happiness is in part derived from a pleasant environment.

She comes over to my desk and picks up a photo of Kate. "Pretty," she says. She looks miffed about it, takes a seat across from me.

"Want anything?" I ask. "Coffee, soft drink, water?"

"What are you, a stewardess? I told you before, you've gone to a lot of trouble to see me. If you wanted to meet for coffee, you could have just called."

She has a certain desiccated look. I often see it in wealthy female tourists. Fortyish, and making a desperate attempt to stop the aging process with overexercise and self-starvation, treatments, expensive lotions and makeup. It seldom works, and it hasn't in Heli's case. She looks older than her years and bitter. I can't connect the woman in front of me with the girl I fell in love with.

"Let's cut to the chase," I say. "Your common-law husband butchered a girl he was having an affair with."

She crosses her legs, folds her hands in the lap of her designer jeans and looks amused. "Yes, let's cut to the chase. My ex-husband has a thirteen-year-old vendetta and concocted some half-assed attempt at revenge."

I try to get this revenge theory she and Seppo have out of the way. "With your ego, you might find it hard to believe, but I've hardly thought about you for years." I point at the picture of Kate. "I have a good life. You're not worth wrecking it over."

She smirks. "You're right, I don't believe it. When I call the newspapers and explain the history behind your investigation of

Seppo, I doubt others will believe it either. What I did was for the best. You must realize that by now."

I'm being dragged into a conversation I don't want to have, but I can't seem to stop it. "What you did was cruel. I didn't deserve it."

"Deserve," she says. "Nobody gets what they deserve. If we did, we'd all burn in hell. We're all fucking guilty."

"You're quite the philosopher."

"Just admit that you hate me for what I did."

I ask myself if this is true. "I don't hate you. You want to know what I think? I'll tell you. I don't think about what you did to me anymore, but when I did, I used to remember when we were about fifteen. It was summer, you were in my folks' house and I was doing something outside. I heard you scream and you kept screaming. I thought you were hurt. I ran in, and you had a sparrow in your hands. It had flown into the house and got tangled in flypaper hanging in the kitchen. It thrashed around trying to get loose and tore most of its feathers off. When I got there, you held it up to me. 'Help it, help it,' you said. I always wondered how you could have had so much pity for that bird, but so little for me."

We sit in silence and look at each other. A good three minutes go by. I feel old pain resurfacing and try to suppress it. I have no idea what she's thinking. She uncrosses her legs, crosses them again, smoothes an invisible wrinkle on her pants leg. "I've wondered that too, but I didn't."

I wait.

"I don't remember. What did you do with the bird?" she asks.

It's an ugly memory. I'm surprised she doesn't recall. She followed me outside and watched me kill it. "I took it out to the front yard and stomped on it to put it out of its misery."

Another minute passes. "I'll take that water now."

I pour it from a carafe on a sideboard and give it to her.

"Tell me what you want to know," she says.

"Did you know Seppo was having an affair with Sufia Elmi?"

"No."

"Not a clue?"

She sighs. "Seppo has affairs from time to time. I ignore them. They always blow over."

"This doesn't bother you?"

"That's not your business."

She's right. I should keep the questions focused on Seppo. I know he has family money and that because of it, he used to sit on the boards of various corporations and institutions, but he seems to have gone off the radar. I don't know what he does at present. "Does Seppo have any kind of work, any responsibilities?"

She shakes her head. "Not anymore. He's rich, he doesn't have to do anything."

"Has Seppo ever been violent toward you?"

"Seppo is incapable of violence. The sight of blood makes him sick. If he cuts himself shaving, he cries."

This is the man she left me for. Amazing. "He drinks a lot?"

"Yes, he drinks."

"Does he exhibit psychotic behavior when he's drunk?"

She puts on a facade of boredom. "He giggles and gets cuddly."

"The murder occurred the day before yesterday, at about two P.M. It appears that your BMW was used in Sufia Elmi's abduction. She may have been raped in the backseat. Do you know where Seppo and the car were at that time?"

"No, I was in church all afternoon."

"Church?"

"That's why I'm in Kittilä, to rediscover my religious roots."

I try to hide my surprise. Heli's antagonism toward religion used to be extreme. That was a long time ago. I remind myself that I don't know her anymore.

"What makes you think she might have been raped in our car?" she asks.

"Blood and semen."

She looks at me like I'm stupid. "Have you stopped to consider that maybe he fucked her and she wanted it?"

"I have, but thanks for your input."

She stands up. "I'm leaving now. Can I have my house keys?"

I toss them to her.

"What about the car?"

I might want to sit in the garage and listen to Miles Davis again. "In due course."

"My advice to you," she says, "is to release Seppo before you make things any worse for yourself. Good luck with your snipe hunt and with the media. I'll be giving interviews soon. You'll be hearing from our lawyer. I'll see to it that Seppo sues you for fabricating a case against him."

"That's your prerogative."

"Good-bye Kari." She leaves, shuts the door behind her with a soft click.

# 13

I DON'T WANT TO see her again, so I give Heli a couple minutes to get out of the building before going out to the common room. Antti and Jussi are sitting there with Esko the coroner. Items from Seppo's house are bagged and spread out over two desks.

"I need to talk to you," Esko says.

"I saw the new edition of *Alibi*. Yeah, we need to talk about it."

"In private."

"Give me a minute." I look at the potential evidence. There's a lot of it. "Anything good here?" I ask.

"Could be," Jussi says. "We found two pairs of boots he could have worn, and a bunch of clothes. We figured they should all go to the lab."

"Yep."

"We got a hammer and a couple *puukko* and some knives out of the kitchen too."

I pick up the bag with the *puukko*, Finnish hunting knives. They're less curved than the skinning knife used to kill Sufia, so

I don't make too much of them, and besides, almost every Finnish home has at least one or two lying around. Statistically, they're the nation's most popular murder weapon. Twice, I've investigated murders in which a group of men got drunk together and passed out. They wake up and one of them is dead with a knife in his chest. All of them have fingerprints on the knife, but nobody remembers what happened. Neither case ended in a conviction.

Antti points at Seppo's computer. "Seppo likes to look at porn."

If looking at porn were a crime, most men in this country would be in prison. "What kind?"

"I didn't go through it all," Antti says, "but I didn't see anything violent."

"Anything with Thai girls?" I ask.

Antti's face goes red.

"And we got this." Jussi picks up a bag with three half-liter Lapin Kulta bottles in it. "They were in the fridge. We figured we ought to check and see if they came out of the same lot as the one, you know, in her vagina."

"It wouldn't surprise me." I look around. "Where's Valtteri?"

"He said he had to go home," Antti says.

I look at my watch. It's a quarter after six. "Maybe you guys should go home too. This stuff needs to go to the lab. Could one of you take it to the airport and get it to Helsinki on the next plane?"

"I can," Antti says.

"By the way, I processed the car and got a lot of forensics. I think this case should be over soon."

Antti looks sheepish. "Think I'll be able to go on vacation?"

"Odds are good. Let's see what happens tomorrow."

"Can we talk now?" Esko asks.

I motion toward my office. "About obstruction of justice, you bet."

I shut the door and we sit down. I toss the magazine at him. "The fucking diener," I say.

"I'm embarrassed about that but . . ."

"But nothing. The photos were irresponsible and disrespectful. Details were released that could impede the investigation. I'm going to charge him."

"There's no guarantee it was Tuomas. There are other workers, cleaners, it could have been any one of a dozen people."

"You know goddamned well it was the diener."

"Will you forget the fucking diener!"

I've never heard Esko yell before. It shuts me up.

"I'm not here to talk about that," Esko says. "I got the DNA results from the crime scene and autopsy back from the lab."

I feel like a jerk, light a cigarette. "What did you get?"

"Can I have one?"

To my knowledge, Esko doesn't smoke. I slide the pack over and he lights one, takes a couple drags, collects his thoughts. "The lab results turned up semen samples in and around her mouth. DNA testing shows it came from two separate sources."

I get a queasy feeling in my stomach that tells me the case has gone wrong. "How do you interpret that?"

"She had to have performed oral sex on two different men on the day of her murder."

"So you're saying Seppo had an accomplice?"

"I can't say Seppo was involved at all. I don't have a DNA sample from him for comparison."

"I can't force him to give one until I charge him. You can have a sample from the evidence collected from his house. It comes back from the lab tomorrow."

"There's more."

I press the stress out of my eyes with my fingertips. "What?"

"There's a third set of DNA from the crime scene. You remember the sample I took from her face? You asked me to collect it."

I nod.

"Teardrops."

"Are you sure?"

"Of course I'm sure."

"I didn't know teardrops have DNA in them."

"Well, they do."

"If it's minus forty and I spit, it freezes before it hits the ground. Why didn't the tears freeze and just bounce off her face?"

"I looked it up. Tears are a saline solution and depress the freezing point of water. They only have about a tenth or a twelfth of the salt content of seawater, depending, interestingly enough, on the cause of the tears. It was enough salt to keep the tears liquid while they fell, until they struck her face. They spattered and then froze instantly. The lowest possible temperature for a saline solution is minus twenty-one-point-one degrees. It was minus forty outside, so the salt crystallized out of the water. That's how you were able to notice it. Your flashlight made the salt crystals sparkle."

"No shit." I don't know what else to say.

"That's not the real news. The tears don't belong to either of the men she performed fellatio on."

I hang my head in my hands. "That can't be true."

He stubs out the cigarette. "It's true."

I sit up straight, compose myself, chain another cigarette off the last one. "She performed oral sex on two men, who may or may not have murdered her, either individually or together. Then, a third individual, I presume male?"

"Yes, male."

"A third man cries over her face while she's being slaughtered, or maybe after."

"Correct. There's still more."

This has gone so awry that I laugh. "There can't be."

"One of the men she performed oral sex on was identified from the sex offenders' DNA database. I recognized the name, Peter Eklund. His father is one of the wealthiest men in Finland. He owns a bank."

I know who Peter is, but I didn't know he's a registered sex offender. His residence is in Helsinki, so there's no reason I would have been informed. He's twenty-three years old and already drinking himself to death. He's been a guest in our drunk tanks several times. I've also given him speeding tickets. He drives a BMW.

"What are you going to do?" Esko asks.

I want to scream out of frustration. This case should be winding down, but now it looks like this may just be the beginning. Too much has happened today. If I find Eklund and interview him tonight, I might make mistakes. "I'm going home."

# 14

KATE IS ON THE BED, watching TV. I lie down beside her and pat her belly. "How are you and the kids?"

She turns and kisses me. "We're okay. That boy, Heikki, came by today."

"Was he any help?"

"Not exactly. He wouldn't speak to me in English. Doesn't he have to take it in school?"

"Yeah, but you know how we Finns are. If you can't do something to perfection, you don't do it at all. He's just shy."

She looks like she just tasted something bad. "He's not just shy, he's creepy. The way he looked at me made my skin crawl."

I laugh a little. "It's the religious thing. I guess they're something like American Pentecostals."

She raises her eyebrows. "You mean they speak in tongues?"

"I don't think they do anymore, at least not frequently, but it used to be common. They believe the same thing about being entered by the Holy Spirit, and they have the same kinds of strict codes of dress and behavior. Laestadian women go for the natural look, tend to be on the plain side. Makeup is against the rules. He's probably never been in the same room with a beautiful woman like you."

"I told him I didn't need anything today. I'd rather he didn't come back."

I don't know how I could explain this to Valtteri. "If he tries to speak English, will you give him another chance?"

She looks skeptical.

"If he gets used to being around you, he'll stop staring at you."

"All right, I'll try one more time. But if he makes me feel icky again, he's got to go."

"Fair enough. You could try speaking Finnish with him. If you both practice languages, it might make him more comfortable."

"I thought he was here to make me comfortable."

"Of course you're right, but you've got some downtime. Maybe you should use part of it to study Finnish. Getting better at speaking it would make your whole life more comfortable."

"Kari, I'm trying. Finnish is just so hard. Even simple things are difficult, because we just don't have those sound combinations in English. Every sentence is like a tongue twister. Like saying good night. *Hyvää yötä*. See what I mean? I sound stupid."

"You don't sound stupid, just strange because your pronunciation is so soft. The more you practice, the more natural it will sound."

I'm being kind. No matter how well foreigners speak Finnish, no matter how good their grammar, it just sounds wrong to me. Still, improving her Finnish would make her more functional and comfortable in everyday life.

"It's like trying to learn Chinese," she says, "except it has a Roman alphabet."

"People learn Chinese too."

She looks put out and changes the subject. "Tell me about the case."

I don't know how to begin, so I just blurt it out. "You remember I told you my ex-wife left me for another man. He's the suspect."

She sits upright and looks at me. "You must be kidding."

"I wish. Things would be much simpler."

"Are you sure he did it?"

"I was, until about an hour ago."

She lies back against propped-up pillows. I tell her most of the story, about the BMW and the money trail connecting Seppo to Sufia.

"Wow," she says. "What karma."

"Valtteri tells me it's the will of God."

She smiles. "You never know."

"I have to tell you some other things too. I think they'll be public soon, and I'd rather you hear them from me."

She raises her eyebrows.

I tell her how Seppo threatened her, how I pulled off the road and stuck a gun to his head, shouted in his ear and scared him, made him piss himself and faint.

She shakes her head in disbelief. "I just can't picture you doing it."

"You didn't see the murdered girl. I got this mental picture of you being killed like her, and I lost it."

She puts an arm around me. "Emotions make us do things. Maybe nothing will come of it."

I relate my interview with Heli. "She says they're going to sue me. If our past comes out in court, it could look like it's not an honest murder investigation, and they might win."

"Does she have any basis for suing you? Don't you have to do anything like question people and check their alibis before you arrest them?"

"No. With such a violent crime, it's pretty much left up to the arresting officer. Besides, I only followed instructions from a superior."

"Unbelievable. After all this time, she's going to try to hurt you again."

"It's because of the way she hurt me before that they could win. A lot of people would think it's a good motive for revenge."

She runs a hand through my hair. "Want to tell me about it?"

"Not really, but I'm going to anyway. After I got shot, I was in the hospital for almost a week. She didn't visit or answer the phone. When I got home, her stuff was gone. A note on the kitchen table said she wouldn't be back."

"You told me that much before."

"I guess that's all I was ready to tell you."

"In the States, dating is like going to confession. If people don't have any traumas, they'll invent them just so you won't think they're shallow. I had a first date once, and this guy tells me that when he was a kid, his mother had an obsession that made her lick the floor clean. I'm sitting there thinking, if that's what he's willing to tell a near stranger, what's he hiding? It's like people think they have to give you a secret before you'll trust them. I've always liked it that you believe in privacy, both yours and mine. I admire it."

"Kate, I had just killed a man. I thought my shattered knee would cripple me. I couldn't get in touch with my wife and I was worried sick about her. Then I go home and find out she left me."

"What did you do?"

"She filed a change of address. That's how I found out she was living with Seppo. Since she wouldn't talk to me, I called him. I meant well—I was still worried about her. I told him that Heli had a lot of problems, that I was her husband and to send her home to me."

"What kind of problems?"

"Eating disorders. Self-image problems. Depression. I've known Heli since kindergarten, she's always been an emotional mess."

"Were you her husband or her caretaker?"

This sounds harsh, but I see her point. "I started dating Heli when we were thirteen. We'd been together for fourteen years, married for seven. I was both."

I lay my head on Kate's breast and she wraps an arm around me.

"Seppo told me she wasn't my responsibility anymore, to forget about Heli. I told him I'd like to meet him to talk. He said he couldn't see any point in that. I was so heartbroken and angry that I told him I'd find him, hunt him down and kill him, stab him in the fucking heart. He hung up the phone, and I never spoke to him again until two days ago, when I clapped handcuffs on him."

She strokes my face. "But you didn't hurt him. You didn't do anything wrong."

"I got so depressed I was nearly suicidal. I'd wake up and think, 'Today is the day I kill him.' But it was like that was all I had to live for. Once I'd killed him, I'd have nothing left. The days passed, I never did, and then one day I just didn't want to anymore."

She kisses the top of my head. "It's a good thing. If you'd killed him, you'd have ended up in prison and we'd never have met."

"I was lucky. If you kill someone in the line of duty, you have to see a therapist. I talked more about the divorce than the shooting. It helped a lot."

"Why didn't you want to kill *her*?"

A fair question. I laugh a little at my ridiculous answer. "I couldn't kill her because I loved her. I needed someone else to blame."

"Why do you think she left you?" The tone of her voice says she's afraid she's prying, but I understand her curiosity.

"I blamed myself for a long time, asked myself what I'd done or hadn't done. Maybe it was partly my fault. She had her friends at music school, I had my cop buddies, and we didn't spend much time together or have much in common anymore. We drifted apart during our last couple years together. I didn't see it and let it happen. Still, though, after a while I realized that her leaving didn't have much to do with me. She left because I had nothing left to offer her."

"What do you mean?"

"In high school, I was a good hockey player, and she studied piano. Heli was a dreamer. She thought I'd be a big sports celebrity and she'd be a famous pianist. I broke my knee and couldn't play anymore. I decided I wanted to be a photojournalist. I got out of high school—you know here we get out at nineteen—and had to do mandatory army duty for eleven months. Just before I left, Heli told me she was pregnant, so we got married. I came home on leave and she said she'd lost the baby."

"Was she really pregnant?"

There are things I don't tell Kate. I cheated on Heli a couple times when we were teenagers. I think Heli knew, but we never talked about it. My brothers told me there were rumors that Heli cheated on me. If she was pregnant, I don't know if the baby was mine. Heli and I never talked about that either.

"Maybe. I doubt it. Heli got accepted into Sibelius Music Academy, in Helsinki, so we agreed that after the army I'd work while she studied, then it would be my turn. In the army, I was in the military police. Afterward, I did what seemed like the natural thing and became a cop. Heli went to school. Six years later, she graduated with her master's degree. At the time, Seppo was on the board of directors of the Finnish national opera. When I talked to her friends later, I figured out that she had started her affair within a week or two of her graduation, just as I was about to start my education. I guess she thought her relationship with Seppo would do more for her career than supporting me while I studied. Heli only takes. She doesn't do things for other people."

"It took you thirteen years to figure that out?"

"I was young and stupid, and love makes you blind."

"It's hard to believe she could be so callous."

"It took me a long time to believe it. Sometimes you don't know people until after they're gone."

She strokes my hair again. "You know I would never do that to you."

I suppose fear is the reason it was so long before I could be in a serious relationship again, but I'm not afraid anymore. "I know . . . "

This is hard to talk about. I pause, try to find the words. "This seems funny when I look back. At first, my plan was to kill Seppo and just turn myself in. We Finnish police are competent. I didn't think I could get away with it."

In fact, three murderers have turned themselves over to me. They said they were sorry and asked me to arrest them. It's common here. "I decided to study law enforcement and learn how to commit a murder. It's not easy to get away with. Murder investigations here have a ninety-five-percent success rate. Of course, the real reason I didn't kill him was because deep down, I never wanted to in the first place, but that's what I told myself. I was insane with grief."

"How long were you in therapy?"

"About a year, but I gave up on the idea of murdering Seppo long before that. I found out I liked studying. I couldn't work as a beat cop with a bad limp, but I could be a detective. I decided to get my master's degree and make a career out of it. I worked while I studied."

Next to medicine, law enforcement is the most admired profession in Finland. The national police force is one of the best in the world and almost free of corruption. As an inspector, I'm one of the most respected members of the community. It may be egotistical, but I enjoy that status.

She laughs a little. "So if you hadn't wanted to be a killer, you wouldn't have become a detective."

"I already was a killer, and because of it, guilt contributed a lot to my depression, but yeah, the irony is great."

She hugs me tight. "You were just a human being in a lot of pain. You're a good man Kari, and I love you for it."

Funny that I'd been so afraid to tell her the truth. There was no reason for it. "Thank you Kate. I love you too."

"It sounds like Heli has some kind of narcissism disorder," she says.

"That's what my therapist thought."

"You don't have to worry about all this old bad business being dredged up in a lawsuit. You were the good guy. She'd come off like the queen bitch of all time."

"You think?"

"I'm certain of it."

She pushes herself out of bed and hobbles on her crutches to the kitchen. She brings me a bottle of beer. All that effort to bring me a beer makes me smile.

"I'm ordering us pizza," she says.

I look at the beer bottle. It's a Karjala. Thank God, because I'm never going to be able to drink Lapin Kulta again.

# 15

In the morning, I call the national chief of police to give him the update he asked for. He must have my name and number in his mobile phone and know it's me when it rings. He wouldn't be so rude if I were someone more important. He barks at me, "What?"

I bring him up to date on new developments, tell him about the three sets of DNA found on Sufia's corpse.

"So she blew the Eklund boy before she got killed," he says.

"And he has a BMW."

"A tough situation," he says. "His father could make our lives difficult."

"Yeah."

"Go question him, impound the vehicle and process it, but go easy, don't arrest him unless you get hard evidence." He hangs up before I can speak, a fucking annoying habit of his.

———

KATE STILL CAN'T GET used to the idea that during her first year at her new job, she earned four weeks of vacation, not including a bunch of paid holidays. In this country, we work a lot less than most people in the world, an average of around two hundred days a year. Nature is close to the Finnish heart. Most of us like to spend a good portion of that free time in the countryside at a summer cottage. It may be a hut in the forest with no running water, it may be a palace, they all qualify as cottages.

In theory, time spent at a summer cottage is for picking wild mushrooms and berries, for going to sauna and swimming in lakes. In practice, a trip to a summer cottage is often an excuse for us to stay drunk for a week or two at a time.

Some of our more well-to-do also have winter cottages. Peter Eklund's father has a winter cottage set atop a high mountain. It's the most valuable piece of real estate in the area and resembles a small Teutonic castle, except that the entire front wall is made of glass. In the months that we have sunshine, the daylight flashing off it can be seen for miles.

I drive up the mountain along the winding road that approaches the Eklund winter cottage and park next to Peter's BMW. It's new, a black 3 Series sedan. I brace myself for the shock of arctic cold, get out of the car and check out his tires with a flashlight. They're Dunlop Winter Sports mounted on seventeen-inch rims, just like Seppo's. The only difference is that Seppo's car has star-spoked wheels, and Peter's are double-spoked.

I call for a tow truck to impound the car, then take in the view from the mountaintop. It's cloudy, but no matter how dark it is, a

little light always reflects off the snow. The world is cast in a charcoal silhouette. Thousands of lights from Levi and Kittilä glitter
in the valley below. It's nine fifteen A.M., a good time to interview
Peter. If true to form, he'll be so hungover that he won't be able to
think straight enough to lie.

I ring the doorbell and wait. I ring it again. He doesn't answer.
Waiting in the cold pisses me off, so I push the button in and hold
it down. The noise is annoying from outside. Inside the cottage, it
must be making his head throb. After a few minutes, he opens the
door.

Peter is tall and blond, with classic Nordic good looks. His
clothes are rumpled and slept-in. "I-i-in-inspec—"

Peter stutters. When he's nervous, he's incomprehensible.
When he's drunk, the stutter disappears.

"I need to talk to you," I say.

"Co-co-come . . . " He gives up and nods.

I walk past him. The front room is vast, the ceiling looms three
stories overhead. The other floors are constructed as balconies that
look down into this space. The room is dominated by a central
fireplace open on all four sides. A stone hood connects to a massive chimney that rises twenty yards before reaching the roof. The
decor is late-twentieth-century bad taste: everything costs a lot of
money, nothing matches. Peter's father uses it as a fuck pad to get
away from his wife in Helsinki. He lets Peter use it when he isn't.

Three men are passed out on sofas, all in their early twenties.
One opens an eye and looks at me. I tell him to go back to sleep.
Peter looks queasy. "Bad hangover?" I ask.

"Y-y-es."

A half-empty crate of Koskenkorva, Finnish vodka, sits in the middle of the floor. I pull out a bottle. "Got a place where we can talk?"

We go to the kitchen. It's better equipped than some gourmet restaurants, although clearly unused. Empty bottles cover every surface and remind me of the bottles littering Sufia's cottage. I open the Koskenkorva and hand it to him. "Drink it. I need to talk to you."

He pours vodka and orange juice, fifty-fifty, in a glass and downs it, pours another. I make coffee while he gets drunk enough to communicate. He lights a cigarette, a Marlboro Light.

He finishes the second drink, makes a third. I pour myself coffee. We sit at an oak kitchen table. It has traces of white powder on it. I doubt Peter is much of a baker. It's probably not flour.

"Feeling better?" I ask.

"Yeah."

"Tell me about you and Sufia Elmi."

"I saw the paper yesterday."

"Then you should have called me."

He doesn't say anything.

"The autopsy turned up your semen in her mouth."

I expect this to shock and frighten him. He shrugs. "She blew me that morning."

"You're pretty casual about it."

"It's no big deal. I met Sufia about a week ago, in Hullu Poro. I fucked her that night."

"Where?"

He laughs. "Everywhere. In the women's bathroom of the bar, in my car, in her cottage."

"You don't seem too sad that she's dead."

"Well, it's not like I really knew her. I like to drink and fuck. Sufia doesn't drink, but she likes—liked—to fuck. After the second time, she asked me if she could borrow some money. I knew what was up. Every time after that, I gave her one or two hundred. We always called them loans. I guess I met her to fuck like five times, stayed over at her place two or three times. It's hard to remember."

"You're stating that you paid her for sex."

He looks pleased with himself. "Inspector, she was worth every penny. She had this weird pussy, and Jesus, she loved to give head."

"I take it you're referring to her missing labia minora."

"Her what?"

"Her vaginal lips. They'd been removed."

"No shit?" He laughs again. "Whatever."

Peter has to be the most worthless piece of garbage I've ever met. "Where were you at two P.M. on the day of her murder?"

He gestures toward the front room. "My buddies came in from Helsinki and their plane arrived about noon. I picked them up at the airport and we've been hanging out ever since. We were in Hullu Poro all afternoon."

"How did you get to the bar?"

"In my car."

"Do you know Seppo Niemi?"

"A little. I've met him in nightclubs in Helsinki and talked to him in Hullu Poro a couple times. Sufia was with Seppo when I met her. He got too drunk and left. Sufia told me she'd been seeing him. It didn't bother me any, he's a fucking dumbass."

"Her room had a lot of empty liquor bottles in it. Were they all yours?"

He puts on a grin like a five-year-old. "Most of them anyway."

"I have to take your car."

The alcohol makes him overanimated. He stands up and raises his voice. "Hey, come on, I told you what you want to know!"

"Shut up and sit down."

He does it.

"Since you had sex with Sufia in it, the car is a potential crime scene. I'll give it back in a day or two."

He gives me the keys. "It's not fucking fair."

"I might be saving your goddamned life by keeping you from driving, you drunk fucking bastard. Go back to sleep, I'm done with you."

In the front room, I shake his friends awake. They won't move, so I yell at them. They sit up and look at me like I'm insane. I point at one of them. "What time did your plane get in on Tuesday?"

"Who the fuck are you?"

"I'm a pissed-off cop who's going to arrest all of you for the cocaine dust on the kitchen table if you don't answer my god-damned question."

The kid grimaces. Peter registers fear. I would take them all in, but the chief said no arrest without probable cause for murder. I figure I should trust his judgment on this.

"Yeah dumbfuck," I say. "I saw it. You're lucky I've got other things to do right now."

"We got in at eleven fifty-eight," the kid says.

"How did you get here from the airport?"

"Peter picked us up."

"Were you with him all afternoon?"

"Yeah."

"Where?"

"In Hullu Poro."

I check all their IDs and write down their contact information.

Their boots are in the foyer. "Which of these are yours?" I ask Peter.

He points.

I pick them up. They're size tens, the same as the prints at the crime scene and the same size Seppo wears. He and Seppo also both smoke Marlboro Lights. "I'm taking the boots."

He starts to say something, thinks better of it.

I open the front door. "By the way, you're a registered sex offender. Who did you rape?"

"Nobody. She wanted it."

"How old was she?"

He doesn't even flinch. "Fifteen."

I stare at him for a minute.

"I did my community service," he says.

# 16

PETER IS A WASTE of humanity, breathing air somebody else could be breathing. He could have killed Sufia. If so, his friends were probably accomplices. Peter and one of the others could have forced her to perform oral sex, accounting for the two sets of sperm in her mouth. One of them, not inclined toward rape, could have been upset by the spectacle and shed the tears that provided the third set of DNA. I wouldn't put it past them, but I don't consider it likely either.

Peter was already getting what he wanted from Sufia, but maybe Sufia wanted more from Seppo than he was willing to give her. Fear that she might destroy his relationship with Heli provides him with one motive. Sufia's affair with Peter gives him another. Seppo remains the most likely suspect.

Valtteri calls. Seppo wants to talk to me. I go to the police station. News vans from Finland's three major television channels are parked in front of it. Reporters and cameramen pile out into the cold, surround me, shine lights in my eyes and start filming.

Altogether, there must be twenty of them, and print journalists too. I see Jaakko from *Alibi* in the crowd. They shout questions. I decline to comment and push my way through them.

Valtteri is in the doorway. "They wanted to wait inside," he says, "but I wouldn't let them."

"Don't. Except for Jaakko Pahkala. After I talk to Seppo, go get him and bring him to my office."

The three major Helsinki newspapers, all morning editions, are scattered around the common room. Sufia is on the front page of each. I take a few minutes to read them. Two of them specialize in yellow journalism. Thanks to Jaakko, they pick up on the Black Dahlia theme and compare Sufia's murder to that of Elizabeth Short, the Hollywood starlet murdered in 1947, whose gruesome killing still remains a source of fascination for murder buffs today.

Only *Helsingin Sanomat*, a more sober publication, takes a more thoughtful line and focuses on the fact that Sufia is the first prominent black woman to have been murdered in Finland. Even their treatment is confusing. It leaves me unsure if, in some twisted way, they consider her murder an advancement of black women in our society. I check my messages.

Nine Finnish newspapers request interviews, plus STT—the Finnish News Service—and Reuters. At some point, I'm going to have to talk to the press. The story is going international, and if I don't, they'll invent something to keep steam behind it. I had hoped that by the time we got to this point, I could tell them the case was solved.

I go down to the lockup to talk to Seppo. I open the port in his door. "I hear you have something to tell me."

He jumps off his cot. "I figured something out. If I can prove I didn't kill Sufia, will you let me go?"

"That's the way it works."

"Yesterday, when you came down here, you said it had been forty-nine hours since Sufia was murdered."

"So?"

"When we went upstairs, I saw a clock. It was three then, so Sufia was killed at two."

"That's right, Sherlock."

"I was on the phone around that time, you can check."

I start to close the window. "I did check. Nice try."

"Wait." He pushes a hand through the port, holds it open. "I wasn't talking on my cell phone. The battery was almost dead, so I used the landline in the room. I was staying in a cabin in the Hullu Poro hotel."

It's next to the bar and restaurant. He gives me a name. "I'll look into it." I shut the port in his face.

I check out his story. Seppo was registered there. He made a call a little later than he said, at two forty-one P.M., and talked for nineteen minutes. I get the number and call Seppo's friend. He confirms the conversation.

"How would you describe Seppo's emotional state during your conversation?" I ask.

"He was Seppo, nothing special."

"You detected no agitation in his voice?"

"He was happier than I've heard him sound for a while."

"What did you and he talk about?"

He hesitates. "It was pretty personal."

"Seppo is locked in a cell and about to be charged with murder. Is it more personal than that?"

"It's about her, then. You arrested Seppo for it?"

"Are you referring to Sufia Elmi?"

"Yeah."

I wait, but he doesn't say anything. "What did you talk about?"

He sighs. "Okay. Seppo talked about that girl."

"What did he say?"

"Shit. Well, I won't lie for him. The girl had just left. He went on about how she sucked him and fucked him. That's all he talked about the whole time. That's why he called me, to brag about it."

Now I know where Sufia was abducted. The killer must have driven her straight from the hotel to Aslak's reindeer farm.

"Did he say if he had feelings for her outside of their sexual relationship?"

"You mean was he in love with her?"

"I mean feelings. Love, hate, whatever."

"No, I didn't get any of that."

"Well, what did you get? What was his attitude, his demeanor, when he discussed Sufia Elmi?"

He doesn't say anything. I can almost hear him thinking.

"Listen," I say, "a woman has been murdered. Bringing her justice is more important than your concept of duty toward a drinking buddy."

"Jesus, you just don't quit. He called her his nigger. You happy now? He said, 'My nigger got on her knees.' He said, 'Nigger looked up at me with those gorgeous eyes while she sucked my cock. I blew in that beautiful nigger's face. Nigger whore took it in the ass.' He went on like that."

*Nigger whore.* The words cut into Sufia's torso. "He used the phrase 'nigger whore.' You're certain."

"Yeah, but you've got to know Seppo. He doesn't mean anything. He talks shit, tries to act like he's a big man. He does it because he feels small. He's not a bad guy or I wouldn't be his friend."

"Yeah, I'm getting a real sense of his underlying sensitivity. I'll be in touch." I hang up.

# 17

JAAKKO, GOSSIP COLUMNIST and writer of true-crime horseshit, walks into my office. He's a little guy with a scraggly beard, full of energy. "Thanks for giving me the tip about the murder," he says.

I finish the last sentence of my report to the national chief of police and e-mail it before looking up. "I did you a favor," I say, "treated you like a professional journalist. You repaid me by writing about Sufia Elmi with disdain and disrespect. You released details of the crime I didn't want published, and the photos you printed were exploitative. I just called you in here to tell you that. Now get out."

He winces like I slapped him. "If you mean the comparison to the Black Dahlia murder, I meant no disrespect. The two killings are similar."

"Putting a Hollywood spin on her murder makes it seem inconsequential. How do you think publishing those photos made her parents feel? I spoke to her father. They're devastated."

He looks penitent. "Can I sit?"

"No."

"I'm sorry I offended you, but anybody would have published the photos. *Alibi* even held the presses to get the story in. Sales were up sixty percent. And, well, true-crime stories are a hobby for me. When I heard the details, the Black Dahlia was the first thing that came into my head."

"Where did you get the crime scene details?"

"I can't tell you that."

"How much did you pay the diener?"

He ignores the question. "I'd like to interview you about the case."

"I'm busy, go away."

"Your ex-wife called *Ilta-sanomat* today."

I should have expected this. "And?"

"She says she left you for Seppo Niemi, and you arrested him for Sufia's murder. She says you're framing him. Care to comment?"

"No." Something occurs to me. "How did Sufia's murder remind you of the Black Dahlia case?"

"I'll tell you, if you answer a few questions."

"You're out of the loop. I can find out about the Black Dahlia case on my own."

"And I can find out about the murder investigation without you. This thing about you and Seppo Niemi, I'll find that out too."

"Go ahead."

He turns to leave, then looks back at me. "I'm still grateful to you for the lead, so I'll tell you this. The Black Dahlia, Elizabeth Short, was dumped in a vacant lot in Los Angeles. Sufia was killed in a snowfield, sort of a rural equivalent. Short was cut in half and Sufia had a deep slash in her abdomen. Both had a piece of their breast cut off. Both had writing scratched into their skin. The crimes aren't exactly the same, but close enough to make me think of it. Most important, though, Sufia had scarred genitals, and Short had a genital birth defect. What are the odds of that?"

"No interview, but I'll keep faxing you police reports," I say.

ANTTI COMES INTO my office. The results from Seppo's house and car are back from the lab in Helsinki. Antti pulls a chair over next to me and we go through them together. DNA from Seppo's toothbrush matched semen found in Sufia's vagina and mouth. He drank out of a couple of the bottles and smoked some of the cigarettes found in her room.

DNA records from the sex offender database validate Peter Eklund's story. The rest of the bottles and cigarette butts match to him. The blood in the backseat of Seppo's car belongs to Sufia, the semen is Seppo's. Hair samples from the car are both of theirs. The source of the tears recovered from Sufia's face remains unknown.

We go out to the common room. Valtteri and Jussi are eating lunch. "The beer bottles in Seppo's refrigerator and the one used to attack Sufia are from the same lot," Jussi says. "They were sold at a kiosk about half a mile from Seppo's place."

I bring them up to date, tell them about the tears dripped onto Sufia's face, about my interview with Peter Eklund and about Seppo's telephone conversation.

"Let's look at the timeline," I say. "Aslak reported the murder at two twenty-five P.M. He saw a vehicle pull away and made the call when he found Sufia's body. Let's say it took him three minutes to do it. That puts the vehicle on the road at two twenty-two. When I left Hullu Poro, I drove the speed limit and I got to Aslak's place in twelve minutes. If Seppo killed her and drove straight back to the hotel, that puts him there at two thirty-four. He calls his buddy at two forty-one. What do you think?"

"It's tight," Jussi says, "but possible."

"That nigger whore stuff," Antti says. "I don't think that's a coincidence."

"Me neither," I say, "but I wouldn't call it damning."

"My problem," Valtteri says, "is that I don't think Seppo is capable of butchering a girl, then going back to his room and laughing it up with his friend to give himself an alibi. If he was a serial murderer, used to killing, then maybe, but Seppo?"

"I see your point," I say, "but it's a mistake to think you know him. I don't know anyone, including murderers I've put away, that I think capable of committing this kind of crime. Do you?"

"No," Valtteri says, "I don't."

"But somebody did it," I say. "It could have been Seppo, or Peter, or the third man who cried in her face. I'm inclined to think it was two men. The evidence against Seppo is piling higher all the time. Maybe he had an accomplice."

My cell phone rings. It's the national chief of police. "I just got a call," he says, "from a reporter named Jaakko Pahkala. He says the guy you're holding for murder had an affair with your ex-wife. She claims it's an attempt at revenge. The reporter claims you refused comment. Would you care to tell me about it? It might have been courteous to mention it."

Jaakko screwed me because I wouldn't give him an interview. The chief is right, I should have told him. "He's my ex-wife's common-law husband. I didn't tell you because it seemed like a simple case. I thought when the DNA test results came back yesterday, they would prove him guilty. It's turned out to be more complicated than that."

"You didn't tell me because you thought I would remove you from the investigation."

It's partly true. I don't say anything.

"Are you?" he asks.

"Am I what?"

"Carrying out a vendetta?"

"Of course not. I think he did it."

"I'm trying to be fair here. Assuming you didn't manufacture the evidence, which I don't think you did, he seems guilty, and I would have thought it was an open-and-shut case too. But now the Eklund boy is in the picture, and I'd say there's enough evidence to hold him for the crime as well. And this thing about the third man and the teardrops, well, that's just fucking weird."

"Yeah," I say, "it is."

"So, we've got a public relations problem. There's evidence against one man, and he's in a jail cell. There's evidence against another, and he's not. The man in jail screwed your ex-wife, the one who's not is the son of a wealthy financier. This could be construed as more than a little biased, wouldn't you say?"

His sarcasm grates on me. "I did what you told me to do. I arrested Seppo, let Eklund go free for the moment."

"But you didn't tell me about your ex-wife and Seppo. I would characterize that as a major fuckup."

"Yeah, I can see that."

"When it comes out in the newspapers today that you arrested the man who broke up your marriage, you're going to look like an asshole."

"I know."

"Your best bet is to cite conflict of interest and recuse yourself from the investigation."

"Then it looks like I framed him and got caught. I still look like an asshole."

"It's called cutting your losses."

"I don't want to."

"I know you don't. I also know you've done a good job and collected a mountain of evidence in a short time. The case is in its fourth day. To be honest, I'd replace you, but if I send somebody up there to take over, it's going to take him a couple days to get up to speed. That's a lot of lost time, and I want this case solved now."

"I'm going to solve it. When I locate the third man, the one who cried on Sufia Elmi, he's going to connect to either Seppo Niemi or Peter Eklund."

"Here's what you're going to do. Issue a written statement to the press. Give enough detail to show that Niemi's arrest was warranted. Talk about his affair with the victim and about the blood and semen in his car. Paint him black to make you seem justified."

"That's unethical."

"It's a tough world. Do it."

I'm not going to. "Okay."

"Then you say he has an alibi and release him. You come off looking fair and honest."

"Are you out of your mind? I'm almost certain he killed her. If he did, he's fucking psycho, and I'd be unleashing a danger on the community. It would be worse than irresponsible."

"If you don't, I'll replace you, and he'll be released anyway."

I'm backed into a corner. I don't bother to respond.

"Call me and report tomorrow," he says and hangs up.

Valtteri, Antti and Jussi look at me. "We have to release Seppo," I say, and try to imagine how I can explain this to Sufia's father.

# 18

I UNLOCK SEPPO'S CELL DOOR and lie to him. "Your alibi checks out, I'm considering setting you free. You should have told me about the phone call earlier—you could have been out yesterday."

"Considering?" he asks.

"Your buddy says Sufia had just left when you called him. Besides her killer, that makes you the last person to see her alive. You're a material witness in this investigation. I want you to coop-erate with me. I can still hold you for another day."

"I still think I should have a lawyer present."

"For what? You're no longer a suspect."

"I don't want certain things to get out," he says.

"Heli knows about your affair."

"She does? Fuck."

"So you don't have anything to lose," I say.

We go to my office. I give him coffee and cigarettes. Seppo's smiling, happy. "About what happened yesterday," he says, "I under-stand that you were upset. You thought a murderer threatened your wife. I'm not going to tell anyone about it. What Heli and I did to you was terrible. Maybe we can just call it even."

I scared him. He played a hand in destroying my marriage. He can't be stupid enough to consider those things equitable. He probably just doesn't want anyone to know he pissed on himself.

"That sounds fair," I say. "Let's forget the past and start over. Who knows, if we met under different circumstances, we might have been friends."

This gratifies him. He offers his hand and we shake.

"Are you comfortable?" I ask. "Want anything?"

"Thanks, I'm fine."

"Are you ready to talk about the case?"

"Anything to help. I guess you know Sufia and I were close."

"Tell me about you and Sufia." I start a tape recorder.

"Do we need that?"

"Yeah, we do. Is it a problem?"

He processes the ramifications of being taped. It takes him a while. "I guess not."

"Good. Tell me about you and Sufia."

Seppo's pause tells me he's thinking about how to present himself in the best possible light. "Sufia was different."

"How so?"

"I met her at a cocktail party about three months ago. She had the most gorgeous eyes I had ever seen. We talked for hours. She was interested in me, she listened to me."

"Did she talk about herself?"

"Not much, she liked to talk about me. It seemed like she really cared if I was happy, like I was important to her."

"Had you been unhappy?"

"Not exactly."

"It sounds like she gave you something you felt you were missing."

He thinks about this. "You know Heli. She can be charming when she wants to. She hasn't wanted to for a while."

I don't know her anymore, so I don't say anything.

"That doesn't mean I don't love her," he says.

"Of course not."

"It's just that some other companionship was nice."

"Sufia was young and beautiful. That must have been nice too."

His voice intimates that we're talking buddy to buddy. "You have no idea."

I mimic his tone. "I bet the sex was pretty good."

He looks proud of himself. "The best I've ever had. She loved doing it with me. The girl came like a rocket."

"Let's talk about Tuesday, the day she was killed," I say.

"She came to the hotel at about twelve thirty. We didn't talk much. You know."

"I can only imagine."

"She left around two, said she had things to do."

Maybe to see Peter. "Why did you rent a room at Hullu Poro instead of going to her cabin? After all, you were paying for it."

"She said it was a mess. She was too embarrassed to let the maid clean it and wanted to do it herself, but kept putting it off. Sufia wasn't exactly domestically inclined."

I give him a just-us-guys smile. "I guess she had other talents that made up for it."

"Yeah." He snickers. "Besides, I stay at Hullu Poro when I've had too much to drink in the bar there, so I don't get behind the wheel."

"You're a good citizen. When was the last time you were in Sufia's room?"

"About a week ago, I suppose."

"Where was your car while she was in your room that day?"

"Outside in the parking lot."

"Does anybody else have access to it? Do you ever loan it to your friends?"

"Just Heli. She has her own set of car keys."

"Did you ever let Sufia borrow your car?"

"No."

"I found your semen and her blood in the backseat. You had other places available to have sex. Why in the car, and why the blood?"

He smiles. "Did you ever see Sufia? I fucked her anywhere and everywhere I could, as often as I could. One look in those gorgeous eyes of hers made my dick hard. Maybe she'd started her period when we did it in the car."

"It seems like your feelings for Sufia were genuine. Was there any future in the relationship?"

"She told me she loved me and would like to have something more permanent. I told her things could stay the way they were. Permanently."

"Meaning she could be your mistress indefinitely. Do you think Heli knew about your affair?"

"I was careful to make sure she didn't find out."

It's hard to picture Seppo being careful about anything. "But you talked to other people about Sufia."

"Just a few close friends."

"I'll need their names and contact information."

He nods.

"Because, the thing is, you called Sufia a 'nigger whore' during a phone conversation, just about a half an hour after somebody carved 'nigger whore' on her abdomen. That strikes me as more than coincidental."

"He told you what I said?"

"Yeah."

He looks down at the desk, starts to fidget. "What are you getting at?"

"You pretended like you cared about Sufia, but you called her a 'nigger whore' behind her back. You bragged about coming on her face and fucking her in the ass. Some people might take that to mean you were using her. If you talked about her, using that exact phrase, to various people, one of them could have used that information to set you up. Or somebody could have overheard a conversation and used it to frame you. That's what I'm getting at."

He looks relieved. "I see what you mean—I'll make a list."

"There's another option," I say. "The phone call was later than you said and doesn't entirely clear you. There was enough time after the murder for you to get back to your room and call a friend to give yourself an alibi."

He scratches his head, thinks about it. "If I did that, why would I call her a 'nigger whore' and mess up my alibi?"

"That's a good question. A better one is why you ever called her that at all."

"If somebody tried to frame me," he says, "like you think they are, it wouldn't have been too hard. Somebody could have borrowed my car for a while and put it back. Everybody knows I don't get out of bed till four when I've been drinking the night before."

"What time do you get out of bed when you haven't been drinking?"

He hesitates. "Four."

So he's drunk every night and sleeps through his hangovers. I change gears. "Did you realize that Sufia's clitoris had been removed?"

"I knew there was something strange down there but didn't ask her about it. Why would someone do that?"

I don't bother to explain. "She didn't enjoy sex with you as much as you think, maybe not at all."

He looks unbelieving.

"Peter Eklund was having an affair with Sufia," I say. "That's why she wouldn't let you go to her room. Peter's liquor bottles were all over it."

I gauge his reaction. He looks injured, as if the idea of Sufia betraying him is both hurtful and mystifying. I wonder how good an actor he is. "No shit?" he asks.

"No shit. I think she wasn't satisfied being your mistress, I think she used you."

"That ungrateful bitch," he says.

"Some people don't know how good they have it," I say, then cut him off. "That's enough for now."

I thank Seppo for his cooperation and apologize for the inconvenience. I give him his car keys and walk him out to the garage. "Anything you need," he says. "Anything. You just ask."

I open the garage door and reporters start swarming toward us.

"I'll see you soon," I say, and wave as Seppo drives away.

I didn't bring my coat. It's fucking freezing outside. The reporters start questioning me, but my statement is brief. "That was Seppo Niemi you just saw leaving. He provided an alibi and I released him. We're now pursuing other avenues of investigation."

They keep shouting. I shut the garage door in their faces and go back into the station.

**BACK IN THE COMMON ROOM,** I relate my interview with Seppo and lay out what we've got to do next. "We've made a lot of progress. We know where Sufia was when she was abducted. Since, by his own admission, Seppo's vehicle was in the parking lot, it could have been used in the commission of the crime. The tears are the key. Because of them, it appears Seppo had an accomplice. Whoever shed them is linked to Seppo. It's possible Seppo wasn't even present when the crime was committed. Sufia's affair with Peter gives him motive. Seppo could have had her killed."

I'm pretending confidence I don't feel. Yesterday, it looked like we'd broken the case in forty-eight hours. Now we're at a standstill.

"We have to pursue the Peter Eklund lead with the same thoroughness as our investigation of Seppo. Peter's car was in the parking lot too. Antti, you process it."

He looks demoralized. I don't have to tell him he can't go on vacation.

"Jussi, you go to Hullu Poro. Check out if Peter was there at the time of the murder. Question the staff and everyone who's been hanging around the bar over the past few days. If his car turns up evidence or we can't confirm his alibi, we'll treat his house as a crime scene. Valtteri, you go back to investigating locals. Known racists, sex offenders, men prone to violence. I'll take photos of Seppo and Peter with me and re-canvass Marjakylä. And Valtteri, come into my office, I want to talk to you."

When we're alone, Valtteri says, "About Marjakylä, your father wasn't at work in the bar when Sufia was murdered. You asked me to check."

"Then I'll ask him about it myself. I want to talk to you about Heli."

"What about her?"

"When she left Kittilä, she shook the dust off her feet and never came back. As far as I know, she hasn't been here since we divorced. She hated her family. When we were married, she only came here when I wanted to see mine. Seppo always came here alone. She tells me, as she put it, that she's 'rediscovering her religious roots.' Have you seen her in church?"

He nods. "It's true, she's been attending regularly."

"Why didn't you mention it to me?"

"I don't like to bring up your ex-wife, it's not my place." He pauses. "You don't think Heli could have had anything to do with it."

"She's gone for years. Then she shows back up, and her common-law husband's mistress is murdered. She had keys to his car, she had motive. It's a natural line of questioning."

"Maybe you're not taking the possibility that Peter and his friends killed Sufia seriously enough," he says. "He and Seppo have nearly identical vehicles and they were both in the parking lot. They smoke the same brand of cigarettes, even have the same shoe size."

"I'm taking it seriously. If Jussi finds blood in his car, it will provide sufficient grounds to seize his house and treat it as a secondary crime scene."

"Arresting Seppo has already caused you a lot of trouble. If you accuse Heli, it might cost you your job."

"I'm not accusing her. It's a line of inquiry we have to pursue, because it's our duty. And I'm not investigating her, I'm asking you to do it."

"How could Heli have done it? I mean physically. She's a woman. She can't commit rape."

"We haven't proven that Sufia was raped."

"Heli is so small, how could she have forced Sufia into the car? Don't you remember how Sufia looked? I can't imagine Heli inflicting those kinds of injuries."

"Just nose around," I say. "Find out what Heli's been doing and who she's been associating with. Discreet questioning. That's all I ask."

"This is going to lead to no good end," Valtteri concludes, and walks out.

# 19

I WRITE A PRESS RELEASE, but not the way the chief wanted it. I don't mention my previous marriage to Heli, or that she left me for Seppo, and I don't write anything to tarnish his image. I keep it simple, say he provided an alibi and was released. I e-mail it to all the major Finnish newspapers, STT and Reuters.

The photocopy of Sufia's address book is on the desk in front of me. I start making phone calls again. After an hour, I get a hit.

"That bitch fucked my boyfriend. She sucked his cock in my own goddamned house. I'm glad she's dead."

"Who's your boyfriend?" I ask.

"You mean, who was my boyfriend. That bitch wrecked everything."

"Yes, that's what I mean."

She gives me the name of a Finnish television star. I call him.

"Fuck," he says. "What did you hear?"

I play him. "Never mind that. Just give me your version of events."

"Maybe it's wrong to speak ill of the dead, but the blackmailing bitch said she was gonna get me."

"How did she say she was going to get you?"

"She was never anything to me. I had a girlfriend and Sufia was a side thing. Excuse me for being blunt, but Sufia was an incredible fuck. The girl could suck an egg through a straw. And gorgeous, Jesus, just looking at her could almost make me come. My girlfriend caught us. Sufia was happy about it because she said we could see each other out in the open, but I wanted to get rid of Sufia so I could patch things up. Sufia got angry. She said she'd claim I raped her and told me I had to give her money."

"Did you?"

"I told her to go fuck herself."

"Have you been to Levi lately?"

"Not for two years. Am I a suspect?"

"Not at present. Thank you for your cooperation. One last thing, what kind of car do you drive?"

"A BMW. Why?"

I ignore the question and hang up. I can understand Sufia's attraction to rich and famous men, but I'm left wondering about her obsession with BMWs. I've talked to around thirty people about Sufia. No one knew her, not even the men she'd had affairs with. It seems no one cared enough to bother, but I want to. I decide to watch her movies.

I PRINT OUT SEPPO'S arrest photo and one of Peter from the sex offender database, then go to the BMW website, download and print pictures of star-spoked and double-spoked wheels and drive to Marjakylä. I decide to get the worst over with and go to my parents' house first. I knock, and Dad yells for me to come in. He's sitting in his armchair smoking an unfiltered North State. A glass of *piimä*, buttermilk, sits on the end table beside him. I take this to mean he's not drunk. I'm relieved.

"Hello son," he says.

The television is turned off, the curtains are drawn. The only light spills out from the kitchen. He's sitting in the dark and what would be silence, except for the incessant ticking of clocks.

Mom's dentures are in a water glass beside Dad's *piimä*. She got them as a present when she was confirmed into the Lutheran church at the age of fifteen. Years ago, dentures were the traditional confirmation gift. There was little or no dental care then, and most people's teeth rotted out of their heads not long after they reached puberty.

"Where's Mom?" I ask.

"Upstairs taking a nap."

Despite his drinking, Dad's health is good. Among other ailments, Mom is overweight and has high blood pressure. She tires easily. I sit across from him, in her chair.

"I'm not trying to piss you off," I say, "but I have to ask you where you were at two P.M. on Tuesday, when Sufia Elmi was killed."

He takes a drag off his cigarette. "That girl was killed across the road," he says. "You think I did it, then came back here and talked to you and your mother?"

I've never figured out why my father is such an argumentative, aggressive jerk. He has four sons, and we all left home as soon as we were old enough. He drove us away with his drunken rages and beatings. My three brothers did pretty well for themselves though.

When Finland's economy collapsed in 1989, my oldest brother, Juha, went to Norway to look for work and got a job in a fish canning factory. Now he's married and makes good money working in the Norwegian oil fields. After Timo's short stint in jail for bootlegging, he settled in Pietarsaari, on the West Coast, and works in a paper factory. Jari got into medical school, and now he's a neurologist in Helsinki.

Dad is always putting Jari down, says he thinks he's better than everybody else. Dad is just jealous of him. Jari is one of the nicest people I know. My brothers are all nice guys, but we're not close. Maybe because we shared so many bad experiences, it's easier to limit contact so we don't have to think about our childhoods.

Mom has put up with Dad going on fifty years. I don't know how she's managed it. Then again, she had no money, no education. I suppose after she got married and figured out what she'd gotten herself into, she didn't have many options. Still, I wish she had tried to do more to defend us kids from him.

"I know you weren't at work," I say. "If I don't know where you were and somebody asks later, it'll look like I'm hiding something. I'm trying to protect you."

"It's not your business where I was."

"If you were drunk somewhere, I don't care." It occurs to me that maybe he's having an affair. "If it's something you don't want Mom to find out about, I won't tell her."

He finishes the *piimä* in a long gulp. "I was fishing," he says.

Now I get it. It was the anniversary of my sister Suvi's death. He spent the afternoon sitting on the frozen lake, visiting the spot where she died. Dad and I look at each other. I feel embarrassed because I intruded on something so private to him, and the sadness I always feel when I think of Suvi wells up.

I stand and put a hand on his shoulder. "Thanks for telling me."
I head toward the front door.

"You gonna come by on Christmas?" he asks.

"Yeah. Kate and I will come over."

I realize I haven't told him Kate broke her leg or that she's pregnant. "Kate took a bad fall skiing," I say. "She fractured her femur."

"Her thigh bone?"

"Yeah."

"She gonna be okay?"

"The cast is awkward for her, but she's okay. And she's pregnant. We're going to have twins."

He laughs to himself. "Twins huh?"

"Yeah."

"You're gonna have your hands full."

He doesn't seem to have anything more to add, so I leave.

# 20

I SHOW THE PHOTOS of Seppo and Peter around the neighborhood. No one recognizes them. I visit Eero and Martta. Eero invites me in and I accept. The scents of cardamom, melted butter and sugar waft out of the kitchen. The Christmas tree is lit. A fire burns in the hearth. Martta comes out from the kitchen and greets me, then brings coffee and warm *pulla*, sweet coffee rolls, for all of us. I sit in a recliner, while they sit together on a love seat and hold hands. I ask Eero if the car he saw pulling out from Aslak's reindeer farm was graphite or black.

"Too dark, too dark," he says. "Besides, I was busy talking on the phone, so I wasn't paying attention."

I lay pictures of star-spoked and double-spoked wheels on the coffee table between us. "Do you happen to remember," I ask, "what kind of wheels were mounted on the car?"

He points at the star-spoked wheels. "This kind."

"It must have been hard to tell," I say. "Wasn't the car moving?"

"It stopped at the top of Aslak's driveway," he says, "before it pulled out onto the road. Even in the dark, they were shiny."

Martta's *pulla* is delicious. I help myself to another. Sulo, their Jack Russell terrier, hops into my lap. I pet him, and we gossip about the neighbors.


ON THE WAY HOME, I stop at the video store and rent Sufia's movies, then go to the grocery and pick up potatoes and a couple steaks. I catch Kate up on events while I cook. She sits at the kitchen table, her broken leg propped up on a chair.

"Eero sounds like a real character," she says, "but if he's schizophrenic and talks to imaginary people, he's probably not medicated. Isn't he a danger to himself?"

"Martta keeps him out of trouble, and besides, we're a small community. Everybody is used to him. People tend to think of him as more eccentric than sick."

She laughs a little. "In the States, they have TV commercials for Viagra, cosmetic surgery, antidepressants. They ask, 'Are you tired in the morning, stressed at work, have trouble sleeping at night?' By the time they run through the list of symptoms, they've included everybody. People believe they're depressed and go running to the doctor begging for drugs. Here, you've got a guy talking to imaginary friends on a pay phone, and they not only don't treat him, they disconnect the line but leave the phone booth so he can be happy. That's real community and I like it."

"Northern Finland has its good points," I say.

"About the case," she says, "what do you think about this Peter Eklund guy?"

"I think I hate him," I say. "His family has been rich for centuries, since Finland was a province of Sweden, and it gives him a feeling of entitlement he's done nothing to earn. It's because of the same mind-set that I had to learn Swedish in school, even though only five percent of Finns are part of the Swedish-speaking minority. I've got nothing against Swedish-speaking Finns in general, but a lot of the rich Helsinki ones in particular believe the rest of us are supposed to cater to their whims. As they say in Swedish, Peter thinks he's *bättre folk*, and he can do anything he wants without regard for others."

"You're right about Heli," Kate says. "She had a motive, but do you really think she could have committed such a brutal murder?"

"I can't imagine anyone doing it, but like I told Valtteri, somebody did. Let's see what he turns up. Besides motive, she needed opportunity. It would have been hard for her without an accomplice."

"Valtteri is right too," she says. "If investigating Seppo caused you so much trouble, investigating Heli might get you fired."

"I know."

"You don't have to. You could hand over the evidence to another detective. Like the chief said, cite conflict of interest."

The steaks sizzle and I flip them. "If it goes far enough, I'll consider it."

I put in *Unexpected*, the first movie of Sufia's trilogy, in the DVD player. We eat in front of the TV and watch it.

Sufia plays a sexy but innocent young woman, adrift in Helsinki's nightlife. She becomes involved in an affair with a young, successful and attractive—but morally arid—man who uses her. Ultimately, she ends up with a young, successful and attractive man who values her. In addition to love, she finds herself and happiness. Sufia's acting is good. She's a bright spot in a bad film.

Kate falls asleep before the end of the movie. I carry her to bed and put in *Unexpected II*. It's much the same as the first one. It poses as a multiplot story that exposes the social mores of young, single professionals in Helsinki. This thin veneer masks a soft-core porn flick in which seven people have a revolving sexual relationship. Some of them find happiness, some don't.

In *Unexpected III*, Sufia's romantic and sexual desires conflict with her studies. She intends to become a Lutheran minister. I fast-forward through it and watch only the scenes in which Sufia appears. In the majority of them, her flawless dark skin is set off by see-through white lingerie. Her great love from the second film winds up in prison, but in the final scene, Sufia marries yet another suitor and finds even greater love and deeper self-fulfillment. The happy couple drives away in a BMW 330i.

The movies aren't low budget, but the producer didn't spend a fortune on them either. Many of the sets and props are reused throughout the trilogy. I take another look at *Unexpected* and *Unexpected II*. In all three movies, happiness is marked by a couple in a BMW 330i. I'm guessing it belongs to the producer or director.

Now the recent events of Sufia's life seem clear. I think she had been trying to make reality out of the fiction of her movies, even to the extent that she searched out men who drive BMWs. I wonder if she was even aware that she did it. The car seems—perhaps unconsciously—to have symbolized wealth, success and happiness for her. No one knew her, maybe she didn't even know herself. Sufia the snow angel, whoever she was, is lost forever.

# 21

I'M GETTING READY FOR BED. My cell phone rings. I look at
the clock: eleven forty-five P.M. It's Valtteri. I answer and hear him
crying. He's trying to talk but I can't make out what he's saying. He
sobs in big heaving gasps.

"Valtteri, I can't understand you. Try to calm down."

"I can't help him," he says. "He's gone."

"Who?"

"He's cold, and I can't help him."

Now I'm scared. "Valtteri, what's happened?"

"My boy, Heikki, he hanged himself."

He wails so hard that he chokes.

Valtteri loves his family beyond all things. He's living a nightmare. "Shit. I'll be right there."

He forces out words. "What do I do? Can I take him down?"

"No. Is Maria with you?"

"Uh-huh. She . . . she found him."

"Just stay with her and wait for me."

"Thank you," he says, "I'm sorry." We click off.

I wake Kate up. "There's an emergency. Valtteri's boy, Heikki, killed himself. I'd like you to come with me, to be with his wife, Maria, while I sort out what happened."

We bundle up and go out into the cold. When we get to Valtteri's house, he's barefoot, sitting on his front porch steps in a T-shirt and sweatpants. It's minus twelve out. I help Kate out of the car and onto her crutches. They slip and slide on the ice and she has a hard time staying on her feet. I help her to the porch and sit next to Valtteri.

"I'm so sorry," I say.

He turns and puts his arms around me. He bursts into tears. He cries and cries, and I hold him until he gets it out.

The three of us go inside. Maria is sitting on the couch, weeping. Her long gray hair is matted to her face from tears. Kate hobbles over to her side and embraces her. Maria sobs on her shoulder. They've never met.

"Where is Heikki?" I ask.

Valtteri wipes his face. "In the cellar. Maria found him when she went to put clothes in the dryer."

"Where are your other kids?"

"I sent them to the neighbors."

"You stay here, and I'll go down and take care of Heikki. Would that be all right?"

"No," he says. "No no no. You can't take him down by yourself. I have to help you. He's my boy."

He bursts into tears again. He's getting hysterical, starting to hyperventilate. Maria's not much better.

"Okay," I say.

I put my arm around him and we go down to the cellar together.

It's a combination laundry and junk room, dank and lit overhead with a single bare bulb. Heikki used a section of laundry line and hangs from a rafter in the center of the room. His feet dangle over an overturned stool. His face is black, his tongue protrudes from his mouth. The cellar smells like feces. Heikki voided himself when he died.

Valtteri stares at him, sits down on the floor, rocks back and forth and cries.

Heikki is a big boy, but I don't need any help. I set the stool upright and stand on it, lift Heikki enough to take the weight off the cord and cut it with a pocket knife. I lay him down on the floor, cross his arms and close his eyes, then drape him with a clean sheet from a laundry basket. When I do, I notice a half sheet of paper on the floor and pick it up: *Hän sai minut tekemään sen.* The Finnish language has no gender marker, so Heikki's suicide note reads either "He made me do it" or "She made me do it."

Further, it could mean that someone drove him to kill himself, or that he committed an act so terrible that he felt only his death could atone for it. His religion guarantees an eternity in hell for the sin of suicide. What could have been so heinous as to cause him such guilt? An internal alarm goes off. Out of gut instinct, I wonder if he was involved in Sufia's murder.

I form a mental picture of Heikki crying over Sufia's corpse. He was in my house, alone with Kate. I suppress an irrational surge of anger toward Valtteri for sending him there.

I sit down on the floor beside him. "Did you see this?"

He nods.

"Do you know what it could mean?"

He shakes his head.

"Valtteri, I'm sorry. This may be an admission of murder."

He nods, he thought of it too, and that reinforces my suspicion.

When Valtteri called me, he said he was sorry. A possible reading of the note is that one of his parents drove him to kill himself after finding out he was a murderer. Valtteri and Maria love their kids more than life, but still, I can't discount the possibility.

"I'm going to have to investigate," I say.

He looks at me and his upper lip quivers. "Does that mean me and Maria have to go?"

"No. With your kids coming and going all day, there's no reason to treat the house as a potential crime scene. But I'm going to have to look in his room, take some of his things."

"I know," he says.

I take Valtteri upstairs and call for an ambulance. EMTs take Heikki to the morgue. Before they leave, they give Valtteri and Maria tranquilizers. Kate sits with them. Nothing she can say will soothe them, but her presence forces them to be strong.

Heikki shared a room with a younger brother. I quickly process it, take some clothes and his computer. I go back down to the cellar and look through boxes of junk, hoping I won't find Sufia's missing clothes or a murder weapon. I don't.

It's three thirty A.M. when we leave. Valtteri and Maria are on the living room couch, asleep in each other's arms. We put on our coats, and I help Kate across the ice to the car. I start it but can't drive yet. Kate and I look at each other for a long moment. We don't speak. There aren't any words. I think Kate has just discovered the meaning of Finnish silence.

# 22

THE NEXT PLANE FROM Kittilä to Helsinki leaves at four forty-six. If I'm right, and Heikki participated in Sufia's murder, the DNA samples I'm sending to the lab will prove it. Kate and I drive straight from Valtteri's house to the airport. I tell her about the suicide note and what I think it might mean. She looks distraught. We don't discuss it further. It starts snowing, and the monotonous slap of the windshield wipers destroys the quiet I need to mourn the death of the son of a trusted colleague and dear friend.

I keep picturing Heikki crying over Sufia, his tears freezing and spattering on her battered face. Possible scenarios flicker through my mind like different edits from the same film. Maybe the boy was a sociopath: he stole Seppo's car, abducted and murdered Sufia alone. I see him hit her in the head with a hammer. He cuts her clothes off and carves "nigger whore" on her belly in the parked car, drags her naked and unconscious into the snow and brutalizes her, twists a broken beer bottle into her vagina. She wakes up blind, writhing and screaming. He cuts her throat and cries at the sight of his fantasy become reality.

Or perhaps Seppo held some kind of power over Heikki and forced him to become an accomplice. They parked in Aslak's driveway. Heikki stood by while Seppo sodomized, maybe raped Sufia in the car, and then dragged her into the snowfield and committed atrocities. Heikki knelt over her and cried while witnessing the aftermath.

I imagine it the other way around. Heikki and Seppo are in the car together, but Heikki commits the brunt of the crimes. I see the same things over again, except Peter Eklund replaces Seppo. This scenario seems implausible. A Laestadian like Heikki and hedonistic scum like Peter would likely detest each other and everything the other stood for.

Then I picture Heli orchestrating the murder. She could have met Heikki at church. She could have been behind the wheel and relied on Heikki's size and strength for the abduction and murder. She could have motivated him in some way, given him the keys to Seppo's BMW and been absent during the commission of the crime. I consider the sexual forms her encouragements may have taken. If he had been true to his faith, Heikki was inexperienced, vulnerable.

These visualizations make me shudder. Whatever Heli may have done to me, I once loved her and want to think of her as good. The idea that she might be capable of such evil hurts me in deep places, makes me remember the way I felt about her when we were young. My gut reaction is that it's not possible, but then I remember what I said not long ago: I can't picture anyone committing such a murder, but someone did. I could never have imagined the way she betrayed me either, and I ask myself if, on a subconscious level, I'm skewing the investigation to punish her for that betrayal.

I don't think so. Seppo's affair with Sufia gave Heli motive. Valtteri was right. Overexercising combined with dieting have left Heli a skinny bag of bones, too small and weak to have carried out the murder by herself. The addition of Heikki to the picture gives her means and opportunity. Maybe Kate was right, maybe I should cite conflict of interest and recuse myself from the case. I can't though, and I'm not sure why.

By the time we get home, it's five thirty in the morning. I take Heikki's computer from the trunk of the car, then bring it and the car battery inside. Kate sits down on the couch, throws her crutches on the floor. She hasn't taken her shoe off. Snow melts on the rug. I don't say anything, sit down beside her. She stares straight ahead. A few minutes go by, then she buries her face in her hands and starts sobbing. I wonder if I should hold her and comfort her, but I have the feeling she doesn't want me to, so I wait.

"I can't do this," she says without looking up.

This night has been hard on her, maybe harder than I realize. I put an arm around her. "What?"

"Did you see that boy?" she asks.

She had seen him on a gurney as the EMTs took him out. I cut him down. "I saw him."

"I spent the night comforting a woman I had never met before. We don't even speak a common language. I'm glad I was there for her, but where were her family, her friends?"

I can't explain the Finnish concept of privacy. When we grieve, often we can't talk about it. Maria may have been more comfortable with a stranger. "You're the best friend she could have had."

"That boy, Heikki, I told you he was creepy, and now he's dead. I feel so awful that I said those things about him."

"You don't need to."

"The note he left. He killed Sufia Elmi, didn't he?"

The more I think about it, the more I'm convinced of the likelihood. If he murdered Sufia, I ask myself again if Valtteri and Maria knew. He might have confessed to them. Talk of the Bible and deserving punishment, of fire and brimstone, could have driven him to suicide. My hands start to shake. He was alone in the house with Kate, and I brought him here. "Probably."

"Even I noticed he was strange. How could his parents not have known there was something wrong with him?"

"They have eight kids. In a family that size, children don't get much individual attention. Things go unnoticed."

She starts to cry harder. "I want to leave this place. I want to go home."

I equate "leaving this place" with leaving me. I don't fear much, but this scares me. "What do you mean?"

"I don't want to live here anymore."

"Where do you want to go?"

"Back to the States, to Aspen."

In my mind's eye, I see Kate every moment of the day. Her cinnamon hair, dove-gray eyes so light they're almost without color. Since we met, our relationship has been something self-contained, both a beginning and an end, like I picture death must be. I thought nothing could ever come between us. I get the same feeling I had when Seppo threatened her. My heart pounds, my ears ring, my vision goes blurry.

"In the States," she says, "I never met anyone who committed suicide, never even knew anyone who had a suicide in their family.

In this little country, it seems like someone does it every day. Finns are like lemmings rushing off a cliff."

It's true. Most years, Finland has the world's highest suicide rate. Last year, it was twenty-seven out of a hundred thousand citizens. If I lost Kate and the twins, I would feel like joining the statistics.

Kate looks at me and reads the panic in my face. "Oh God. Kari, I'm so sorry. I didn't mean it like that. I want you to come with me. I would never leave you."

I start to calm down. She puts her arms around me and kisses me. "We could leave here," she says. "You speak and write almost perfect English. You're educated and a decorated officer. Any police department in the U.S. would be privileged to have you on its force."

Her opinion of me is higher than my own. "Why do you want to leave?" I ask.

The sadness in her face tells me she's going to speak from the heart. "When I first arrived here, my picture of Finland was different. Nature and the environment seemed wild and beautiful, life seemed orderly. I thought people were happy."

"You were mostly right," I say.

"No, I was wrong. This is an ugly place. The silence, the misery, the months of darkness. It's too extreme, like living in a desert made of snow instead of sand."

Sometimes I think this too.

"When I talk to people," she says, "they hardly ever laugh or even smile unless they're drunk. Finns are inscrutable. I have no idea what they're thinking or feeling. Sometimes I feel like people hate me for being a foreigner, like the nurses at the hospital when I broke my leg. I'm uncomfortable. Worse, I'm terrified because

I'm pregnant. I'm at the mercy of people I don't and can't under-stand."

I didn't know how deep her cultural alienation had become. I try to explain. "What you perceive as silence, we view as peace-ful solitude. Most of us aren't miserable, but our approach toward life is serious, maybe because of our extreme environment. People don't hate you, they respect you because you're successful. Finns are afraid of making mistakes. If we can't do something perfectly, it's hard for us to try to do it at all. The people that work for you speak fluent English and are proud of it, but a lot of people are too scared to try."

"That's no excuse for the way they treated me at the hospital."

"You were in pain. Sometimes, people here ignore suffering so the sufferers can maintain their dignity. When you give birth, your medical care will be excellent, for the same reason the nurses wouldn't speak to you. Health care professionals expect themselves to excel at their work. Our educational system is one of the best in the world. There's no better place for our children to grow up."

I've given a speech that sounds like an advertisement selling the Finnish way of life. Hearing the words come out of my mouth, even I don't buy it.

She looks frustrated. "Are we living in the same country? We just watched a teenage boy, probably turned psychotic murderer, be carted off to the morgue after hanging himself. I run places that sell booze. Do you think I don't see how rampant alcoholism is here? People are drunk because they're depressed. They get so depressed that they become mentally ill and kill themselves. You say this place is safe? You want our kids to grow up in this environment?"

Almost everyone in Finland knows a suicide. The normal way of dealing with it is to allow ourselves to grieve, to speculate about why and talk about our love for the departed. Then we bury the dead and seldom mention them afterward. I don't know if it's because of our pain at their loss, or because of guilt, the feeling that we didn't give them the help they needed to stay alive. Suicides get only a tiny obituary in the newspaper, a minimalization of our loss, a form of denial. The minuscule death notices speak of our shame.

"There's a lot of truth in what you say. I can't defend life in the north against its flaws, and there are many, but this is my home and I love it. If you stay here long enough and learn the language so you can understand the culture, you may come to love Finland for some of the reasons you hate it now—the silence, the solitude, even the melancholy—like I do."

She's getting angry. "The language! I don't speak Finnish, but I know enough about it to see that it's a reflection of the culture. In colloquial speech, you refer to other people as 'it.' That tells me a lot."

"Kate, I'm a cop in early middle age with a bad leg. I don't know if I could get a job in the U.S. or not, but I'm pretty sure that even if I did, I wouldn't be any good at it. I speak English, but I don't understand your culture. I can't catch crooks if I don't know how they think. Those few months I spent in the States working on my master's thesis, I felt like a fish out of water, just like you do now."

"My income is six figures. It doesn't matter if you work or not."

"It matters to me. Besides, after the twins are born, you'll be on maternity leave. We could figure it out then."

"What difference does my maternity leave make?"

"It's a hundred and five workdays, that's a long time."

"What are you talking about? I'm not going on maternity leave for months."

"Why not? Everyone does."

"Does that mean I'm required to?"

As much as I love Kate, sometimes the cultural differences between us mystify me. "I guess not, I just never heard of anyone not wanting to before. What do American mothers do?"

"We take a few weeks, get child care and go back to our careers, and that's what I'm going to do. Are you saying no to moving? Won't you even think about it?"

My automatic reaction, when someone tries to make me do something, is to do the opposite. I try to stay reasonable. "This feels like an ultimatum."

"Kari, it's not an ultimatum. I would never leave you, I just want to know if you'll consider it or not."

I don't want to say it, but Kate's happiness is more important to me than my own. "I'll consider it."

We drop the subject and get ready for bed. Kate always goes to sleep with her head on my shoulder, our arms wrapped around one another. We do the same now, but I can still feel the tension between us, like magnets forcing each other apart instead of pulling each other together. I've never felt that way with Kate before, and it worries me.

# 23

MY PHONE RINGS at nine A.M. "Where are you and Valtteri?" Jussi asks.

I tell him about Heikki's suicide, the note and my suspicions.

"Fuck," he says.

"He and Maria are torn to pieces."

"Do you really think the suicide note was a confession?" he asks.

"Maybe. Probably."

"Why would he do it?"

"It doesn't pay to speculate. Let's wait and see if DNA places him at the crime scene. What have you and Antti turned up?"

"Antti processed Eklund's car and found blood and semen. He sent them to Helsinki for testing. Eklund's alibi checks out, but I'm not convinced. If he slipped out of Hullu Poro for a little while, killed Sufia and then came back, I'm not sure anybody would have noticed."

The case is entering day five and I haven't had a decent night's rest since it started. "Listen, I've only slept for two hours. We're all tired. Let's take the morning off and get together this evening, after the DNA reports come back."

"Should I check on Valtteri and Maria? I don't know what to say to them."

He means it's hard to console your boss about his son's suicide, especially when the boy may have killed himself in the aftermath of a sick murder.

"No. I'll stop by and check on them later."

We hang up. Heikki's suicide and my conversation with Kate take turns whirling through my head. It's hard to get back to sleep, but the next time I look at the clock, it's three P.M. Kate is propped up on the bed beside me, reading a book. "I made coffee," she says.

I go to the kitchen, get a cup for myself and sit on the bed beside her. She puts a hand on my knee. "I'm sorry I made you feel bad," she says.

"This is a hard time for both of us. The whole world seems turned upside down."

"Yeah, it does."

I put my coffee down on the floor and hug her. "I want you to be happy."

"I'm happy with you," she says.

"Just let me get this case finished, then we can figure out what we can do to make things better for you."

She nods and kisses me.

In the far corner of the room, I've got a little table set up with my home computer. I connect my monitor to Heikki's computer and power it up.

When I was a kid, there was a myth that Laestadians aren't

allowed to own washing machines with windows in the doors, because you can see underwear through it while it's spinning. Strict Laestadianism forbids dancing and music, movies, television and video games, sports, most of the entertainment content average users clutter up their computers with. Plus, Heikki had no Internet connection at home, so I'm guessing going through his machine won't take long.

It's an old computer loaded with only a few basic programs and no encryption software. I sift through the folders and files, mostly school stuff. I open a folder titled BIBLE INTERPRETATION. There are four files in it—the first is labeled SONG.

Heikki has typed out the Song of Solomon, all one hundred and seventeen verses of it. I can tell by the spelling mistakes that he didn't copy and paste it from somewhere. Another file is called MY SONG. He's rearranged fragments of lines from the Song of Solomon to make a poem of his own:

> upon the mountains of Bether
> the young stag feeds among the lilies
> the scent of your perfumes spreads its fragrance
> your lips drip with honey
> your breasts are like towers
>
> lovesick, my hand is by the latch
> set about with lilies
> my head is covered with dew
> I have drunk
> of the honey and milk under your tongue
> Do not stir nor awaken love until it pleases

The poem is a curious mixture of religious fervor and sexual desire. To have written it, Heikki must have been a very sensitive young man—and very much in love with someone. The next file is titled THE ACCURSED. It reads:

> Must we hear now that you too are doing all this terrible wickedness and are being unfaithful to our God by marrying foreign women? Nehemiah 13:26–27
>
> For we have disregarded the commands you gave when you said: The land you are entering to possess is a land polluted by the corruption of these peoples. Their detestable practices have filled it with their impurity. Therefore do not give your daughters in marriage to their sons or take their daughters for your sons. Ezra 9:10–12
>
> And Ham, the father of Canaan, saw the nakedness of his father. And Noah awoke from his wine, and knew what his younger son had done unto him. And he said, Cursed be Canaan. Genesis 9:21–25
>
> Ham=nigger
>
> *Jumala vihaa neekereitä*, God hates niggers. Niggers should die.

My stomach churns, and I consider again if Valtteri knew how disturbed Heikki was. Valtteri will be destroyed when I tell him what Heikki thought, what he did. He'll blame himself, maybe even blame God. Maybe he already does. Part of me wants to delete the folder, let the case go unsolved. I ask myself if exposing the truth will serve any purpose, if it will bring Sufia justice. The answer is yes, and it makes me sick. I open the last file, called BABYLON:

> And upon her forehead was a name written, Mystery, Babylon the great, The Mother of Harlots and Abominations of the Earth. Revelation 17:5
>
> If she profanes herself by harlotry, she profanes her father; she shall be burned with fire. Leviticus 21:9
>
> The men of her city shall stone her to death because she has committed an act of folly in Israel by playing the harlot in her father's house, thus you shall purge the evil from among you. Deuteronomy 22:21
>
> *Jumala vihaa huoria*, God hates whores. Whores should die.

The words shock me. My mind is a blur of questions. Where did he get these ideas? He expressed love in his poem. Who did he focus it on? He expressed hatred. Why, other than the color of her skin, did he focus it on Sufia? How could he have known about her promiscuity? Given the quotations in the BABYLON file, it seems he would have chosen burning or stoning as the method of Sufia's execution. Why did he murder her in the manner that he did? I browse through the computer and look for answers.

I find a downloaded folder from a true-crime website titled "The Black Dahlia: the True Story of the Murder of Elizabeth Short." I don't know a lot about the case beyond what Jaakko mentioned, so I read through it. It's a thorough treatment, offers theories about the murder and discusses the crime in great detail.

I hook my own computer back up and visit the website. It's

massive, with articles on dozens of serial killers and notorious murders, but I focus on just the Black Dahlia case. Sufia's murder seems to be a clumsy attempt at a copycat crime with some personalizations.

Short was killed, cut in half and her body washed before the killer dumped it. Sufia was killed on-site, and it appears that an inept effort to cut her in half failed. Short had three-inch gashes cut into both corners of her mouth, giving her a death smile reminiscent of a demented clown. Sufia didn't, but her eyes were gouged out. Seppo talked about her gorgeous eyes to both me and a friend. This seems an improbable coincidence.

Short and Sufia were left in the same positions after their murders: arms raised at forty-five-degree angles and legs spread. Both had a superficial section of skin removed from the right breast. It remains an unsubstantiated rumor that Short had the letters "BK" carved into her torso and that grass had been inserted into her vagina. Sufia had "nigger whore" carved into her torso and a broken bottle inserted into her vagina.

Most striking to me, as Jaakko pointed out, is that both Elizabeth Short and Sufia had genital deformities. In order for Heikki to have known about Sufia's genital mutilation, either he'd seen her vagina himself or someone told him about it. The latter is about a thousand times more likely.

Heikki could have chosen to emulate Albert DeSalvo, Ted Bundy or Jeffrey Dahmer, someone famous. The Elizabeth Short murder was never solved, and the number of vicious details makes it unwieldy and complicated in comparison to a normal homicide. I can think of no other reason to copy it, other than being inspired by their common genital abnormalities.

Heikki had no Internet access at home. How could he have

imported the Web files into his computer? He either downloaded them using someone else's computer or someone gave them to him. I go through his floppy discs and CD-ROMs. They don't contain any true-crime files.

My cell phone rings. The display reads DAD. He never calls unless he's in a drunken rage or Mom is sick. I'm afraid it's the latter, so I answer. "Hi Dad."

"Hello son. I think you'd better come over here."

"Is something wrong with Mom?"

"No. It looks like Pirkko Virtanen just couldn't take it anymore. She's killed Urpo."

I can't picture it and don't trust him. "Are you drunk?"

"I wish I was."

I hang up. A crime-scene photo of Elizabeth Short shows on the monitor. I remember Sufia in the dark snowfield, then think of Heikki crying, splashing tears on her face. Pirkko can't speak, can barely get out of her chair. How could she kill Urpo? There must be something in the water. Our whole community has gone insane.

# 24

I DRIVE BETWEEN HIGH, looming snowbanks, down the narrow lane into Marjakylä. The sixteen houses that comprise the village sit on plots identical in size and shape: longer than they are wide, big enough for a house, an outbuilding or two and a sizeable garden. The homes are all wooden A-frames painted barn-red. They were built on land given to war veterans made homeless by the Germans.

Near the end of World War II, the Germans adopted a scorched-earth policy as they retreated through Lapland. They burned down Kittilä almost entirely, only the church was left standing. Our grandparents cleared away the charred remains and rubble, dug into frozen earth and granite, rebuilt the town.

The houses line a single dirt road, eight to a side. My parents occupy the last house on the right. The mother and daughter, alcoholic Raila and anorexic Tiina, live across from them. Big Paavo lives next to my parents, and the Virtanens live on the other side.

Big Paavo is the neighborhood entrepreneur. He owns five of

the houses in Marjakylä, including my parents' place. He converted the house across the road from him into a general store, which his wife runs. He also owns the bar downtown that Dad works in.

A crowd of about twenty has gathered outside the Virtanen house. I catch Eero in my headlights. He's dapper as always, holding his dog Sulo, wearing a coat with a fur collar. A silk dressing gown sticks out beneath the coat, and below that, long thermal underwear pants are tucked into unlaced boots.

I park in my folks' driveway. Big Paavo is in his shed with Dad. They're leaning against a worktable, smoking cigarettes.

"Tell me," I say.

"I was out here working," Big Paavo says. He motions toward a bicycle frame leaning against the table and a few piles of sprockets and gear parts. "Urpo was yelling at her so loud, I could hear him all the way out here. He wanted her to get up and make him dinner. He kept on for a long time, then he kind of shrieked and went quiet. I figured I'd better go check on them."

Big Paavo is also the Virtanens' landlord. "I knocked and nobody answered, so I went inside. He's dead on the floor. She stabbed him in the neck. I went over to your dad's place and told him to call you."

For us, the Christmas season isn't just dark because of the lack of daylight. It's also the dark time in regards to domestic violence. If I hadn't grown up a couple doors down from Urpo and Pirkko, I would be almost glad to investigate this killing. After the bizarre events of late, it would seem like a normal December workday.

"Where is Pirkko?" I ask.

"When I left, she was sitting in her chair like always, except she had a butcher knife in her lap. She didn't say anything. As far as I know, she hasn't spoken in a long time."

"What are all those people doing outside?"

"A couple people came over because of the screaming and I told them what I saw. I guess they spread the word. I shouldn't have said anything, but I was shaken up. Sorry."

"It's okay," I say. "Both of you come with me and keep everyone outside while I check things out."

We walk over. They stand guard and I open the door. Pirkko is in her armchair. She doesn't look up. Her dress and face are spattered with blood. Urpo is on the floor beside an overturned coffee table, still clutching his neck. She missed his windpipe but hit the artery. Blood spray is all over the floor and walls.

I kneel down beside Pirkko, take the knife out of her hand and set it on the floor beside me. "Can you talk to me?" I ask.

She offers no sign of recognition.

"It's going to be okay. Nothing bad is going to happen to you."

She doesn't move, but tears run down her cheeks.

I open the front door and hand Dad my car keys. "Would you bring the tackle boxes out of the trunk for me?"

When he comes back, I bag the knife and take a few pictures of Pirkko, but not many, because I don't want to embarrass her more than I have to. I call emergency services and request two vehicles. While I wait, I sit beside Pirkko and hold her hand to comfort her.

I've seen a lot of these situations, deal with them at least a couple times a year. I have a good idea of what happened. She was in her chair, he stood over her, screaming in her face. I'm not sure how she came to have the knife. Maybe she went to the kitchen, got it and sat back down, maybe she already had it hidden under the seat cushion. I'm sure she was afraid of him. I would have been. Who knows, she might have had the knife hidden there for years, just in case.

He screams at her until she can't take it anymore, then she

holds up the knife. He might have been so drunk that he didn't even notice. She has so little strength, she couldn't have done more than poke it up at him, but it was sharp and went through his neck, severed the left carotid artery.

From the blood spray pattern, I can see that he spun in a circle, fell across the coffee table onto the floor, bled out and died. It couldn't have taken long.

The EMTs arrive. I tell them to sedate her and take her to the hospital. She's fat. With effort, they lift her up and put her in a wheelchair. Her empty chair is wet and the smell makes me gag. Pirkko had been pissing in it for a long time. She couldn't take care of herself, but nobody cared.

After she's gone, I walk around and take more photos. The whole house smells like a mass grave. Bootleg Russian medical alcohol bottles stand empty on the kitchen counter. His brand of choice was Royal American Spirit. A bootlegger brought thousands of liters of the stuff into the country and was bold enough to make his own label. I take some close-ups of Urpo. He's malnourished, has been living on booze and not eating much all winter. His corpse reminds me of a plucked dead chicken.

When I'm done, emergency workers take his body away on a gurney. I walk out with them. Mikko's work lamps give us enough light to see by. The crowd is still out in the yard, milling around in the snow, stamping their feet and rubbing their hands together to stay warm.

Raila, alcohol psychosis in full sway, sees the body and begins shrieking. She points at the Virtanens' front window and screams over and over, "They couldn't even iron the curtains! They couldn't even iron the curtains!" She starts clapping her gloved hands in time.

Tiina has a droopy mouth and eyes, an upper lip thin as a razor, and no groove between her nose and lips: typical characteristics of fetal alcohol syndrome. She takes her doll out of its carriage and coos at it. "Be quiet Mom, you'll wake the baby," she says.

Raila keeps shouting about curtains. Tiina keeps telling her to shut up. Tiina walks over to Big Paavo's shed, comes back with a plastic bicycle pump and hits Raila on the head with it.

Blood runs down Raila's face, she starts to cry. She has thin gray hair. Tiina reaches over and pulls out a clump of it, throws a bloody wad of hair and scalp onto the hard-packed snow.

I grab Tiina, the EMTs leave Urpo on the gurney and tend to Raila. When Tiina is calm, I tell her to go home. She pushes the baby carriage in front of her and trudges back to her house. It strikes me that what I just witnessed doesn't surprise me in the least. Psychosis has become run of the mill. Maybe the cold and dark have driven us all crazy.

Dad and Big Paavo walk over to me. We all light cigarettes.

"Strange day," Dad says.

"You have no idea." I look up at Big Paavo. "Did you know Pirkko and Urpo were living like that?" I ask.

"Urpo's been drunk and Pirkko's been miserable in that house for thirty years," he says. "What was I supposed to do about it?"

A lot of people drink bootleg medical alcohol because it's cheap, but it's nearly a hundred percent pure, makes people crazy and mean, especially during *kaamos*. Urpo didn't need booze to be an asshole though, he was crazy and mean when he was sober too. I shake my head. A woman had to kill her husband to get some help.

A car pulls up and Jaakko gets out. "I heard about it over the scanner," he says. "What happened?"

I don't want to deal with Jaakko right now, but he's a reporter and this is a crime scene, so I don't have much choice. "Urpo Virtanen is dead. His wife killed him."

"What happened?"

"I'll file a police report in the morning."

"Give me something, an official statement."

"Honestly Jaakko, I just don't have the strength right now."

"Mind if I take a few pictures?"

"Do what you want outside, but stay out of the house."

He looks pissed off. "I understand your sergeant's son commit-ted suicide yesterday."

"Yes, he did. The past couple days have been sad ones for this community."

"Finally," he says, "something quotable. Do you have any rea-son why?"

"Do we ever really know why people kill themselves?"

"Fair enough. Care to comment on your ex-wife's marriage?"

He catches me by surprise, as I'm sure he intended. "What marriage?"

"She and Seppo Niemi were married today at the magistrate's office. You arrested him for murder, released him and he married Heli the next day. I find that intriguing."

I do too. I need time to process the information and consider the motivations behind their marriage.

"She called me this afternoon to make a statement," he says. "She says Seppo has been asking her to marry him for many years, and that she finally did so today as a show of support in light of his wrongful arrest."

"That's noble of her."

"She also says that when you arrested him, you pulled the car over to the side of the road and put a gun to his head. Is that true?"

Seppo just couldn't keep his fucking mouth shut. "You should ask Seppo."

"I did."

"What did he say?"

He pauses, takes a minute to try to think of a way to trap me, but he can't. "He says it never happened."

"Then why ask me about it?"

He reminds me of a dog trying to dig a rabbit out of its hole. "Because I think it's true. I think there's a lot going on here. I think the investigation of Sufia Elmi's murder is compromised by personal feelings and old hatreds."

"You're welcome to your thoughts, but be careful what you print. A lot will become clear to you in the next day or two."

"You're being circumspect. What are you hiding?"

My cell phone rings. I turn away from Jaakko and answer it. "The DNA tests just came back from Valtteri's house," Antti says. "They place Heikki at the murder scene, and also inside Seppo's home."

For the second time in as many minutes, I'm caught off guard. "Inside the house."

"Yeah."

"Okay, thanks. I'll call you later."

"What do you think . . . "

I cut him off. "I can't talk right now."

The EMTs drive Urpo's body away in an ambulance. Raila stands by herself, looking miserable. Maybe she's afraid to go home.

I turn to Dad and Big Paavo. "Thank you both."

Jaakko starts in again, but I cut him off too. I walk Raila home and make sure Tiina is calm, then head to my car. I've got to see Valtteri and tell my friend that his dead son is a murderer.

# 25

As I reach the intersection in the road leaving Marjakylä, the aurora borealis appears. Instead of turning onto the highway, I drive across the road to Aslak's reindeer farm, park in his driveway and get out of the car.

It's about twenty below zero. In this kind of cold, the sense of smell is almost useless, but I smell the northern lights. I'm told it's not possible, but I've always been able to. The scent is like copper and burned cinnamon. A couple times I've heard them. The sound was like constant humming thunder.

I light a cigarette and watch the northern lights dim and brighten, wavy green serpents of light. Fresh snow has turned the field where Sufia's body lay into a clean white funeral shroud. Around twenty reindeer saunter toward me, curious.

It occurs to me that I haven't spoken to Sufia's father since Seppo was released. He's going to be upset and the conversation won't be pleasant. I take my phone out to call him and it rings in my hand. "Good evening Inspector," Abdi says. "I have read in the newspaper that there has been an unpleasant development in the investigation of my daughter's murder."

"You mean the release of Seppo Niemi."

"Exactly so."

"I apologize for not calling you about it earlier. The investigation has moved so fast that I haven't had time. Seppo was released for political reasons. It has no bearing on his guilt or innocence."

"Will my daughter's murderer go free for, as you say, political reasons?"

I don't mention my suspicions about Heli's involvement. If it proves that she coerced Heikki to murder, Abdi will still be satisfied that justice was done. "I can rearrest him at any time. A new development has come to light that suggests it may be soon."

"What development?"

"A teenage boy committed suicide yesterday. Forensics place him at the crime scene and also in Seppo's house. It appears the boy was an accomplice to the crime."

"I remain unconvinced. When we last spoke, you had Sufia's killer in custody and believed her case would be brought to a speedy conclusion. Now you talk of political considerations and teenage accomplices. I begin to lose my faith in you Inspector."

"Mr. Barre, I promise you . . ."

He cuts me off. "The Koran instructs, 'There are guardians watching over you, noble recorders who know of all your actions.' Do not let Sufia's murder go unavenged."

The line goes dead. I look up. The northern lights have disappeared, and I'm staring into a dark and lifeless Arctic night.

———

I KNOCK ON VALTTERI'S door and Maria answers. She looks like she's aged ten years in a day. I step in and give her a hug, take off my boots in the foyer. Valtteri walks into the living room. He looks frightened, maybe because of what I'm going to tell him.

"Maria, why don't you make us some coffee," he says.

"He was my son too."

"Maria, go in the kitchen."

She doesn't argue and walks away. He and I sit side by side on the sofa. "I have to tell you some difficult things," I say.

He folds his hands, rests his arms on his knees, stares at the floor, waits.

"Heikki was present at the murder scene. The tears on Sufia's face belonged to him."

Valtteri doesn't look up.

"I went through his computer today. There was no admission of guilt, but I found strange things. He wrote, 'God hates niggers' and 'God hates whores,' almost like we saw on her body."

Valtteri cries silent tears. They fall between his knees, splash on the rug between his feet. "Why did he do it?" he asks.

"I don't know."

"You're telling me Heikki thought God wanted him to kill that girl. I raised my children religious. I thought God would make them good strong people. Now you're telling me what I taught Heikki made him sick, a killer."

"I don't think that. I could tell from what he wrote that Heikki was disturbed."

"And I made him that way."

"No you didn't. You raised him right. What Heikki did had nothing to do with you. I've known you a long time, you're a good man, a good parent."

He looks up, holds his hands out toward me. I don't know what he wants me to do. His voice trembles. "Then why?" He yells it. "Dear God, why!"

Maria comes in from the kitchen. She's carrying a tray with cups of coffee and slices of cake, which she sets down on the coffee table in front of us. She's crying. "Valtteri, I heard what was said. He killed that girl, didn't he?"

He wraps his arms around himself, rocks back and forth. "Maria, we raised a monster."

She stills her tears, kneels down on the floor and wraps her arms around Valtteri, tries to calm him. "Why?" she asks me.

"Heikki was in love with a girl. He wrote a poem about her and I found it in his computer. Do you know who she is?"

"No," Maria says.

"Some of the things he wrote give me the feeling that somehow this girl and Sufia Elmi are connected. There's something else too. We found his DNA in Seppo Niemi's house. Did he and Seppo know each other?"

"Heikki did odd jobs for Seppo and Heli. Shoveled snow, carried firewood, things like that. He met Heli at church. It's no surprise that he was in their house."

Maria's comforting worked, Valtteri is calmer, but now I know that he withheld information. My doubt about whether he knew Heikki killed Sufia renews itself. "Why didn't you tell me?" I ask him.

"You don't like to talk about Heli, and I didn't see any point in telling you my son shoveled her driveway."

An idea hits me so hard that I curse out loud without meaning to. "Goddamn it."

They look stunned, must think I'm mad at them for not telling me Heikki knew Heli and Seppo. "Sorry," I say.

I've just realized the most economical solution to Sufia's murder. Heikki and Seppo knew each other. My investigation into Seppo's life has suggested to me that he's morally arid enough to plant his dick in anything with a pulse. If he swung both ways, it wouldn't surprise me. Maybe he seduced the boy who did his odd jobs.

Heikki was young, sheltered, most likely inexperienced. He could have been exploring his sexuality. Heikki and Seppo could have had a homosexual affair. If they were lovers, it would have given Heikki access to Seppo's car keys. Heikki might have killed Sufia out of simple jealousy.

I put a hand on Valtteri's shoulder to let him know I'm not angry, and feel sudden shame for thinking Valtteri and Maria could have had anything to do with Heikki's suicide. They loved their boy so much. "Is there anything else you haven't told me?"

He shakes his head.

"I guess you know I can't keep this out of the papers."

Maria gulps back a cry. She must have just realized she and Valtteri are about to take on new identities as the parents of a psychotic murderer. They'll endure humiliation that neither they nor the community will ever forget.

Valtteri takes her hand but looks at me. "I'm sorry about all this," he says. "I've embarrassed you and the police department. I'll turn in my resignation after the funeral tomorrow."

I grasp at words, they're all inadequate. He loves his job. "Damn it Valtteri, what Heikki did isn't your fault, and I won't accept your resignation."

He lets out a whimper. "I raised him, it's my fault. You'll accept it and you'll be glad you did."

"You're in a lot of pain and you're being foolish."

"I don't see that I have any choice."

"Resigning isn't an option for you. You have seven other children and a wife to take care of."

He starts to cry again. "What do I do then?"

"You're going to grieve for your boy, then you're going to go back to work and do your job while I figure out why Heikki did what he did."

He looks at Maria, she nods. "I'll try," he says.

I get up to leave. "I'm so sorry that I had to tell you these things. I'll see you tomorrow at the funeral."

"Don't come," he says. "We don't want anybody there except us and his brothers and sisters."

"I understand," I say, but I don't. No one can understand their torment. They've suffered the emotional equivalent of what was done to Sufia, and it fell to me to deliver this burden upon them. I hope one day they can forgive me. I leave without another word.

# 26

THE FACES OF VALTTERI and Maria, their grief and horror, are frozen in my mind. I want to be alone, so I take my time driving back to the police station. I can sit in my office, write reports. The national chief of police has been like an ax hanging over my neck. Maybe letting him know the case is drawing to a close will pacify him. But first I need to read the report about Heikki's DNA results.

At a stop sign near the station, a car pulls up beside me in the wrong lane. Seppo's BMW. Heli waves at me from the driver's seat. The passenger-side window rolls down, and I roll down my window to hear her. She shouts at me to follow her.

She guns the engine, wheels spin on the ice, the BMW shoots past me. I wonder who's been killed this time, pull out fast and hurry to keep up with her. She blows through a red light, I do the same. After a few blocks, she turns a corner and parks. I stop behind her.

She gets out of the car and leans against the door. She's tiny and shivering, bunches up her coat at the neck to keep out the cold. My hands shake from adrenaline. "What the fuck?" I ask.

She points at the neon sign of a diner flashing in the dark. "I saw you driving and thought we could have that cup of coffee we talked about."

"I didn't talk about it, you did. You drove like a bat out of hell and ran a red light. Are you insane?"

She laughs. "I was just having fun, teasing you a little. Gonna give me a ticket?"

She pissed me off, but I don't want her to see it. "I need to talk to you anyway. Go inside, I'll be there in a second."

From the warmth of my car, I call Antti. "I'm in a hurry," I say. "You found Heikki's DNA in Seppo's house. What was it from and where did you find it?"

"Pubic hair," he says, "on the rim of the upstairs toilet and in their bed. On the mattress under the sheet."

"No DNA on the sheet?"

"The bedclothes were fresh. There was a load of sheets and towels in the dryer. They'd been washed in a detergent with bleaching agent. No chance for DNA."

I click off, take a tape recorder from the glove compartment and put it in my coat pocket.

She hasn't chosen just any diner, it's our diner. We came here together when we were kids, when we were first dating. The place hasn't changed in thirty years. You can still get an ice cream float here. I find Heli looking at the magazine rack. We hid behind it and shared our first kiss when we were thirteen.

"Let's get that coffee," I say.

The same guy that waited on us almost thirty years ago is still behind the counter. It looks like he's still wearing the same bow tie. The place smells like he hasn't changed the French fry grease either. He's about sixty years old and owns the place now. He's surprised to see us together, raises his eyebrows but doesn't comment. "What can I get you kids?" he asks.

"Two coffees," Heli says. "Mine with milk, black for Kari."

She pays. We sit down in a booth.

"Congratulations on your marriage," I say.

"Thank you. It was long overdue, seemed like the right time."

Heli no longer seems like the raging woman that spit on me, or the ice queen that sat in my office. She's got on worn boots and jeans, an old sweater. She's without makeup and her long blond hair is braided in pigtails. She's smiling, and I recognize the girl I fell in love with. I suspect this is her intention.

"You have a flair for the dramatic," I say.

"The diner seemed appropriate," she says, "after all this time."

"After thirteen years, I don't see any reason to relive old memories."

"It seems like a good place to create new memories. I apologize for the way I acted. I was a bitch. There's no excuse for bad behavior, but you barged into our home and shocked me, and I thought you were out to get Seppo. I can see now that those things aren't true."

Sarcasm creeps into my voice. "You can, can you?"

"Yes, and I'm sorry. I also want to thank you for releasing Seppo so quickly when his innocence became clear."

"You thanked me for releasing Seppo by telling a reporter I threatened him."

"Seppo was angry at me for that. I was still mad at you then."

"But you're not anymore."

She smiles, stirs her coffee, clinks the spoon against the inside of the cup. "No."

I set the tape recorder on the table. "Then you won't mind help-ing me out with the investigation and answering a few questions."

She grimaces. "Do we need that? It makes me nervous."

It's my turn to smile. "My memory isn't what it used to be. I need it."

She looks thoughtful, sips her coffee. "How's the investigation into the girl's murder going?"

"It's drawing to a conclusion. I understand you knew Heikki."

She puts on a sad face, an appropriate tear wells up. "He was such a sweet boy, I was shocked when I heard. How are his parents?"

She reaches toward my hand, as if she's trying to share a moment with me. I move mine away. "They're like you'd expect. What did you hear?"

She fiddles with a salt shaker, like she didn't mean to take my hand. "There's talk around the church that he hung himself, and that he," she pauses, sniffles, "might have had something to do with the girl's murder. It's so tragic. Is it true?"

"That's confidential. Let's get to what I wanted to talk to you about. How well did you know Heikki?"

"Not well, but we were sort of friends. He needed some money, he was saving for a car and college. I gave him some jobs to do around the house."

"That's all?"

She thinks about it for a minute. "After he shoveled the snow or whatever, we'd have hot chocolate, talk about the Bible."

"I forgot you're here to rediscover your religious roots. How's that working out?"

She looks hurt, guides the subject back where she wants it. "You don't have to be mean. People change, you know. I was on the way home from a church meeting when I saw you driving. I'm serious about my religion. I just wondered how a nice boy like Heikki could have done such a thing."

"You seem pretty concerned."

"Maybe it's morbid curiosity, but it's not every day that a boy you have in your home turns out to have done something like that. It's hard to believe."

Heli always did have an inclination toward the macabre, loved crime and horror films. I remember when she watched me stomp that little bird to death: she didn't look upset, she looked fascinated.

"Heikki had some unusual religious ideas," I say. "Did he ever say anything that struck you as odd?"

She shakes her head. "He seemed like a fine young man."

I start to home in. "I'll satisfy your morbid curiosity. We've placed Heikki at the crime scene. We found his tears on her face. Imagine, he butchered her like an animal, then felt such remorse that he cried on her face as soon as he'd done it and committed suicide a couple days later."

She sheds a couple tears of her own. "Poor her. Poor him. He must have been so disturbed."

"It's generous of you to sympathize with the suffering of a woman that had an affair with your husband."

She sighs. "Whatever she did, she didn't deserve to die like that."

I nod in agreement, try to gauge the level of her sincerity. "How many times did Heikki come over to your house?"

She shrugs. "I don't know, a few."

"Where did you sit when you had your Bible talks?"

"At the dining room table, on the living room sofa." She looks into my eyes, probing. "What are you getting at?"

"We found his pubic hair in your upstairs bathroom and on your bed. I was wondering how they got there."

Her eyes go dull like a snake's, then they start to dance and she sits back and laughs at me. "Kari, are you suggesting I had an affair with a sixteen-year-old boy?"

She keeps laughing until tears roll down her cheeks. I wait for her to stop. "I'm not suggesting anything, why would you think that?"

"It seems to be your implication."

"I asked you a simple question. How do you think his pubic hair made its way into your bedroom and bathroom?"

She gives me the look she gave me when I interviewed her in my office. The one that says I'm stupid. "Let's use our imaginations, shall we? He has to pee, a couple pubes come loose. One stays in the bathroom, the other sticks to my or Seppo's feet and gets tracked into the bed."

"You have a bathroom downstairs. Why would he go upstairs?"

"I don't know, but which story sounds more plausible, a hair tracked into a bed, or me fucking the boy? Think about it."

"I didn't accuse you of fucking the boy. He used your car to commit the crime. Now it's your turn to think about it. Tell me what conclusions you draw."

She rests her elbows on the table, her chin on her hands. Time goes by. The idea hits her like it hit me. She sits bolt upright. "No fucking way," she says.

"You've got a dirty mouth for a churchgoing girl."

"Old habits die hard." She starts laughing again. "You can't seriously believe Seppo had a homosexual relationship with that boy."

I don't say anything, stare at her and wait.

"It's impossible," she says.

"Why?"

She has no answer. We stare at each other. I let her win and speak first. "Have you ever known Seppo to be involved in a gay relationship?"

She gulps down the rest of her coffee. Her lack of an answer is an answer.

"Heli, if you know something, you should tell me. You could end up being an accessory, which would mean jail time. I'm not threatening you, I'm trying to help you."

She stands up, winds her scarf around her neck, puts on her coat. "I know you're concerned about me, but you're barking up the wrong tree. You're a good guy, you always were. I'd forgotten."

We step out into the dark together. The diner door has a bell on it that makes a friendly ring. The cold takes my breath for a second. "Thanks for the coffee," I say, and head for my car.

She calls after me, "Kari."

I turn toward her. She opens the door of the BMW, looks at me. "I'm sorry I hurt you when I left you. I loved you once."

I'm not sure why, but I'm glad she said it. I nod at her but don't know what I mean by it. Maybe it's thanks—maybe it's simple acknowledgment.

Heli starts the BMW. I have to test something out. I walk over, she rolls down the passenger-side window and I stick my head in while I talk to her.

"A couple days ago," I say, "this crazy idea occurred to me that you learned about Seppo's affair and decided to get rid of Sufia. You and Seppo were unmarried. If Seppo left you for Sufia, by Finnish law, you'd get nothing. You seduced Heikki and played on his religious beliefs, convinced him that Sufia was a nigger whore, a sinner that deserved to die, then you and he colluded in Sufia's murder."

I pause. Heli's face registers nothing. I continue.

"You and Heikki used Seppo's car and framed him, then you convinced Seppo to marry you, fed him some song and dance about how your solidarity would speak of his innocence. Marriage would assure your financial well-being. You drove Heikki to suicide by telling him the truth, that you used him and intended to discard him. Of course, I can see now that all this couldn't be true. Seems like a stupid idea, looking back."

Her expression doesn't change. "You have a wild imagination."

"Yeah, I do. A homosexual love affair between Seppo and Heikki is a far more economical solution. It's all there. Motive. Opportunity. Still, you can see how all the pieces fit in the scenario with you and Heikki as well, it's just more complicated that way."

Heli smirks and starts to close her window.

Something hits me. "Hey, wait a second," I say. "How do you spell *lasi*, glass, in English?"

"Why?"

"I have to send my wife a text message and can't remember."

"G-R-A-S-S."

She rolls up her window and drives away. I light a cigarette. The cold makes my eyes run and blur. Her taillights streak red and fade away. Heli's English always sucked. Could Sufia really have had a broken bottle stuffed into her vagina because Heli read a website wrong and mistook "grass" for "glass"? I stand under a streetlight, smoke and think for a while.

# 27

I BRUSH THE SNOW OFF my shoes and leave them in the foyer, then walk into the living room. Kate is sitting up in the bed reading, wearing only black panties. Modern Finnish homes are so well insulated that no matter how cold it is outside, you can always hang around the house in your underwear in comfort. She holds up her book, *Finnish for Foreigners. "Mitä kuuluu?"* she asks.

I kneel down on the floor beside her. Her skin is white, as colorless as snow. The veins under her skin cast bluish shadows on its surface. I touch her breast, trace the azure map with my index finger. *"Rakastele kanssani,"* I say.

"I tried to ask how you are," she says.

"And I said make love to me."

She giggles. "How do we do it with my cast in the way?"

I start peeling off my clothes. "We'll figure it out."

We figure it out. After the third time, I lay my head in her armpit and nuzzle her breast.

"If this was a scene in a romance novel," Kate says, "they'd write that you were furious with desire."

My mouth is full of her breast, I have to turn my head to answer. "I've been around so much ugliness lately, I needed something beautiful."

She kisses my lips. *"Minä rakastan sinua,"* I love you, she says. Her accent makes her sound like a child learning to speak. It makes me grin.

"I've been thinking about the conversation we had," I say. "What if, instead of going to live in the States, we moved to Helsinki? It has a big international community, a lot of people speak English there. You might not feel so isolated."

"Would they let you transfer back there?"

"I think so."

"Would you be happy there?"

"I don't know, and I don't know if you would be happy there either. We might be. But the big ski resorts are in the north. You'd have to manage another kind of business. It's just an idea."

She frowns. "I think you were right before," she says. "Let's figure it out after you solve Sufia Elmi's murder."

"The case should be closed soon."

I tell Kate about everything that's happened since I left the house earlier today. About how Pirkko murdered Urpo, about the chaos at the murder scene, Tiina attacking Raila. How I had to tell Valtteri and Maria their son was a killer and that I realized Heikki may have had a homosexual love affair with Seppo. About talking to Heli.

"That's a nightmare of a day," she says.

"Yeah. The good part is that if Seppo admits to an affair with Heikki, I can close the investigation. The Lone Gunman theory."

"Why do you think Heli wanted to talk to you?"

"All that talk about making amends was bullshit. She tried to pump me for information about the case. She's scared of something."

"Do you really think she and Heikki might have murdered Sufia together?"

"I believe she knows more than she's telling. I wanted to see her reaction when she realized she could be a suspect. The woman I knew had emotional problems but didn't fit into a sociopath-murderer profile. But that was a long time ago. I don't know her anymore. Her confusion about spelling 'glass' and 'grass,' and the glass and grass in Sufia's and Elizabeth Short's vaginas, if it's a coincidence, is just plain weird. When you think about it, this whole case is just plain fucking weird."

For me, a criminal investigation is like playing a card game. When I get more to work with as the game progresses, my imagination rearranges the cards. Discussing the case with Kate makes the whole deck reshuffle.

"I just got this mental picture," I say, "of Seppo, Sufia and Heikki in a bedroom. Seppo fantasizes that he's the Sheik of Araby, Sufia is his Nubian dancing girl, Heikki his teenage catamite. That would explain how Heikki knew about Sufia's genital mutilation. He saw her vagina, maybe even had sex with her, while having a ménage à trois with her and Seppo."

"But how did Heikki make the connection between Sufia and the Black Dahlia case?" Kate asks.

"I don't know that yet. Maybe Seppo can tell me. Maybe that's why Heli tried to pump me for information, to see how much I know about Heikki's relationship with Sufia and Seppo. Maybe she blackmailed Seppo into marrying her by threatening to tell me the truth. Who knows, she could have read about the Black Dahlia murder and talked about it with Heikki."

"Maybe," Kate says, "but given that Peter Eklund and Seppo know each other from Helsinki, Sufia's relationship with Peter seems more than coincidental, like too much of a loose end. If you're right and there was some kind of sex circle, is it possible that traces of his semen could be found in her mouth alongside Seppo's, without his playing some part in all this?"

The deck reshuffles again. "Peter admitted to having met Seppo a few times in nightclubs in Helsinki. Maybe they discovered they have a mutual thing for teenage boys. It could be that Sufia wasn't cheating on Seppo with Peter. Seppo could have introduced Sufia to Peter, more or less pimped her out to him. Seppo and Peter could have been fucking Sufia and Heikki together. Maybe it didn't go exactly like that, but some variation on the theme."

Kate takes it all in. "Then who killed Sufia?"

The deck won't reshuffle for me this time. I can't imagine the sequence of events that led to her death. "I don't know, maybe they all did."

My cell phone rings. It's Antti, he's on call tonight. I pick up. "Fuck Kari," he says, "you have to come here quick."

"Where?"

"The lake where you and your dad like to fish. Somebody's dead, burned to death on the ice, looks like a child. I can't fucking believe it."

I can't believe it either. The clock reads twelve fifteen A.M. The investigation of Sufia's murder just entered its sixth day. Three murders during that time period. I hear Antti choke back a sob. He's tough, it must be bad. "It's still burning," he says.

"Get a fire blanket out of the cruiser and put it out. I'll call Esko and be there soon."

Naked beside me, Kate waits for me to tell her what's wrong.

"Antti says a child's been burned and murdered. I'll be gone all night."

She winces. "No," she says.

My feelings exactly.

# 28

DAD AND I NEVER fish together, but we fish in the same spot, and I'm pretty sure for the same reason. It's where my sister Suvi died. It's a way of being with her. Sometimes I talk to her when I sit there on a crate, dangling a fishing line through a hole in the ice.

The starry night casts the frozen lake slate-gray. A half moon silhouettes a thin column of smoke rising into the sky. Antti stands near the source, not fifty feet from where Suvi fell through the ice and drowned. It makes me shudder. I get my fishing-tackle boxes out of the trunk, head down the bank and onto the lake.

Walking toward the body with a flashlight, I can't quite take in what I'm seeing. The smoking figure in the beam doesn't look like a person, more like a blackened candle that's burned halfway down and been snuffed out. Antti and I nod at each other but don't speak. I look at the victim, blink, look again. Part of me just won't accept that it's true.

A tire was hung around the child's chest and arms and set ablaze. The smell of petroleum and scorched flesh is overwhelming, sickening. Someone filled the ring inside the tire with gasoline, lit it and watched the child burn. A rumpled fire blanket lies on the ice a few yards away from the body. Antti extinguished the flame, but the rubber is still smoldering.

The victim sat cross-legged while the killer attended to the details of his or her murder. Somehow, the body stayed upright while it burned. Because the tire was draped around the top half of the body, flame shot up and burned nearly all the skin away from the chest and head. Only fragments of charred and desiccated muscle and ligament remain attached to bone and a blackened skull.

From the waist upward, the body is shriveled by heat. Soot and ash cover the body from the waist downward, but in relative terms, the lower portion remains unscathed. Antti assumed the victim is a child because heat and flame caused a diminutive appearance, steamed out liquid, removed hair and flesh, in effect shrank the upper body. He was wrong.

I kneel down with my weight on the balls of my feet and examine the lower body. Under the filth from the burned tire, I see jeans and worn boots. Understanding knocks me backward. I fall on my ass and drop my flashlight. I try to breathe, can't, clench and unclench my fists. I close my eyes, stop looking at the corpse so I can relax enough to speak. When I open them, Antti is standing over me.

"It's not a child," I say. "It's a small adult woman. My ex-wife Heli."

Antti's mouth opens and closes, opens and closes again. "Fuck. Kari. I'm sorry."

He offers his hand, helps me to my feet. We stand side by side on the ice. He picks up the flashlight and shines it on Heli. We stare at her for what seems a long time.

"What do we do?" Antti asks.

I consider the question, can't think, sit down on a fishing-tackle box. "I saw Heli earlier tonight. I might have been the last one to see her alive. I can't do anything, it might contaminate the investigation. You have to process the crime scene. Wait on Esko, he'll help you."

What I said is true, but also, I'm incapable of working and I know it.

He sits down on the other tackle box. "Okay," he says.

Esko arrives, and Antti explains the situation to him. Esko hunches down beside me. "I'm sorry," he says, "we'll take care of it."

Antti needs my crime kit. I stand up, walk a few yards away, chain-smoke and watch them examine Heli's corpse, the husk that remains of her. I should feel something, remember moments from my life with Heli. Her life should pass before my eyes, but my mind is blank, I feel nothing. The cold seeps through me. It feels like ice water flows in my veins. I stare across the lake into the forest's impenetrable shadows, then watch the stars.

After a while, Esko comes over. "You don't need to stay here."

It takes me a second to realize he spoke to me and another to understand what he said. "What if Antti needs something?"

"He won't. Can you drive yourself home?"

I nod.

"Go on then," he says.

I stumble off the lake and wade through the snow up the bank to my car.


I SHUT THE FRONT door behind me. Kate is sitting on the couch with her broken leg propped up on a stool. She's watching an American sitcom with a canned laugh track. I sit down beside her.

"I thought you'd be gone all night," she says.

I stare at the TV, shake my head.

She comes close, looks in my eyes. "What happened?"

"It was Heli," I say.

"What are you talking about?"

Maybe she thinks I'm talking about Sufia's murder or Heikki's suicide. "Heli. My ex-wife. It wasn't a child. Somebody put a tire around Heli's chest and arms, filled it with gasoline and set her on fire. She's dead."

Kate's eyes open wide. She reaches over and takes my hands. "Kari . . ."

I keep staring at the television. I laugh at a stupid joke, look down at my feet. I forgot to take off my boots. I watch snow melt all over the carpet.

I almost never cry. Sometimes I go years without crying. When I was a boy, if I cried, Dad beat me. He must have beaten the tears out of me. I start to cry, just a little, and it surprises me. In a way, it terrifies me. "Suvi," I say.

Kate keeps my hands clasped between hers. "What?"

"Suvi. Heli died where Suvi died."

She turns off the TV. Her voice goes gentle, like she's talking to a child. "Kari, would you like a drink?"

I nod.

She hobbles to the kitchen on her crutches and returns with a bottle of scotch and a water glass. I pour a triple and think of Dad, sitting in his armchair, drinking vodka out of a water glass, getting drunk, yelling at Mom and us kids, hitting us. I down the scotch and pour another just like it.

Kate wraps an arm around me. "Suvi died where Heli died?"

I take another drink. "Yeah."

200 / JAMES THOMPSON

"Who is Suvi?"

I haven't said Suvi's name out loud in thirty years. Tears shoot out of me. I can't see. I try to talk through the snot choking me. "Suvi died because I didn't take good enough care of her. Heli died because I didn't solve the murder. They're dead and it's my fault."

After I finish off the second drink, Kate takes the glass away from me. "Kari, you still haven't told me who Suvi is."

"Suvi was my sister."

I'm crying and choking and choking and crying and through it all I'm spitting out the story of how Suvi fell through the ice and drowned and how Dad and I did nothing and how they dragged the lake under the ice and pulled her body out. In between broken sentences, I'm taking swigs out of the scotch bottle. I've drunk most of it.

Kate pulls me close. I try to push her away but don't have the strength. "Why didn't you tell me about Suvi before?" she asks.

Crying embarrasses me. I wipe snot on my sleeve and sob. "Because I didn't want you to blame me."

She pulls my face next to hers, cradles me in her arms. "Kari, you were nine years old."

I start crying harder again, spread tears and snot on her shoulder. "Do you blame me?" I ask.

"No Kari, I don't blame you."

She rocks me back and forth. I pass out drunk, don't remember anything after that.

# 29

KATE SHAKES ME AWAKE. "Antti is on the phone," she says. "I didn't want to answer your cell phone, but he kept ringing. I told him you needed to sleep, but he says it's important."

My mouth feels like a rat crawled into it, died and rotted there while I slept. My head throbs. Drinking three quarters of a bottle of whiskey like a pitcher of water has given me an awful hangover.

I take the phone. "What?"

"Sorry to bother you," Antti says, "but I thought you should know about what's going on with Heli's murder."

"It's okay, tell me."

"Esko and I processed the crime scene. The tire around her chest was a Dunlop Winter Sport, the ID was still legible. I found a star-spoked hubcap and an empty gasoline can by the edge of the lake."

My stomach churns from guilt more than the hangover. "You're telling me I turned Seppo loose and he killed Heli?"

He refrains from passing judgment. "I went to his cottage and his BMW was in the driveway. The keys were still in it. I looked in the trunk and the spare tire was gone, so I'm pretty sure he used it to kill her. Her purse was still in the car. This was about four A.M."

"Did you find Seppo?"

"He answered the door when I rang, said he'd been asleep and looked like it. Passed out is more like it. He was still pretty drunk. I guess he got tanked, killed his wife, then drove home and went to bed."

"How did he react about Heli?"

"I didn't say anything about it. I arrested him but didn't charge him. I thought I should leave it up to you to decide how to handle him. Being arrested again upset him, to put it mildly, but I just couldn't see leaving him free when his vehicle is evidence in a second murder."

"You did right. I'll call Esko and get his take on things, then come to the station and question Seppo."

"Esko already did the autopsy. I was there with him."

"Why so quick?"

"To tell the truth, Esko was afraid you'd want to attend, and he thought it would be too hard on you, so we met at the morgue at seven this morning."

I look at the clock. It's eleven now. "When did you sleep?"

"I haven't yet. Esko went home and got a couple hours of shut-eye while I went to Seppo's cottage."

"Fuck," I say. "I have to see Heli's parents."

"I already went to their house with Pastor Nuorgam and talked to Heli's father."

"How did he take it?"

"Bad. I told him you were broken up about it, that you'd talk to him when you could."

Having the people I work with try to spare my feelings touches me, but also embarrasses me a little. "Thanks, I appreciate all you've done."

"No problem. You okay?"

I'm not sure yet. "Yeah, I'm okay. Go home and get some rest, I'll talk to you soon."

Kate sits down on the bed. "What are you planning to do?"

I shrug my shoulders. "Go to work."

"Do you remember last night?"

It's a little fuzzy, but I remember more than I want to. I imagine how I looked, crying like a baby. I feel my face turn red. "Sorry, I guess I let things get on top of me."

"You don't need to be sorry, I just wonder why you never told me about Suvi before."

When I lived in Helsinki, I had an apartment on the fourth floor of a nine-story building. About six months after Heli left me, I came home and found a big orange tomcat on my balcony. The only way he could have gotten there was to have jumped from a higher floor. No one inquired about him and I didn't ask. I named him Katt—Swedish for "cat." A stupid name for a stupid animal, but I came to love him.

Katt loved nature shows on TV, seemed to think all the other creatures of the earth lived in a little box in the living room. In the evenings, I would lie on the sofa, he would lie on my chest, we'd share a bowl of ice cream and watch antelopes mate or cougars stalk bison or whatever. He liked the documentaries with other cats in them the best.

I transferred here to Kittilä and brought Katt with me, had him for eight years. One day I came home and found him dead. He tried to eat a fat rubber band and choked to death on it. Katt had shit for brains. It broke my heart. I buried Katt in the backyard in an unmarked grave. Still, every year on All Saints Day, I light a candle on it for him. I never told anybody how much I loved him, and I never told anybody how much it hurt me when he died. I've never told Kate he existed at all. Sharing pain just isn't part of my emotional makeup.

I didn't realize until last night how much I wanted to tell Kate about Suvi. "I didn't know how," I say.

"Is there anything else you haven't told me, anything you want to tell me?"

I think about it. "No."

"I'm worried about you," she says. "I don't want you to go to work."

"What do you want me to do?"

"You know what I want and you know I'm right. Things have gone too far. You told me you would."

I nod. The case has spun out of control, gone to places I never would have imagined, and it's taken a heavy toll on me. I don't want to because it feels like failure, humiliating, but I should give it up. "I'll do it now," I say.

I call the national chief of police. He starts in on me before I can speak. "You didn't write the press release the way I told you. Now things are fucked up."

"Jyri, my ex-wife is dead. She was murdered last night." I tell him about the circumstances.

Momentary silence. "Jesus, I'm sorry. How are you bearing up?"

"Not that well. I'm recusing myself. This has become too personal. I may have been the last person to see Heli alive, and given my relationship to her and her husband, the prime suspect, it's inappropriate for me to continue."

"Are you up to talking about the case?"

"Yeah."

"Tell me what you know and where you think the case is headed."

"The last time we talked, I told you that when we found the third man, the one who shed the tears on Sufia's face, he would lead to someone else and we'd solve the murder. The boy, Heikki, committed suicide, and a DNA test proved the tears were his. He connected to Heli and Seppo, and that left me with four working theories. I figured I didn't have to prove any of them, just disprove the others, and process of elimination would leave me with the truth."

"Let's hear them."

"At first, I thought it most likely that Heli and Heikki did it together. She stood to lose a lot if Seppo left her for Sufia, and she also had a revenge motive. Heikki was young, malleable, impressionable. She could have used sex and his religious beliefs to coerce him. But then I thought Heikki and Seppo acting together was a more elegant solution with fewer working parts. I asked Heli if Seppo is bisexual. She didn't deny it. A homosexual relationship would give Heikki a simple jealousy motive."

"Since Heli is dead now," he says, "that pretty much just leaves Seppo."

"Wait. That doesn't explain the Elizabeth Short copycat aspect of the murder and how Heikki knew about Sufia's genital mutilation." I explain the common features of the two murders. "If Heikki was involved with Sufia and Seppo in a sex triangle, Heikki would have been aware of it. In this instance, Heikki might have acted alone out of jealousy, or he and Seppo might have killed her together, most likely because Sufia tried to blackmail Seppo, since she was known to have attempted it in the past under similar circumstances. Maybe that's what happened. Heli found out about it and forced Seppo to marry her by threatening to tell me the truth about Sufia's murder. That would provide Seppo with a motive for killing Heli."

"But the way he did it, with the tire from his own car, would be an act of complete idiocy. If he killed his wife, he's made himself the main suspect."

"He's not the brightest bulb, but yeah, the stupidity involved makes me question his guilt."

"You said four theories. That's three."

"Sufia's relationship with Peter Eklund is the piece of the puzzle still unaccounted for. She performed oral sex on both Seppo and Peter earlier in the day of her murder, had traces of semen from both of them in her mouth. Peter and Seppo knew each other in Helsinki, maybe they both like young boys. If they both had sex with Sufia, maybe they also shared Heikki. It's ugly, but it's a possibility."

The chief mulls it over. "What do you think now that Heli is dead?"

"I haven't had a chance to think about it."

"Think about it."

"Honestly, my gut feeling was that Heli and Heikki did it, but now I just don't know anymore."

He barks it out, surprises me. "Don't recuse yourself."

"Jyri, that's ridiculous. I may have been the last one to see her alive. It makes me a possible suspect."

"Did you kill her?"

"Of course not."

"Then you weren't the last one to see her alive. Have you seen the papers or watched TV today?"

I've been avoiding them. "Not for a couple days. I haven't had time."

"You're all over the news, national and international. They're flashing pictures of Sufia Elmi, talking about how the handling of the Finnish Black Dahlia case is all fucked up. The implication is that a dumb redneck cop, a reindeer biter from Lapland, abused his authority and used the murder of a sweet and innocent but talented Somali refugee—who worked her way to fame and fortune against all odds—as a way to get back at his ex-wife and the guy who fucked her when they were married. If you'd written the press release the way I told you, been up-front about your relationship to the accused, then painted the shithead black, you would have seemed like a good guy. Now you could end up losing your job over it. Or worse."

Now I see why Jyri is the national chief of police. He understands politics. I knew the media might make me look bad, maybe incompetent, but I didn't expect them to crucify me. "What should I do?"

"Finish the case and solve it."

"My friend's son and my ex-wife are dead. I'm too emotionally involved and I feel like I've lost my judgment and perspective. I've done my best, but I've had about all I can take. You were right in the beginning—I never should have taken the case."

"But you did take it. In for a dime, in for a dollar, they say."

"Let someone who's better equipped take over."

"If you give up the case after already being demonized in the press for malfeasance, you might end up getting prosecuted for your ex-wife's murder. My willingness to let you continue the investigation will demonstrate official belief in you. If you solve the case, you save yourself."

"I didn't do it, so they can't prove it. They can write what they want."

"You can't be that naive."

"I guess I am."

He yells into the phone, hurts my ear. "Fuck you! Do you have any idea how much fucking flack I'm taking over this goddamned murder? I'm trying to help you and you won't let me. When you took this case, against my better judgment, I told you it was on your head. Now I want you to pull yourself together and do your goddamned job."

I don't know what to do. I try to think.

He lowers his voice. "It's three days before Christmas. It would be hard as hell for me to get a homicide team up there, and even if I could, it would take a couple days for you to get them up to speed. You know the statistics. Every minute that goes by lessens our chance of solving this murder. The case will lose momentum, it might even slip through our fingers and go unsolved. Are you willing to let that happen?"

He's pushing my buttons, trying to manipulate me, but what he said is true and I'm not willing to let it happen. "No."

"I realize this is hard for you, but when you told me you wanted this case, you mentioned your career. You solve the murders, both of Sufia Elmi and your ex-wife, and I'll show my gratitude. You can have the job of your choice."

I think about how unhappy Kate is in Kittilä. "Tell me how you think I should continue."

"It's obvious. Everybody else in this case is dead. Seppo Niemi is in custody. Arrest the Eklund boy too. Charge them both with conspiracy to murder. Neither one of them is tough enough to face double-homicide charges. One of them will talk."

"What about Eklund's father?"

"He and I play golf together. I'll deal with him, and I'll get the arrest warrant for you and smooth things over."

He's right about everything. "Jyri, I want to thank you for your faith in me and the support you've given me."

"Thank me by solving the case." He hangs up.

Kate listened to my end of the conversation and understood enough to get the idea. She shakes her head like I'm a child she can't reason with. "It's almost Christmas," she says. "Stay here with me where it's warm and safe."

I shake my head no.

"You're making a mistake."

"It's what I've got to do."

"I didn't tell you because you were already so upset. I saw a report on BBC World about the murder. They're making you out to be a corrupt policeman abusing his authority. They raised the question of whether you're really a hero decorated for bravery, or a cop that got away with murder once before. You're risking everything."

"He offered me any job I want if I do this. You wanted to get away from Kittilä, I'm doing it for you too."

"Don't do it for me, I don't want you to."

"I have to."

Kate turns her back on me. Her voice radiates anger and disappointment. "This will end badly," she says.

# 30

IN DOWNTOWN KITTILÄ, what passes for our shopping district
is decked out for Christmas. The main square has a tall tree, over-
decorated with gaudy blinking lights and laden with thick snow.
Store window banners say *Hyvää Joulua*, Merry Christmas, or some
variation on the theme, and advertise special holiday offers. I hate
the commercialization of Christmas. Maybe because when I was
a kid, we were poor and couldn't afford expensive gifts, maybe
because it just sucks.

Last year, Kate and I spent our first Christmas together. I made
a traditional Finnish Christmas Eve dinner: *rosolli* (a salad with
pickles, beets, onions and herring), a fifteen-pound ham and three
different casseroles made out of potatoes, turnips and carrots. She
said we'd never eat it all, but it was gone in four days. It comes to
me that Heikki was supposed to help out Kate, but he's dead, and
I don't even know if she has anything to eat at home. This case has
made me a negligent husband.

I feel like shit from the hangover, and whatever I do is wrong, damned if I do and damned if I don't. I haven't even considered how my insistence in pursuing my ex-wife's murderer makes Kate feel. Judging by her reaction, I've already ruined her holidays. I don't want to further destroy them by having nothing to eat but takeout pizza on Christmas. Luckily, I bought Kate's gifts weeks ago, but on the way to work, I stop at the grocery and buy all the food for the holidays. I'm afraid if I don't do it now, I'll forget later.

I leave the supermarket and look around. Almost every small Finnish town has the same eight or ten chain stores, and Kittilä looks like all the rest, as if it had been stamped out of a sheet with a cookie cutter. Standing in the cold and dark, looking at my hometown done up in fake Christmas bullshit, I wonder what the fuck I'm doing, why I'm not at home with my wife. Finnish people are obedient, we do what we're told. Maybe I'm as faceless as this community.

It's too late now. I've made my choice. Like the chief said, in for a dime, in for a dollar.

No media vultures hover outside the police station. I guess since I wouldn't talk to them, they gave up and went home for Christmas. I park in the police garage and leave my groceries in the trunk of the car. They'll stay cold enough there without freezing.

Inside, I find Valtteri slumped over his desk, his head in his hands. "What the hell are you doing here?" I ask.

He's a wreck. His appearance is so bad that I think he hasn't eaten or slept, hasn't done very much but cry, since he found his son dead in his basement a couple days ago. He fires my question back at me, his tone is sharp. "What the hell are *you* doing here?"

In seven years of working together, I've never heard Valtteri use a swear word before, even a mild one. "You heard about Heli?" I ask.

"I heard. Antti told me."

"I'm not criticizing you. I just think you burying your son one day and coming back to work the next is too much. You should be at home."

"To do what, sit on the couch with my wife and cry?"

That's exactly what I think. "You should stay home with Maria for a few days. She needs you."

"I can't help her and she can't help me. You told me to come back to work and here I am."

I pull up a chair, sit down next to him and put a hand on his shoulder. "I'm trying to be your friend. Have you looked in the mirror today?"

He brushes my hand away. "You should take a look in the mirror yourself. You look like a bucket of shit without the bucket. You saw Heli, a woman you spent years with, burned to death last night, and you're here at work. If I shouldn't be here, you shouldn't either. We both stay or we both go home."

His behavior is strange but his argument is logical. Maybe work is the therapy he needs.

"Did Antti go home to sleep?" I ask.

"Yeah, and Jussi went out on a call, a car wreck. It's just us for now."

"You talk to Seppo yet?"

"No."

"I'll see if he wants to confess. If he doesn't, we're going to arrest Peter Eklund."

Valtteri nods and stares down at the top of his desk again.

I go downstairs and open the port in the door of Seppo's cell. He stares through it at me. "I guess you think you're pretty goddamned funny," he says, "having me dragged out of my house in the middle of the night and arrested again."

"Stick your hands out so I can cuff you."

He's learned the drill, lets me put handcuffs on him and steps away as I enter. He's wearing his own clothes, looks like less of a buffoon than the last time we met in this cell. "Why did you do this to me?" he asks. "I thought we'd settled things between us."

"Me too, but that was before you killed your wife."

He tilts his head, appears uncomprehending. "What are you talking about?"

I've still never figured out if Seppo is a good actor, smarter than he seems, or if he really is the complete dolt I take him for. I try to bait him into a confession. "Stupid to kill your wife five days after you murder your girlfriend. Even more stupid to use the same vehicle. You might just as well have hung a sign around your neck saying, 'Send me to prison and throw away the key, I'm guilty of double murder.'"

He shakes his head back and forth like a wet dog. "I don't get it."

"Heli is dead. The spare tire from your BMW was filled with gasoline, hung around her chest and arms and set ablaze. She looked like a little blackened doll, her face and hair scorched off, sitting on the ice in a puddle of filth."

He blinks, looks around, blinks again, looks around some more, then a quavering noise comes out of his throat and he launches himself at me. I'm so surprised that he gets his manacled hands around my neck and knocks me to the floor. If I weren't so much bigger and stronger than him, I'd be a dead man. I manage to roll him over and pin his shoulders to the concrete with my knees. He bucks and writhes, tries to shake me off him. He can't and gives up, just lays there with tears streaming, saying "Fuck you, fuck you," over and over again.

I wait awhile. "Think you can control yourself now?"

He doesn't say anything. I let him up anyway.

He wipes snot on his sleeve. "How could you hate her enough to kill her?"

It takes me a second to get it. "Why would you think I killed her?"

"It's been thirteen years. I hurt you, but why would you wait all this time, then take everything away from me? First Sufia, now Heli. You want to send me to jail for life for something I didn't do. It's just not fair."

He believes, or wants me to think he believes, that I committed two homicides to get back at him. I'm dumbstruck. "You can't be serious."

He sits on the edge of the metal cot, buries his face in his hands, bursts into tears again. "Don't do this to me, it's not fucking fair."

Could anybody be this good an actor? I sit beside him, give him a cigarette. "I don't hate you, and I didn't hurt Heli. And if you didn't do it, I'll prove you innocent."

He sniffs, looks up. "You promise?"

It's like dealing with a three-year-old. "Yeah, I promise."

"Tell me what happened to her," he says.

I don't know if he's conning me, but watching him listen while I re-create the crime in graphic detail will give me an opportunity to gauge the effect it has on him. I tell him everything. He cries the whole time I talk.

"I don't know why you think I would kill Heli," he says. "Or Sufia. I'm not a violent person. Until I jumped on you, I'd never even been in a fight, even when I was a kid. I wouldn't know how to hurt someone if I wanted to, like you just saw."

I think about interrogating him and accusing him of sex cabals and homosexual love affairs, of murdering Heli to get out from under blackmail and cover up his murder of Sufia. He'll only start crying again. I decide to investigate further before I press him harder. "Why did you marry Heli after all this time?" I ask.

"She had wanted to get married for a long time. She said if I married her, it would make me look better if I had to go to trial for Sufia's murder. She said I owed it to her for having an affair and humiliating her. Mostly, I did it to make her happy. I loved her. I didn't realize how much until this thing with Sufia happened and she stuck by me. Most women would have left."

It crosses my mind that, if he was going to murder Heli, it would have simplified matters to do it before getting married, rather than burning to death his bride of two days. "Do you have any idea why someone would kill Heli?" I ask.

He shakes his head. "I don't think she had an enemy in the world. Heli could be a bitch sometimes, but she wasn't the kind of person that made people hate her. Except for you. Do you swear you didn't kill her?"

"Yeah, I swear."

He goes silent and thoughtful. "Do I have to stay in here?"

"For the time being."

"How am I supposed to take care of her?"

"What do you mean?"

"I'm her husband, I have to see to her funeral."

"I'll bring your cell phone."

He starts crying again in big sobs, puts his head on my shoulder. In my years as a police officer, I think this is the most ridiculous moment I've thus far experienced.

"You used to love her, didn't you Kari?"

I don't like him using my name. "A long time ago."

"Would you do this for me? I'm not strong enough. If not for me, for her, for the way you used to love her?"

Again, I don't know what he's talking about. "Do what?"

"Make her funeral arrangements."

"You serious?"

"Please, I'm begging you. Get her the best of everything, it doesn't matter what it costs."

My sense of the ridiculous multiplies itself. He took my wife away from me in life, wants to give her back in death. "Sure, no problem."

He lifts his head off my shoulder, gives me a soulful look, like we're brothers sharing the loss of a family member. "Thank you," he says.

I leave him alone to his grief.

I GO TO MY OFFICE and call Esko the coroner. "Tell me about the autopsy."

He hesitates, maybe trying to think how to spare my feelings. Having people try to spare my feelings is getting tiresome. "How much do you want to know?"

"As much as I need to."

"As far as forensics go, I didn't find anything that will help you."

"Was she too badly damaged to gather evidence?"

"No. Given her external appearance, the body was in good condition. Her internal organs, in relative terms, were unscathed."

"She looked burned to a cinder. How could that be?"

He clears his throat. "The intense heat from the gasoline melted her subcutaneous layers of fat. The fat leached out of her body and soaked out into her clothes, which acted as a wick. That's why the fire smoldered for so long after Antti put it out. Rubber fires are hard to extinguish as well. In any case, her organs were well-preserved."

"So you're certain the fire killed her, it wasn't an attempt to cover up another murder method."

"She had soot from the burning tire inside her trachea. She was alive when the killer lit it."

I had hoped she was already dead, had suffered less torment. I'm tempted to thank Esko for his efforts but don't feel like it. "Her husband asked me to check into funeral arrangements. When will you release her body?"

"There's nothing more to learn from it, he can take possession at any time."

I ring off and call Jorma the undertaker. I don't mention I'm calling about burying my ex-wife, so he doesn't offer condolences, for which I'm grateful.

"Funeral arrangements are difficult this time of year," he says, "even grave diggers want to stay home over the holidays. If her family wishes to put this behind them, if it would help with their grief, I could make funeral arrangements for tomorrow. Otherwise, I suggest waiting a few days."

I tell him I'll check with her husband.

"Did you know that Sufia Elmi's funeral is tomorrow?" Jorma asks.

"Here in Kittilä? I would have thought her parents would want to take her home to Helsinki. Why did they wait so long?"

"Her father insisted that her funeral be here and in accordance with Islamic tradition. I had difficulty seeing to all the preparations. There was a ceremonial washing of the body to be performed by the family, certain burial shrouds I had to order, things I'd never dealt with before. Mr. Barre was insistent that everything be done in a most precise way, and it took me a few days."

I say thanks and hang up.

Antti bagged and tagged the contents of Heli's purse. I retrieve them from the evidence locker and sort through them. Just the usual stuff. Makeup, wallet, dirty Kleenex, a hairbrush and her cell phone. I take the phone out of the plastic bag and scroll through the menu. Received calls and dialed numbers, received and sent messages. I find nothing noteworthy.

The phone is a new Nokia N82, which does just about everything and costs as much as a month's rent for an average apartment. It has a Global Positioning System, an MP3 music player, a digital camera and Internet-access capability. I check the downloaded files, mostly a bunch of useless crap from diet and exercise websites, and then finally I find the connection I've been hoping for: the download from the true-crime website in Heikki's computer, about the murder of Elizabeth Short, the Black Dahlia.

Maybe I should be surprised, but I'm not. Ever since I found Heikki's suicide note, my instincts told me that Heli put him up to murder. Not because I wanted to vilify her, but because I thought that she, more than anyone else involved, possessed the requisite tools—her sexuality and knowledge of Heikki's religious beliefs—to turn him into a killer. It makes me sad, because now I'm convinced someone I once loved committed an act so evil.

The question remains, if Heli and Heikki killed Sufia, who killed Heli? The field is narrowing and the chief was right. If I arrest everybody, someone will talk. I send the chief a text message, ask him to have Heli's and Seppo's residence in Helsinki searched with an eye for true-crime material. I don't tell him I'm investigating Heli and not Seppo, so he won't think I'm off on a wild, grief-stricken tangent. The evidence is provocative but not damning. I decide to keep my suspicion of her guilt to myself for the time being, to keep from being accused of chasing ghosts.

My case notes are in a pile in front of me. I browse through them, look for something I've forgotten that could explain why Seppo or Peter, or both of them together, might want to kill Heli. I run across my note to check out Abdi Barre. I never did it.

Things Abdi said come back to me. He claimed he can't pass the Finnish medical boards because his language skills are insufficient. Yet his Finnish is excellent, more proper than mine. He feared Sufia's death would go unavenged, asked me if I believed twelve years in prison was adequate punishment for what was done to his daughter, warned me that I had to find her murderer. I more or less told him Seppo was guilty, then Seppo walked free and married Heli. Abdi had called me, angry, distraught.

I remember reading that in Somalia and Rwanda, filling a tire with gasoline and burning the victim alive has sometimes been used as a form of execution. The method was popularized in South Africa by the African National Congress during the eighties. They called it a tire necklace, the verb is necklacing. It was also used in the Mogadishu area during the early years of the Somali civil war. Abdi has a potential source of knowledge about how to commit the crime. I know nothing about his activities during the conflict. He could have seen it done or even necklaced others in the past. Abdi has motive: an eye for an eye. He could have taken from Seppo as he believed Seppo had taken from him.

We have minority populations in Finland—Lapps, Gypsies and Swedish-speaking Finns—but they're all of a long-standing and homegrown kind. Between five and six thousand Somali refugees poured into the country in the early 1990s, our first major experience with foreigners. A lot of us had never seen a black person before the Somalis arrived.

At first, popular feeling was benevolent. Most Finns were

pleased to have an opportunity to help the downtrodden. Then we realized the refugees had to be supported by our rather generous welfare system. They got apartments, televisions, an income, all on the public dole. They often wear more expensive clothes than our working class can afford, because most Muslims don't drink up their money like we do and can use it for other things. Public resentment grew and has never abated.

I remember what I've read about the Somali civil war. The Somalis who took flight during that time were mainly Daarood clan members, escaping violence at the hands of the Hawiye clan. As Somalia disintegrated, the Daarood residents of Mogadishu became the objects of revenge killings. In Somalia there was chaos, clan warfare, genocide, a mass exodus. Few people had passports. It would have been easy to steal an identity and go undiscovered in the flood of refugees. If Abdi had never been a doctor in the first place, it would explain his inability to practice medicine here.

The problem is how to investigate him. Somalia has had no government worthy of the name for the better part of twenty years. The country is ruled by regional warlords, has no infrastructure. There's no one I can call to request a background check or crime sheet. Then it comes to me. Abdi said he studied at the Sorbonne. They should have a yearbook or at least some kind of student photo. Maybe they even keep up with alumni, can tell me something about what happened to Abdi after he graduated. All this is contingent upon whether the man who calls himself Abdi Barre committed identity theft. Maybe he really is Dr. Abdi Barre. Maybe there never was a doctor with a practice in Mogadishu by that name.

I call Interpol and get lucky. I talk to a cop who tells me he's seen what a beating I'm taking from the world press. He's sympathetic and anxious to play a part in a glitzy homicide investigation. I explain what I need, tell him I'm in a hurry. He promises to help me out. Then I call Finnish passport control, ask them to e-mail me a photo of Abdi. It occurs to me that maybe I should even just question Abdi about his past myself. I call him and ask him if he would allow me the privilege of attending his daughter's funeral. I say I'd like to pay my final respects. This is true.

"Are you a Man of the Book Inspector?" he asks.

"What do you mean by Man of the Book?"

His tone suggests I'm an uneducated moron. "According to the Koran, the term describes non-Muslim peoples who received religious scriptures before the time of Muhammad. The Koran completes these scriptures and is God's true and final message to the faithful. However, because People of the Book recognize the supreme Abrahamic God, as do Muslims, they practice revealed faiths based on Divine ordinances. As such, a certain level of tolerance is accorded them under Islamic law. If you are a Man of the Book, I will allow you to attend Sufia's funeral. If you are not, I must regard you as unclean and will not permit you to defile her last rites."

At first I excused it because of his grief, but with every interaction I've had with him, Abdi's arrogance and superior attitude have grown more tiresome. "You may consider me a Man of the Book," I say. "I'm a baptized Lutheran and I've read the Bible."

"Very good then, you may attend." He gives me the time and place and hangs up without saying thank you, fuck you or good-bye.

# 31

I GO OUT TO the common room. Valtteri is still sitting at his desk, still staring at nothing. "How did it go with Seppo?" he asks.

"Not well."

Abdi is a possibility but a long shot, so I don't mention it. Most likely, this will end with Seppo or Peter or both tried and convicted. "Did search and arrest warrants come for Eklund?" I ask.

"Yeah."

I wish Valtteri would go home. "Then let's pick him up," I say.

We take a squad car and I drive. It's snowing hard—wind drives it toward us in blinding sheets. My head hurts from the whiskey, my mouth is still sour. My hangover magnifies everything: the hiss of tires slicing through snowdrifts on the road, the drumming of the windshield wipers. The headlights penetrate the dark, light up the falling snow and the glare burns my eyes. Even the silence between Valtteri and me seems amplified.

In the passenger seat beside me, he drums on the dashboard with chewed fingernails. He grinds his teeth and bites his lip.

I doubt if he knows he's doing any of it. I catch my reflection in the rearview mirror and barely recognize myself. I can't help but think that in our current conditions, we're not fit to be dog catchers, let alone law enforcement officers. But I've investigated enough crimes to know this is almost over. Soon, Valtteri and I can rest, maybe in time for Christmas. When Kate's cast comes off, I'll take her somewhere warm on vacation, maybe the Canary Islands. I can make this up to her. We'll put all this behind us.

The recurring image of Heli's burned body resonates through me, makes me shiver. The significance of my sister and ex-wife dying within a few yards of each other seems too great to ignore. I ask myself who might remember Suvi's death thirty years ago, and who might also have hated Heli enough to not only kill her but to destroy her with fire. Only a few old men who helped recover Suvi's body might even remember where she died. And Dad. He was at that very spot on the lake just a few days ago. He has emotional problems and a violent streak, but I never thought he gave a damn that Heli left me. He never had room for the pain of other people.

I remember Valtteri's reticence when I told him to find out where Dad was when Sufia was murdered. It hurts me to think of it, but maybe pursuing Seppo and Peter is the wrong track. I have to ask. "Do you know anything about my father you haven't told me?"

He looks at me, emotionless. I can't read anything in his face. "I've lived in this town my whole life and I'm a policeman. I know lots of things about people."

"Is there anything I should know?"

He sighs. "Some things are best forgotten, sometimes hurtful things best never known."

I'm scared, but I press it. "Is there something about my father I don't know that has a bearing on these murder cases?"

He shakes his head, indulgent, as if he suffers a fool. "No."

"At the beginning of this, you said we shouldn't look at family, like you were trying to protect me."

"I said we shouldn't waste time investigating family when we know they're innocent."

I don't point out that Heikki wasn't innocent. "Would you tell me if there was something?"

He stares straight ahead. "I'm not sure."

Time passes. "Do you believe in God?" he asks.

We've never discussed religion before. "Yes."

"My faith teaches that what my son Heikki did, committing murder and suicide, condemns him to hell without hope of redemption. Do you believe that?"

I wish I could find words to console him, but I don't have them. I answer his question as best I can. "I think our God is one of forgiveness, and that there's always hope for redemption. If Heikki asked for forgiveness in his last thoughts, I believe he received it."

"I wish I could believe that too," he says. "Heikki always loved hunting more than anything. I thought he was a born outdoorsman. Now I think he just liked killing things."

We ride on in silence. From the foot of the mountain, even through the snowstorm, I can see the multicolored lights of Christmas decorations in the glass front of the Eklund winter cottage. When we pull up the drive, I realize Peter must have had it professionally done. They're as elaborate as those of any department store. We get out of the car, and I look down the mountain into the dark. Below us, Kittilä is almost hidden from view, the lights of the town blurred, nearly obliterated by the pouring snow.

We walk up to the house, and I ring the bell. Peter doesn't answer. I twist the knob, the door is unlocked. Beside the massive hearth stands a Christmas tree nearly as tall as the one in Kittilä's main square, and even more garishly decorated. Christmas music booms through the house. Bing Crosby croons "The First Noël."

Peter comes out of a second-story bedroom, wearing pink silk pajamas, closes the door and locks it behind him, puts the key in his pocket. "What the fuck are you doing here? Get the fuck out!" He doesn't stutter—he's drunk.

"We have a warrant," I say.

He trots down the stairs to head us off.

I hear a muffled cry. It sounds like it came from the room he just left. "Who the fuck was that?" I ask.

We start toward the stairs. Peter blocks our path, tries to keep us out of the room. He's upset, near tears. "You can't go in there, that's Daddy's room."

"You were in it."

Another muffled scream.

"Give me the key," I say.

He doesn't want to. I shove him against the wall. He takes the key from his silk pajama pocket and hands it over. Valtteri cuffs his hands behind his back. I go upstairs and unlock the door.

Two girls are in the room. One is about seventeen and naked. She's manacled spread-eagle to the bedposts with four sets of velvet-lined handcuffs. She's got a red ball gag in her mouth, fastened around her head with nylon straps. If the other girl is in her teens, she's only just barely. She's wearing jeans and socks, but her shirt is off. She sits on the edge of the bed, her arms folded tight across partially formed breasts, rocks back and forth. She stares, vacant, at an invisible fixed point in front of her.

I look around, take in what's happened. Peter's father set up "Daddy's room" with a digital video camera on a tripod, connected to a computer and a big monitor on the wall, so he can watch himself fuck and record it at the same time. I see the keys to the restraints on top of a dresser, beside a collection of dildos, vibrators and lubricants. I take the gag out of the girl's mouth and unlock her. She sits up, starts crying, jabbers fast at me in Russian. She's so upset that she doesn't even think to cover herself.

I tell her to slow down. She speaks a little Finnish, I speak a little Russian. I piece the story together. She came from Kuolo-yarvi, a village not far across the border, to do some prostitution and get some money from the holiday tourists. It's a common tale. A lot of Russian hookers come to Levi, raise some cash and go back home. They can make as much in a week by hooking in Fin-land as they can by working at a straight job for a year in Russia. She takes care of her little sister and brought her along, she says, because there wasn't anyone else to look after her.

Peter cruises the bus station, picks them up there. He seems like a nice guy, is good-looking, has nice clothes, a nice car. She says she doesn't have a place for her sister to stay yet. No problem, he says, she can have something to eat and watch movies while we attend to business. He brings them here, shows the kid the fridge, parks her in front of the TV.

He brings big sister here to Daddy's bedroom. He wants to tie her up, make a video. He offers extra money. He's still smiling, makes it sound like fun. She thinks it will be okay. He ties her to the bed and gags her. He fucks her in the ass, not part of the deal. He doesn't use a condom. Then he drags little sister into the room, takes off her shirt, makes her suck his cock while big sister watches. Big sister wails and sobs, tears at her cheeks with her fingernails, cuts herself. She screams that he didn't even wash his dick before he stuck it in little sister's mouth.

I'm sitting on the edge of the bed next to big sister. Valtteri stands in the doorway listening, Peter behind him.

I walk out into the hall, shake my head and look at Peter. "Boy, you're in big trouble."

Panic sets in. I see it in his eyes. He turns and starts to run. I don't know where he thinks he's going in handcuffs and pink pajamas. I guess he's so drunk he doesn't know either.

Valtteri takes a step forward and grabs him by the collar of his pajama top. He jerks Peter toward him, then punches him in the back of the head. Peter reels, hits the balcony railing, teeters on the edge. He's about to fall to the floor, twenty feet below. Valtteri makes no move to help him.

I reach out and catch Peter, pull him toward us, away from the railing. Valtteri delivers a devastating punch to his face. The crunch of cartilage is loud and sickening. His nose shatters, flattens against his face. He issues a high-pitched squeal. Valtteri punches him in the head again. Peter falls to his knees.

I never could have imagined this scenario. I don't know what to say. "Valtteri?"

"I can't abide violence against innocent women," he says.

There's movement behind me. The little girl comes out of the bedroom into the hall, still topless. She kicks Peter between the legs. He screams. She positions her leg for another kick. I don't try to stop her, can't make myself do it. She kicks him in the face, further crushes his already broken nose. He shrieks in agony and collapses to the floor, hands chained behind him.

He makes a perfect target. She delivers another kick to his crotch with a stockinged foot. He vomits, pulls his knees up to his stomach, tries to protect his testicles from further violence, cries like a baby. She goes back in the bedroom, sits down on the bed beside her sister, stares at the invisible fixed spot again.

Peter's nose requires medical attention, but I don't feel inclined to get it for him yet. He was a handsome boy, maybe too handsome, so pretty he was almost effeminate. Valtteri and little sister cured that problem, but then again, no doubt Daddy will have a plastic surgeon put it back the way it was. I leave him on the floor of the hall. Puke drools out of the corner of his mouth. Blood runs out of his nose and puddles on the floor around his head. He's curled into a fetal position, bawling his eyes out.

Prostitution isn't a crime in Finland, and neither is procuring the services of a prostitute. Prostitution only becomes a matter for the law when it's organized, involves human trafficking and slavery. Big sister is at least sixteen, the age of consent in this country, and is taking part in prostitution of her own volition. Little sister, however, is well under the age of consent. Peter has raped and sexually assaulted a minor.

The law states that people entering the country for the purpose of prostitution must be deported. But not today. I'll get the girls medical and psychiatric care first, and take their statements, but they'll never return for trial. Daddy will buy Peter a good lawyer, and in the end, Peter might walk on the rape and assault charges.

I call for EMTs and search while I wait. I find cocaine and Rohypnol, the date-rape drug, and pills which I think are probably GHB or ecstasy. I check out Daddy's computer. Some of the video files are encrypted, some aren't. I guess Daddy had the sense to encrypt his videos, but Peter found the key to the secret lair, used the equipment and didn't have the brains to cover his ass.

There's footage of him having sex with a variety of people, some male, some female, some adults, some children. In a folder labeled BROKEN ANGELS, I find downloaded kiddie porn, Japanese videos of violent sex with abused and damaged children. Peter is already a convicted sex offender, and possession of child pornography is a serious crime here. In essence, Peter's fucked, and Daddy can't help him without incriminating himself.

Two ambulances arrive, the sisters and Peter travel in separate vehicles. Through driving snow, Valtteri and I trail behind them in the cruiser without speaking. At the hospital, I find a nurse fluent in Russian. She translates and I take statements from the girls. We sit in the waiting room and I take a short nap, until a doctor says we have to leave Peter because he has a ruptured testicle. Both the testicle and his nose require surgery. He won't be able to walk for a week. I suggest he test Peter for HIV/AIDS, because he has unprotected anal sex with prostitutes from Russia, where the disease is rampant.

I'm not worried about leaving Peter unguarded. He's temporarily crippled and anyway, I have his passport. He has nowhere to run. We drive back to the station. "He resisted arrest," I say, "and it was your duty to stop him, but you overreacted and you were going to let him fall over the rail. You almost killed him. And there was no need to hit him like that."

He stares straight ahead, repeats what I said to him a few days ago. "If you feel like you have to report what I did, I won't hold it against you."

I'm not sure if he's mocking me. "I guess we're even now," I say, "but are you sure you're ready to be on duty?"

"I wouldn't have let him fall."

I don't press it.

# 32

BACK AT THE POLICE STATION, I go down to the lockup and open the port in Seppo's cell door. He's sitting on the edge of his cot, crying, looks like he hasn't stopped since I left him there hours ago.

"You have two options," I say. "You can hold Heli's funeral tomorrow, or wait until after Christmas."

He looks up through eyes swollen almost shut. "What do you think I should do?"

My patience with him is gone. "For fuck's sake, she was your wife. What you do with her isn't my decision."

He whimpers. "I can't think, just do whatever you think is best."

Maybe we should just get it over with and put her burial behind us. At least then I won't have to discuss it with him anymore. "Let's do it tomorrow."

He starts bawling again in big sobs and shouts through his tears, "My wife is dead and I can't even go to her funeral because I'm in jail."

I've already considered this. "You can go. I'll take you."

He pauses, wipes his eyes. "Thank you," he says, then gets down on the floor on his knees, folds his hands and starts begging. "I'm innocent, please help me. I'm innocent, please help me." He keeps repeating it over and over again.

I ignore him, shut the port in his door and go up to my office. I call Jorma to make Heli's funeral arrangements, then check my e-mail. Luck is with me. Interpol sent me a student identification photo from the Sorbonne. It's twenty-six years old, but the man in the photo bears little resemblance to the man in Finland claiming to be Dr. Abdi Barre. The last the Sorbonne heard of him, Abdi Barre was practicing medicine at Karaan Hospital, to the north of Mogadishu. It wasn't so much a real hospital as a group of villas that were converted to form a collective center for emergency surgery for those suffering acute war injuries. Dr. Barre was last heard from in 1990.

Since there's no agency in Somalia I can turn to, I consider who might be able to trace Dr. Barre. If he was killed, maybe his death was recorded and listed somewhere. Murdering a physician treating civilian wounded might qualify as a war crime. Finland is a member of the European Union, and international cooperation between EU police departments is good. However, the EU has no jurisdiction over war criminals. That responsibility falls to the International Criminal Court, in The Hague.

When I call the ICC, they give me the bureaucratic runaround. After a while, I get a minor functionary on the phone who explains to me that they've been talking about holding war crimes tribunals for genocide in Somalia for some years, but haven't done anything about it yet. They haven't even assembled an official list of suspects, let alone put together a list of victims. I ask why not. He doesn't have an answer.

When Serbians committed genocide in the Balkans, the ICC took their prosecution of war criminals seriously and is still tracking them down. The message is clear: Europeans find their own lives of great value, but African lives of little or no worth. I ask if any agency might have assembled a victims list. He says the Human Rights Commission monitored violence in Mogadishu during that time frame and suggests I check with them.

I phone the HRC and speak with a helpful and concerned woman. I give her the year and name of the hospital and she checks their records. There is no victims list, but physicians from the expatriate staff of Médecins Sans Frontières provided emergency assistance. She has a list of MSF doctors that were there, and can e-mail me their contact information. Two minutes later, I get it and notice that one of the doctors is a Finn. I call her up.

Yes, she remembers Abdi Barre, his death was very sad. In the first weeks of heavy fighting, it was common for groups of armed soldiers to bring their wounded to the hospital. They dictated triage decisions and forced doctors to operate with guns held to their heads. The president's own bodyguards, the Red Berets, notorious for torture, subjected Dr. Barre to such treatment. When his patient died on the operating table, they took him outside, filled a tire with gasoline, placed it around his arms and chest and burned him to death.

I'm thinking maybe a Red Beret took his passport before they killed him and used it to get out of the country. The picture of the man claiming to be Abdi Barre has arrived from passport control. I e-mail it to her while we talk and ask her if she can identify the person in the photo. She's sorry, but the moment was so shocking, there was such chaos and confusion, that she couldn't identify any of the murderers if they were standing in front of her. I thank her for her help.

The pieces of the puzzle are coming together. The problem is that I don't know how to prove any of it. I decide it's time to call it a day and go home.

I WALK INTO THE living room carrying bags of groceries. Kate is on the couch, typing on her laptop. I lean over for a kiss, but she doesn't return it. "I put on the sauna," she says, "I thought it would do you good."

"Thanks, I could use it."

Sauna relaxes me more than anything else in the world. Like most Finns used to be, I was born in one. Mom had an emergency birth. Dad wasn't home, they didn't have a phone then, and a neighbor woman acted as midwife. Maybe going to sauna is like a return to the womb for me. God willing, I'll die in one too.

"I got everything for Christmas dinner," I say.

She still hasn't looked up. "Who's going to cook it and eat it?"

I want to make amends, so I ignore the slight. "What are you doing?" I ask.

"Catching up on e-mails. If you're going to work through Christmas, I might as well do it too."

She's pissed off and I don't blame her. "I don't intend to work through Christmas."

She keeps typing. "No?"

"I'm close to solving this. It should be over tomorrow."

She closes the laptop, and with effort moves her broken leg from the couch to a stool. She pats the seat beside her. "Sit down and tell me about it."

I tell her about the day, about Seppo and what I learned about Abdi, about arresting Eklund and what Valtteri said about my father.

"So to sum up," she says, "you conclude that in Helsinki, before they came to Kittilä, Heli overhears Seppo on the phone, bragging about fucking Sufia, his nigger whore with the beautiful eyes. He talks about her strange vagina. Heli learns he's going to Levi to be with her. She's worried he's in love with Sufia. If he leaves Heli, she'll lose everything. She follows him to nip this in the bud. Am I right so far?"

"Yeah."

"She starts thinking about teaching Seppo a lesson. She covers her real purpose for coming here with a story about rediscovering her religious roots. She's a crime buff. Seppo talking about Sufia's strange vagina inspires Heli to copycat the Elizabeth Short killing. She meets Heikki, opportunity presents itself. She uses his beliefs against him, tells him niggers and whores are sinners. She sucks his cock, tells him it's not intercourse and so not a sin. She knows Seppo and his big mouth. He's been going on about his gorgeous nigger whore to anyone who will listen. Am I still on track?"

I don't like where this is going. "Yeah."

"She gets Heikki to cut the words into Sufia's belly—damning evidence—so that if she has to, she can blackmail Seppo into marrying her, insurance in case he falls in love with another young beautiful girl. She also has the boy gouge out Sufia's eyes, a way of punishing Seppo because he loved them. Afterward, she pushes Heikki over the edge to suicide by rejecting him, forcing him to the realization that he committed murder and will suffer eternal damnation for nothing, and so all the evidence against her is gone. It's a well-executed murder. She just didn't count on being murdered herself for revenge."

"That's about it," I say.

"And then the father of the victim," she says, "who pretends to be a doctor, is actually a former torturer, a deranged man. He kidnapped your ex-wife and burned her to death to exact retribution for the loss of his daughter."

"I think so."

"But if that's not the way it happened, it could have been your father, because your distraught coworker said cryptic things about him, and your father is the only one who would remember where your sister died."

"I don't want to think that, but I have to consider everything."

"But just in case it wasn't your father either, the murders might be the result of a sexual cabal, involving several people, for reasons unknown."

I can't understand why she's doing this. "You're not being fair. You're trying to make me sound stupid."

"And yet you're close to solving this case and you'll be here with me for Christmas dinner."

She's backed me into a corner, made me uncomfortable. "I know you're angry, but you don't need to insult me."

"Who's your next suspect? Your mother? Where was she at the time of the murder? Maybe she set this diabolical plan in motion, waited years for the opportunity to exact revenge on the people who hurt her son. It could have been me. Jealous of your ex-wife, I seduced Heikki and we murdered Sufia together as a cover for our final intent. I drove him to suicide to erase all traces of my crime, then destroyed Heli with fire. Maybe it was Pirkko Virtanen, and stabbing her husband to death was the final act in her murder spree."

I'm not just insulted, I'm furious, but I don't want to show it because this is my fault. I've let this case interfere with our relationship. She has cause for her anger and I can't muster a worthy response. "You have no right to talk to me like this," I say.

"Let's look at what you've got here. A theory about a copycat murder. Why? Because your ex-wife can't spell in English and two women killed sixty years apart both had genital deformities. I read about the Elizabeth Short murder on the Internet. Yes, there are a few similarities in the cases, but the differences far outweigh them. You've got Abdi Barre, a grieving father with a bad personality who said a few untoward things. Nothing suggests he's a killer who's been hiding in this country for the better part of twenty years. Your sister and your ex-wife being killed in the same approximate location was most likely coincidence. Stranger things have happened."

I'm trying hard not to yell at her. I've never done it before and I don't want to start now. "All right genius, since you're the cop all of a sudden, you figure out the murders and explain them to me."

"Before, you talked about finding the most elegant solution. Let me tell you what I think happened. Sufia had the semen of two men in her mouth. There was no sex cabal. She had two lovers. She was a slut and sucked them both off within a few hours. Heikki's suicide note said he or she made me do it. He meant Seppo. They killed Sufia together, for love or money or whatever, and then, for some reason we don't know, Seppo killed Heli. Maybe he's just fucking crazy. You don't seem to have thought of that."

"That leaves too many things unexplained," I say. "I'm looking for the truth."

"Then I'll give it to you. You're an emotional mess. You look like shit. Last night, I watched the strongest man I've ever known fall apart because he never came to terms with the death of his sister, and probably never truly dealt with the fact that his ex-wife left him. Instead of grieving for her, you're demonizing her rather than admit to yourself that you loved her and she hurt you. You're tearing yourself apart."

She takes my hand, puts my palm on her belly. "The truth is in here. You have two children growing inside me and you're going to be a good and wise father to them." She puts my other hand against her cheek. "And here you have a wife who loves you. You need to heal, to give these murders to another investigator and to be here with me so I can take care of you."

I love Kate so much. Sometimes I wish I could crawl inside her, be a part of her, flow in her veins, drown in her blood. I wish I could say this to her.

My cell phone rings. It's the national chief of police, so I answer. He tells me they searched Seppo's Helsinki residence. A computer contained a number of true-crime files downloaded from the Internet. They also found a copy of *The Black Dahlia*, the novel by James Ellroy, based on the murder of Elizabeth Short, and also a video of the movie based on the book. I tell Kate what he said.

"You're not going to stop, are you?" she asks.

I don't respond.

"You can't, can you?"

I shake my head no.

She sighs and holds my hand. We sit in the quiet for a few minutes.

"When it's over," she says, "I'll be here, and I'll help you put yourself back together."

I realize that I know how to end this. I know it's irresponsible and I shouldn't do it, but I'm equally certain I'm going to do it anyway. I go to the sauna to be alone, to prevent myself from telling Kate what I intend to do.

# 33

THE NEXT MORNING, I put on a sweater and wool socks and step out to the back porch for a cigarette. The weather turned even more severe overnight and the cold hurts me, like somebody threw a handful of razors in my face. It almost drives me back inside. The thermometer reads minus forty, like it was a week ago today when Sufia was murdered, but now the bitter cold is accompanied by a driving wind that makes it almost impossible to bear. By the time I finish my smoke, my ears are numb and burning.

I have two funerals to attend today. I put on a black suit and a thick, full-length wool coat over it. My dress hat is made of heavy fox fur. I pull down the inner ear flaps and steel myself for a miserable frozen day.

At the police station, I bring Seppo up from his cell to my office and call Valtteri in to join us. Seppo looks bad, but he doesn't cry or beg, and his lack of emotion surprises me. I suspect he's gone through so much that he's numb inside. I pour us all coffee and we sit around my desk. Seppo and I light cigarettes.

"Seppo," I say, "unless something changes, you're going to be convicted of double homicide."

His expression stays flat. "I know."

"Both your girlfriend and your wife are going to be buried today, Sufia at eleven this morning, Heli at four this afternoon."

He nods.

"I don't know if you killed them or not. Do you want to confess and make things easier for yourself? If you do, you'll shave time off your prison sentence, still have some good years left when you get out."

He sips coffee. His voice doesn't change as he replies. We could be talking about what we're going to have for lunch. "I didn't kill them."

"Then who did?"

"I don't know."

"If what you tell me is true, I want to help you, not because I care what happens to you, but because I want to see justice done. Do you understand?"

"Yes."

"I have an idea. It's risky, but if you agree, we'll try it."

He takes a drag off his cigarette. "What is it?"

I explain what I learned about Abdi Barre. "Sufia's father thinks you killed her," I say. "I believe he killed Heli as an act of revenge, to pay you back. I think if he has the chance, he'll try to kill you too."

He raises his eyebrows, his first show of emotion. "You want to let him try to kill me?"

"I'm going to tell him that even though I know you murdered Sufia, I can't prove it, and if he doesn't kill you—the man who first defiled and then brutally murdered his daughter—you're going to walk free, that you'll never be punished for what you did. I'll tell him I know he's not who he claims to be and that he killed Heli. I'm going to say I'm glad he did it because what the newspapers say is true: I hated her, and I hate you for what you did to me. That I want you dead and I want him to kill you. And I'm going to give him the chance to do it. I'll tell him we'll make it look like you committed suicide."

I turn to Valtteri. "The point of this is to elicit a confession, and I need your help. I'll take Seppo out to the lake where Heli was killed, and tell Abdi to meet us there. I want you hidden in your army winter camouflage, a little way into the forest. I'll wear a wire. You bring recording equipment and a video camera. And a rifle, in case things go wrong. I get the confession, you document it, and we arrest Abdi."

He looks confused, uncertain.

"I'm sorry," I say, "but I think you and I both know Heikki and Heli killed Sufia. We just don't know if Seppo killed Heli. If Abdi confesses to the second murder, and further investigation of forensic evidence clears Seppo of the first one, as I think it will, he can go free. Justice will be served."

I sit back and look at them. "What do you think?"

"Do you really hate me?" Seppo asks.

"I don't give a shit about you."

"What would prevent you from taking me out there and letting him kill me?"

I shrug. "Nothing could be easier. I could just say you escaped from my custody while I escorted you to your wife's funeral, and I don't know what happened to you afterward. You can take your chances in court or with me. It's easier for me if you just stand trial for double murder. Either way, I'm done with this today."

"What happens if Sufia's father doesn't take the bait?"

"You go to prison."

Seppo stares at me for a long moment. Maybe he still thinks I killed Sufia and Heli, and now I'm going to kill him too. "Okay," he says.

"If it works," Valtteri says, "when it comes out how we did it, we'll be reprimanded for an irresponsible act. We could even lose our jobs."

"That's right."

"But we could solve all this today," he says, "put all this behind us forever."

"Exactly," I say.

For the first time since the death of his son, I see Valtteri smile. "I like it," he says.


AT ELEVEN, I go to the cemetery. I find Sufia's mother, Hudow, in a far corner by herself. She's shivering in the cold and dark, next to an open grave with a modest tombstone at its head. I grew up here and even for me this weather is punishing. I can't imagine how painful it must be for her. I express my sympathy for the loss of her daughter.

"I glad you come," she says. "Thank you."

"Where is everyone else?" I ask.

She stifles a sob. "Abdi come. He explain."

It's too cold for life, human or otherwise. Besides the sounds of wind and snow crunching under our feet, the graveyard is silent. No birds sing, no animals stir. My eyes run and the tears freeze before they can roll down my cheeks. I brush the ice off with gloved fingers. The wind cuts into us, hurts us. My face aches, then goes numb. Wind in this part of the country is seldom this fierce. It feels like a bad omen. A frozen tree branch breaks. The noise makes me start.

The hearse pulls up. Abdi steps out, motions me over. He doesn't offer his hand but gives me a slight bow. "Thank you for coming," he says. "Whoever attends a *janazah*, a Muslim funeral, until it is finished will earn a *qirat*, and whoever stays until the burial will earn two *qirat*s." He offers a weary smile. "A *qirat* means a reward as big as a mountain."

"Thank you for allowing me to attend," I say. "I'm sorry for your loss."

"No one dies unless Allah permits," Abdi says. "We must pray for God's mercy on the departed in the hope that they may find peace and happiness in the afterlife. We must strive to be patient, and remember that Allah gives life and takes it away, at a time appointed by Him. It is not for us to question His wisdom."

Jorma gets out of the driver's side, opens the rear of the hearse. I'm taken aback, because there isn't a coffin. Sufia's body is wrapped, with obvious precision, in cloth as white as the snow that blankets the graveyard.

"There were many difficulties in preparing for Sufia's parting," Abdi says. "As a Muslim, she may not share a burial ground with infidels. I purchased a plot in the corner of the cemetery, and those plots surrounding it, so that her resting place may remain separate and undefiled. The grave must be aligned on a northeast-to-southwest axis, facing Mecca. It was most difficult to communicate the importance of this to the grave diggers."

"Jorma told me there were complications," I say.

He sighs. "More than I would have imagined. Proper burial garments and bindings were difficult to obtain. Her body should not be embalmed or placed in a coffin, but this is not in accordance with

Finnish law. I had to obtain special permission to forgo the casket and instead place her in a grave with a concrete liner. Women may not accompany the departed to the site of burial. As such, my poor wife has had to wait here and suffer in this frozen graveyard."

I'm surprised and touched by his candor. I would never have expected it of him. "Are there no other mourners or clergy?" I ask.

"There is no mosque in this town, no Muslim community. We have no friends here. As her father, it is permitted that I serve as imam and offer the spoken prayers. It will not be difficult for you. They are similar to the five daily prayers, but most are silent. No bowing or prostration is required. Would you assist me in taking her to rest?"

He means will I help him carry her body. With care, we take her from the hearse.

"We must place her in the ground on her right side," he says. "It should be so that I remove the veil from her face, but because of her condition, I choose to leave it covered. I do not believe this will be displeasing to Allah."

We carry Sufia through the snow on our shoulders. It's not easy and we move with slow care. Hudow looks on as we place Sufia in the concrete liner. Abdi adjusts the arrangement of Sufia's body in minute ways and looks up at Hudow. She nods, saying without speaking that Sufia's final resting place is to her satisfaction.

The grave was dug with a backhoe, the earth piled up in a neat mound. Abdi takes three clods of earth, which he must have broken up beforehand, because the dirt is frozen rock-hard and there's no way he could have done it otherwise, and drops them in the grave. Hudow does likewise. He offers three clods to me and I toss them onto Sufia's shrouded body. He says a short prayer in Arabic. He translates for me and asks me to recite it. "We created you from the earth, and return you into it, and from it we will raise you a second time."

I say the prayer and he offers some others. It doesn't take long. "Now we must pray for the forgiveness of the dead," he says.

We do it in silence. I'm so moved by the service that I'm tempted to abandon my plan to lure him into a confession. I remind myself that no matter the cause, Heli's murder was a monstrous act that must be punished.

When it's over, he takes me aside. "We must not linger long," he says, "because Hudow suffers greatly. The Prophet said that three things continue to benefit a person after death. Charity given during life, knowledge imparted unto others, and a righteous child who prays for a departed parent. Now, after our own deaths, Hudow and I will not benefit from the prayers of a righteous child. You cannot know, but my daughter was a warm and delightful person. She brought us great joy and did not deserve what befell her in this evil place. I believe Allah will receive her with open arms. In this world though, there must be an accounting. How do you progress?"

"I've failed," I say. "Seppo Niemi murdered your daughter, but I can't prove it and he'll go free. I'm sorry."

He rocks on his heels like I slapped him. "This cannot be, I will not allow it."

"There's another option."

I see rage in his face. "Which is?"

"I'll create an opportunity for you to take your vengeance."

Rage is replaced by curiosity. "Why would you do this?"

"Have you read the papers? Do you know what Seppo did to me, how my ex-wife betrayed me and Seppo made me a cuckold?"

He nods.

"You could take vengeance for both of us, redress all the wrongs done to us."

He studies me. "I see."

"I know certain things," I say. "You aren't Dr. Abdi Barre. He was killed with a tire necklace outside Karaan Hospital in 1990. I think you killed him, stole his passport and used it to escape Somalia with your wife and daughter. I further believe that you murdered my ex-wife to punish Seppo. As you put it, 'eye for eye.' I'm not judging you for this, I'm glad she's dead."

His face betrays nothing. "You must believe yourself quite clever," he says.

"I'll take Seppo to Heli's funeral this afternoon. Afterward, I'll bring him to the lake, to the same spot where you killed Heli. I'll leave him there with you. Give me some time to get back to town and establish an alibi, then kill him. Make it look like a suicide. It's the only way we can make things right."

He lifts a gloved hand and presses a long finger to pursed lips as he contemplates. "Why have you investigated me?"

I shrug. "It's my nature. Meet me at six P.M."

"You must think me foolish," he says. "Forgive me for saying that you do not have my full trust in this matter. I must decline."

"I don't think you have much choice. If you refuse, I'll arrest you for Heli's murder. You'll serve a lengthy prison term, and afterward you'll be deported back to Somalia."

"I see."

"Are we agreed?"

He doesn't answer.

"I'll be there," I say. "Do as you will." I start to walk away.

He calls after me. "Inspector, it is unfortunate that you were not as assiduous in the investigation of my daughter's murder as you have been in your inquiry of me. Much would have been spared us all."

"I'm sorry for that, I did my best."

I turn and don't look back. My bad knee has stiffened from the cold. I limp across the windswept graveyard through the crackling snow and drive away.

I GO TO SEPPO'S house and look for clothes appropriate for a funeral. I pick out a charcoal pinstripe suit for him, find him a long heavy wool coat so he doesn't get frostbite during last rites at the cemetery. Back at the station, I let him use our sauna and shower room to prepare himself, clean up and shave.

I talk to Valtteri. He's been on the phone, calling people from the church, trying to make sure Heli gets a proper send-off. He's gotten everything together: his white winter camouflage suit, a video camera, recording equipment and a scoped AK-47. I let Seppo sit in the common room without handcuffs. It seems too cruel to make him linger in his cell while he waits to bury his wife. I sit in my office alone for a while and smoke cigarettes.

When it's time, Seppo and I drive to Kittilä's church in my car. The day is wretched. Cold, dark and miserable. He sits in the passenger seat beside me and maintains his composure. He attempts conversation, wants to commiserate over Heli. I let him know, in no uncertain terms, that I don't feel like chatting.

Like in many small Finnish towns, our church is simple and wooden. The turnout is good, maybe sixty people. Some knew Heli when she was a girl, some come out of obligation because a member of the congregation has died. Her family is there. Her mother and father barely acknowledge Seppo, but hug me like I'm still their son-in-law. Jorma did a good job. Her casket is white with polished brass handles. There's no clue that preparations were made at the last minute.

Pastor Nuorgam, a Laestadian, holds the service. He goes through the ritual parts, then begins the sermon. It starts nicely enough, mourns the loss of a daughter of the church who was for a time a lost lamb but who thanks be to Christ recovered her faith before her passing. Then it devolves into a rant, low-key and in a calm voice, but a rant nonetheless, about original sin and the tortures of hell. It ends with the expression of hope that Heli won't suffer such torments.

I'm asked to be a pallbearer. I decline. We tramp out into the frozen graveyard, my second trek through it today. Heli's burial plot is about seventy-five yards from Sufia's. The wind has died down, a small blessing. Heli is lowered into the ground, a few more prayers are offered, and then it's over. Seppo cries a little, but overall comports himself well. There will be no wake.

We get back in my car and pull out onto the road. "I'm going to take you to the lake now," I say, "to the place where Heli was killed."

"Is Sufia's father coming?"

"I don't know."

"What did he say?"

"Not much."

We ride in silence for a few minutes. "I suppose you don't think so because of the things I did," Seppo says, "but I loved Heli more than you imagine. I don't know how I'll live without her."

I keep my eyes on the road, but out of the corner of my eye, I see Seppo shed a tear. "I'm certain you'll find a way," I say.

"You're a strong man," he says. "You must have loved Heli after so many years together, even after what happened between you at the end, but no one could have guessed how much pain you were in at the funeral."

This is the second time in two days I've been told I still loved Heli, and it's fucking annoying. "Yesterday, you were convinced I hated her enough to kill her, now you think I still loved her. Which is it?"

The dimwit puts a consoling hand on my shoulder. "Both."

I push his hand away. "You're wrong. I didn't hate Heli. It took time and self-discipline, but I did something worse to her. I forgot her, deleted her from my mind like she never existed. I threw out every picture of her. If I had something I thought she might even have touched, I got rid of it. If I had seen her on the street, I wouldn't have acknowledged her presence. I would have looked past her like she wasn't there. If she was starving and came to me begging, I wouldn't have given her pocket change for something to eat. If her lungs were on fire, I wouldn't have pissed down her throat to put it out. If it hadn't been for this investigation, I would have never, ever, spoken to her again. You get it now?"

He takes this in. "I would have liked it better if you hated her," he says.

He stays quiet after that.

# 34

We get to the lake and I pull off to the side of the road. The sky is overcast and the snow reflects only the dimmest of light. A small fire is burning on the ice where Heli died. I clip a microphone to the inside of my fox fur hat, chamber a round into my Glock and slip it into my coat pocket. I snap cuffs on Seppo to make it seem that he hasn't come of his own volition.

"I'm afraid," he says.

I don't comfort him.

We lurch through the snow down the embankment. The lake looks the same as the day Suvi drowned. The wind has polished the surface until it's as slick and clean as a slab of slate. The muted light makes it appear the color of dark pearl. I look off into the woods. The shadows are impenetrable, but it's reassuring to know that Valtteri is there, watching and listening.

We walk across the lake. Abdi has gathered wood and made a small campfire. He's sitting on a tire, warming his hands, a can of gasoline beside him. A few feet away from him, the ice is still scorched in the spot Heli was burned.

We come close to him. I push Seppo down on his knees.

I look at the tire and gas can. "That's a messy suicide you've concocted."

Abdi raises a hand, levels a pistol at my face. This isn't according to plan. "Where did you get the gun?" I ask.

"I'm a businessman and transport quantities of cash. I have a license to carry it."

We stare at each other. I don't know why I'm not afraid.

"You were correct in certain assumptions, wrong in others," he says. "No, I am not Dr. Abdi Barre, my name is Ibrahim Hassan Daud. I did not kill Dr. Barre, in fact, I rather liked him. I did, however, take his passport. After all, he had no further use for it. Your inquiry into my identity has raised certain difficulties."

"Who you are isn't my concern," I say. "It has no bearing on what happens here."

"But it does. Although I did not kill Dr. Barre, I have killed others. I took no pleasure in it, but it was a time of war, something I doubt you can understand. One does what one must in order to survive. I take no pleasure in what I do now, but once again, I do what I must. You have placed us both in a most uncomfortable position. Were I to be deported back to Somalia, I would be summarily executed. Hudow has already lost her only child, and she would be left here alone, incapable of fending for herself. This, I must not allow."

I try to keep him talking, to get his confession. "Who would execute you?"

"I served as an officer in the security service of the now-deceased former president of Somalia, Siad Barre. The doctor and he were not related. Barre is a most common Somali surname. Like you, I was once a policeman. Because of my duties in that capacity, many would take pleasure in my death."

"What you've done in the past doesn't matter to me," I say. "I have no interest in having you deported."

"As I suggested to you earlier today, forgive me if I lack enough confidence in you to place myself and my wife in your hands. Your performance to date has been most unacceptable. Please surrender your weapon."

I don't move.

"I won't hesitate to kill you Inspector, and our time is short."

I set my Glock down on the ice.

He looks at Seppo. "Defiler of innocence and murderer. You are not forgotten. I will deal with you shortly."

Seppo starts to snivel and swear his innocence.

"Shut up," Ibrahim Hassan Daud or Abdi or whatever-his-real-name-is snaps, "or you will be dealt with sooner rather than later."

Seppo shuts up.

"You must be cold Inspector. Please come and sit by the fire."

I do it. Now I'm getting scared, but I think of Valtteri in the forest with the rifle, maybe fifty yards away, an easy shot.

Abdi keeps the pistol trained on me with one hand, sets the tire upright and starts pouring gasoline into the inner ring with the other.

I'm so scared now that I'm shaking, wondering why Valtteri hasn't done something, if he's really out there at all. Kate was right, and I was wrong about everything, and like she said, this is going to end badly. "Why are you doing this?" I ask.

"It is the only solution to my dilemma. It will appear that

Seppo Niemi murdered you, as he did his wife, and then committed suicide. My wife and I will be safe, and my daughter will be avenged."

"I have a wife too, she's pregnant with twins. They need me as much as Hudow needs you."

He sighs. "I am sorry for your family. Blame yourself. You have placed yourself and them in a situation of your own making."

I try to stand, to at least make him shoot me instead of burn me, but my bad knee is locked and I can't get up.

"You are also incorrect in believing that I murdered your ex-wife," he says. "As I told you at our first meeting, I expected you to be my surrogate in seeing justice done on Sufia's behalf. Now you must reap the consequences of your incompetence."

"If you didn't kill Heli," I ask, "how did you know she was murdered here?"

"Your local newspaper published the name of the lake. Ice blackened by fire gave me the exact location. Had wind not swept the new-fallen snow away, I might not have been able to find it."

He has no reason to lie. I've gotten it all wrong. I'm frightened and bewildered. I'm going to die without ever learning the truth. I'm going to die for nothing. Because of my stupidity, Kate will be left alone to raise two children. The children will grow up without a father. It took me almost forty years to find Kate and happiness, and now I'm going to have my life cut short, lose everything, because I'm a fool. I sit on the ice and await my execution. He lifts up the tire to hang it around my neck.

A rifle booms. The bullet whines past my head and strikes Ibrahim in the shoulder. He lurches sideways and falls, still holding the tire, onto the campfire. The gasoline ignites and he bursts into flame. He tries to stand, but wobbles and collapses, a ball of fire screaming and writhing on the ice. It doesn't last long. He lays still and burns. It happens so fast that I can't even try to help him.

Valtteri runs out of the forest onto the lake. In his winter camouflage, he looks like a white wraith streaking out of the darkness. He reaches me in a few seconds. "Oh Kari," he says, "please tell me you're not hurt."

He helps me up onto shaking feet, hugs me and starts crying. I promise him I'm okay, tell him to calm down.

He pulls away from me and nods. A few feet away, Seppo is still on his knees. Valtteri walks over to him and draws his pistol, presses the muzzle to Seppo's forehead.

I'm confused, don't know what to do. "Valtteri," I say, "please stop. Talk to me."

Seppo doesn't move, his mouth opens and closes like he's searching for words but can't find them.

"I've got to kill him," Valtteri says. "Like you said, this ends today."

He keeps the pistol pressed to Seppo's forehead, bends down on one knee to look in his eyes. "Because of you," Valtteri says, "two women are dead. Because of you, my son committed murder and suicide and burns in hell. You're as guilty of his death as if you'd hung him yourself."

Seppo stammers. "I didn't kill anybody. I barely knew your son. Please don't shoot me, I'm not guilty of anything."

I try to talk Valtteri down. "This isn't the way and you know it. Give me your gun before you do something you can't take back."

He screams at me. "This is the way! This stupid bastard didn't kill anybody, but they're all dead because of his lechery, his selfishness and stupidity. His affair with Sufia Elmi, his sins, set all this in motion. His sins resulted in all this death and misery."

"Valtteri, what you say is true, but setting a series of events in motion isn't the same as being guilty of murder."

I step toward him and hold out my hand. "Please give it to me."

He looks indecisive, then frantic, and swings the pistol toward me, I guess trying to keep me away from him.

I start to speak. "Give me the . . ."

The pistol goes off. My head recoils. I feel a burning in my face, put my hand to my right cheek. Something is very wrong. When I pull my hand away, it's bloody. I roll my tongue around. There are hard things in my mouth. I spit out chunks of teeth.

I can talk, but it's hard. "Valtteri, what have you done?"

He looks at me and goes to pieces, screaming and crying and saying he's sorry and he raised Heikki wrong and now he's hurt me and everything is his fault. He goes on and on and I want to console him but I'm dizzy and pain is starting to spread through my head. I roll my tongue around some more and come to the realization that I opened my mouth to speak and he accidentally fired the pistol. The bullet passed through my mouth, blew out my back teeth and exited through my cheek. I think I'm going to vomit.

Valtteri keeps talking, rambling something incomprehensible and saying he's sorry, waving the gun around. He's so upset I'm afraid he'll shoot me by mistake again. Seppo stands up and starts apologizing to Valtteri for his part in events. I manage to punch him in the face to shut him up, knock him off his feet onto the ice.

All of a sudden, Valtteri lowers the pistol to his side. His face sags and he goes calm. "It was me," he says.

Gunshot trauma has caused endorphin release, and my body's natural painkillers are protecting me for the moment, but the agony will start soon. I've got to get Valtteri under control before it begins. "What do you mean?"

"I killed Heli."

This is more than I can take in. "What?"

"That night, after Heli and Heikki killed Sufia, he came to me and told me what they had done. It was just like you thought. Heli seduced him and made him fall in love with her. She told him the girl was a sinner, not even a human being, and she had to die. She said it was God's will, like missionary work, and told him what to do. He said she talked about it all the time, and after a while, he thought it wouldn't be any harder than gutting a deer. Heli sat in the car and watched while he murdered Sufia. He said when he did it, at first it didn't seem real, like a dream. When he was cutting her belly she woke up and screamed. It scared him so he cut her throat and it was like he woke up. When he understood he'd killed another human being for no reason, he started to cry. He told Heli they'd done wrong and she laughed and told him she never wanted to see him again."

Valtteri starts to sob. "Heikki cried and cried and begged me to forgive him. He wanted to confess, for me to arrest him. I wouldn't let him and told him I would protect him. He was a good boy who made a mistake. He promised to never do it again."

"For God's sake Valtteri."

"It's your fault. You're the detective. You were supposed to fix everything and prove Seppo innocent. The murder could go unsolved. No one else would be hurt and Heikki could pretend like it never happened. But you didn't. And then Heikki hanged himself. He died because of that bitch Heli, and she was going to get away with it. She was going to go on with her life and be rich and happy. I couldn't let that happen. Could you have? My boy is burning in hell and she needed to burn in hell too. Heikki suffered the torments of hell before he died, out of guilt. I wanted her to taste the flames of hell on earth before she spent eternity there, so I burned her alive. It was justice as the Bible teaches. 'If she profanes herself by harlotry, she shall be burned with fire.'"

The words Heikki wrote in his computer. Now that I know most of the truth, I want all of it. "Where did you get the idea to use a burning tire?"

"I read about it years ago in a magazine. Aristide's death squads did it in Haiti, and they used to do it in South Africa and Rwanda and Somalia. The article had pictures and they reminded me of hell. Then because Sufia was a Somali, I remembered the story. It seemed fitting and just, like God's wrath. I didn't do it to frame Sufia's father. I never thought you'd make the connection."

"What about the lake? Why did you pick this place?"

"I knew about your sister and did it to hurt you, because you didn't fix everything like you were supposed to. I'm sorry."

"It doesn't matter. Where are Sufia's clothes and the murder weapon?"

"Heikki gave her clothes to me. I burned them, and the clothes he had on too."

He takes a knife out of his pocket and hands it to me. It's a folding survival knife with a rounded serrated blade.

"I gave him this for his twelfth birthday," he says. "He used it to do what you saw to that girl, unspeakable things. I thought my pocket would be the last place you would look for the murder weapon."

He was right.

"I kept it so I would have a constant reminder of my failure as a father and my sin of pride. I couldn't bear to see my son go to prison. His shame would have fallen on the whole family. If I had let Heikki confess, to go to prison and atone for his sin, he would still be alive. He couldn't bear the guilt and killed himself because of me, because I wouldn't let him. I killed him."

"That's not true, he killed himself."

"We all killed him." He looks at Seppo. "That worthless bastard there. Me. You. That bitch Heli. We're all going to hell." He points at Abdi's still-flaming body. "I almost let him kill you. To save myself, because I'm weak. I'm going to be with my boy now."

He puts the gun to his temple. "I'm sorry."

"Please Valtteri, don't do this."

He says the prayer that every Laestadian child says before going to sleep. *"Jeesuksen nimessä ja veressä kaikki synnit anteeksi."* In the name and blood of Jesus forgive us all our sins.

I try to stop him, to grab his hand, but my knee won't work and I'm sick and too slow.

Valtteri pulls the trigger. His blood and brains spray across the ice. The shot echoes around the lake. He looks at me with dead eyes for a second, then he falls.

I slump down beside him on my hands and knees. I pull off his wool cap and run my fingers through his bloody gray hair. I hear myself moan and say, "Oh God, oh God Valtteri. Get up, get up."

I realize I'm going into traumatic shock from my wound. I look around. Abdi is still burning. Even with cold dampening my sense of smell, the stench of gasoline and his scorched flesh is sickening. I threatened him and brought him here and he died for nothing. Valtteri is dead beside me. His blood stains the pearl-gray ice and looks black in the murky light. Seppo sits on his haunches, stares at me, hands still cuffed in front of him.

"Come here," I say. He crawls over, looks like he's about to go into shock himself. I give him the keys to the handcuffs and my car. "Unlock yourself and open my trunk. There's an emergency first-aid kit. It has morphine in it and I need it."

While he's gone, I call Antti, tell him where I am and that I'm shot, that there are two dead bodies here. I tell him to get me help. He tries to ask questions, but I hang up and drop the phone on the ice.

Seppo brings me the kit and I inject myself. "I'm sorry," he says, "I never meant for all this to happen."

"Valtteri was right," I say. "Your affair with Sufia started all this. You used her and brought all this misery on us with your selfishness, your childishness. If he'd killed you, it might not have been justice, but not far from it. If you weren't the worthless piece of shit that you are, all these people would still be alive."

Then I don't see Seppo anymore. I see Suvi. The ice is three feet thick, but I look through it like a window and see her swimming beneath me. She's been there all these years, alive under the surface, waiting for me to find her.

Then I feel Kate behind me, her arms around me. I feel her pregnant belly, big and round, pressed against my back. Suvi isn't under the ice anymore, she's here with me. I hold her hand and we skate through the darkness across the lake. We stop and Mom and Dad join us. They're young again and happy. Dad's not drunk and they're having one of their good days.

Abdi gets up, pats out the flames and stops smoldering. He stands tall and proud in a dress police uniform, medals on his chest. He has his arm around his daughter. Sufia, gorgeous as always, in a cocktail dress, looks up at her dad and smiles. I notice Heli is here. She's thirteen, laughing like she did when she was a kid, and I know she's okay too. I feel warm and safe. Valtteri looks up at me and winks. I lie down on the ice, use his body for a pillow and go to sleep.

# 35

"I KEPT MY PROMISE. I'm home on Christmas Eve."

Kate shakes her head, laughs a little. "Yes you did. And I'll keep mine and help you put yourself back together again."

By some miracle, the bullet passed through my mouth without breaking my jaw. It shattered the next to last two teeth on the upper right side and passed out through my cheek without further damage. I asked the doctor how bad the scar will be.

"You'll look like a tough guy."

"People already say I look like a tough guy."

He laughed. "Well, now you'll look like a tough guy who got shot in the face."

"That's great," I said, "just what I need."

Kate called Dad. When she explained what happened, Mom offered to come over and help make Christmas dinner. Dad said he'd come if I put the sauna on. Christmas isn't Christmas without sauna, he said. It's sweet that Mom is cooking. She's doing it for Kate. I can't eat solid food and will be living on soup for a few weeks.

I start building a fire for the sauna. I can't go with the bandages on my face. It disappoints me almost as much as not being able to eat Christmas dinner. The phone rings. Even with heavy painkillers, my face and broken teeth hurt like hell. It's the national chief of police and I want to find out if I'm fired, so I answer anyway.

"How's your face?" he asks.

"Hurts."

"Fair enough, it's been hurting the rest of us for a long time." He laughs at his own joke. "You're a jackass," he says.

"I know."

"I don't know whether to prosecute you or promote you."

"Me neither."

"When your officers processed the scene, they found the video camera and tape recorder. The whole thing is documented."

I didn't know Valtteri left them running and captured his own suicide. "It was a tragedy. I wish it could be forgotten."

"It can't. I'm putting it on the evening news. To save your ass."

I don't say anything.

"I'm a man of my word and a deal's a deal," he says. "You solved both murders. What job do you want?"

"You serious?"

"What do you think?"

I tell him to wait a second and start to ask Kate what she wants to do, then think better of it. She's been under enough pressure lately. It can wait until after Christmas.

"Can you give me some time to consider it?" I ask.

"I'll give you a week," he says. "You're a jackass, but I guess I'm going to have to decorate you for bravery again anyway, to put the right spin on things. What the hell, it will get me some face time on television." He hangs up.

I tell Kate what he said.

"You were right about the case," she says. "Maybe you're right about staying here too. Then again, Helsinki sounds nice. Let's take some time and think about it."

I wasn't right about everything, and wish I'd been wrong about the rest of it.

Mom and Dad arrive. Mom hugs me, looks like she's going to cry. "You okay son?" Dad asks.

"Yeah."

He hands me two wrapped gifts. One is obviously a bottle. "Open them," he says.

The bottle is Koskenkorva vodka. The other package contains two plastic straws. "They're symbolic," he says. "We're gonna drink it together."

"I shouldn't drink on top of the painkillers," I say.

Mom doesn't speak any English, but Dad's is passable. He looks at Kate. "Do you mind if your husband gets drunk with his father?"

"A little," she says. She looks at me—I shrug. She gives Dad a Christmas hug. "But go ahead anyway."

He looks happy, cracks the top off the bottle, takes a drink and hands it to me. I take a sip.

The doorbell rings again. I'm surprised to find Seppo on my front porch. "Merry Christmas," he says.

He's the last person on earth I want to see. "What do you want?"

He looks sheepish. "If I had done what you told me, left here and never come back, Heli would still be alive. Now I'm leaving for good and I want you to have this."

He hands me a manila envelope. "What is it?" I ask.

"The deed to my winter cottage. I don't want it anymore. I thought it might make up for things a little bit."

Five people are dead and he thinks he can just buy goodwill, fix everything with an expensive gift. I hand it back. "I don't want it."

He doesn't take it. "It's worth eight hundred thousand euros."

I grab his hand and press the envelope into it. "I still don't want it. Go away."

He looks like a sad little kid. "Sorry I bothered you."

Then I realize. "Wait," I say. "Give it to me."

He hands it back. "Why the change of heart?"

"Valtteri left a widow and a bunch of kids, and Sufia's mother is alone now. I'm not sure if she's capable of providing for herself. Selling your winter dacha can take care of them all for a long time."

"Good," he says, "I'm glad."

I shut the door, and for the first time I realize how much better off we all were when Heli left me for him. She got what she wanted—a stupid rich man she could manipulate. He had a woman who stayed with him despite the fact that he's a philandering drunk, and besides, I think he really loved her. Heli wasn't who I thought she was when I married her. Maybe, like Sufia, no one really knew her. I was allowed to go on with my life and find someone I could make happy, someone who makes me happy.

Dad asks me who was at the door. I tell him it was nobody.

Mom takes Kate to the kitchen to teach her the fine art of making *rosolli*. The way they manage to communicate despite not having a common language, mostly with hand gestures, amuses me. People always seem to find a way.

Dad and I sit in front of the television, pass the bottle back and forth. The combination of drugs and alcohol allows me to screw up my nerve and ask the unspoken question. "Dad, do you ever think about Suvi?"

He leans over, arms on his knees, and stares at the floor. It takes him a long time to answer, but when he does, he looks me in the eye. "Every day of my life."

"Should we talk about it?"

"Some things you can never make right. There's nothing to say."

A few silent minutes tick by. "The sauna almost ready?" he asks.

"Almost."

More time passes. "It was a good-looking ham you bought," he says.

"Yep," I say, "a good-looking ham."

Kate comes in from the kitchen. "How are you two doing?"

Dad holds up the vodka bottle. "Couldn't be better. You know Kate, the sun is going to rise tomorrow. Just for a few minutes, but *kaamos* is almost over."

Kate comes up behind me, reaches over the couch and puts her arms around me. *"Hyvää Joulua,"* Merry Christmas, she says.

Merry for whom? Sufia Elmi, a refugee who defied the odds and succeeded in a xenophobic country, felt so hopeless inside that she let herself be abused by men who cared nothing for her. My first instinct was right. Her charm and beauty inspired hatred, and because of them, she was butchered like an animal. I don't know what her father was guilty of, but he had put his past behind him, come to our country and built a new life for himself. I dredged up his past and he died, because of me, for nothing.

My ex-wife, a woman I once loved and believed I would spend the rest of my life with, turned out to be a sociopath and a killer. She manipulated a boy who had led such a sheltered life that he was nearly defenseless. She drove him to murder and suicide, destroyed him, so I believe, with no more thought than she would have given to squashing a bug. Maybe Heli, burned to death on the ice, got what she deserved. I don't know.

Valtteri was a good man who believed his faith would protect him and his family. What God failed to do, he tried to do himself, and he covered up a murder to protect his son. His shattered faith and his own failure drove him to murder Heli, an atrocity that, a week earlier, would have been beyond his comprehension. His widow and seven remaining children are spending Christmas mourning his loss and Heikki's, doubtless mystified, drowning in sorrow, shock and disbelief. Abdi's wife, Hudow, must be doing the same.

I neglected my wife, risked my marriage, nearly left my children fatherless for what I believed was the pursuit of justice. Instead of justice, I got the truth, and it was a poor substitute. Now I don't know what I was looking for. I feel like I failed them all, like I failed myself. I saved no one. And yet, I'm going to be decorated for bravery, labeled a hero, given a promotion if I want it. Maybe there is no justice.

But there are other things. I look around and see all I have to be grateful for. I'm surrounded by family. My wife loves me, has her arms around me. Our babies are growing inside her.

I look up at her. It hurts, but I force a smile. "Merry Christmas Kate."